CARRY ON

CARRY ON

CHRONICLES OF A HIDDEN CITY™
BOOK ONE

AUBURN TEMPEST

MICHAEL ANDERLE

DON'T MISS OUR NEW RELEASES

Join the LMBPN email list to be notified of new releases and special promotions (which happen often) by following this link:

http://lmbpn.com/email/

LMBPN Publishing
2375 E. Tropicana Avenue, Suite 8-305
Las Vegas, Nevada 89119 USA

Version 1.00, March 2024
eBook ISBN: 979-8-89146-018-8
Print ISBN: 979-8-88878-821-9

THE CARRY ON TEAM

Thanks to our Beta Team:
James Caplan, Kelly O'Donnell, Mary Morris, John Ashmore

Thanks to our JIT Team:

Veronica Stephan-Miller
Christopher Gilliard
Deb Mader
Dave Hicks
Wendy L Bonell
Dorothy Lloyd
Diane L. Smith
Jan Hunnicutt
Angel LaVey
Paul Westman

Editor
SkyFyre Editing Team

DEAR READERS

Welcome to the adventures of my mind and heart. I hope these stories offer you an escape from reality and a laugh or two…or three. Michael and I both create fiction, hoping our readers will enjoy the stories enough to reread them again and again.

It's the ultimate compliment to storytelling.

Carry On is the first book in the Chronicles of a Hidden City and I hope I've given you the starting point you need to jump in and find your footing quickly.

If you're the type of reader who needs to start chronologically from the beginning, there are twenty-eight books before *Carry On* that have shaped our journey to this point. If you want to start there, enjoy the ride.

Chronicles of an Urban Druid–15 books

Case Files of an Urban Druid–7 books

Chronicles of an Urban Elemental–6 books

Then…

Chronicles of a Hidden City

Whether you're new to the universe or one of my fantastic Team Trouble Superfans back for more, I'm honored you're here, and thank you for your time.

And as the family motto goes: *Glaine ár gcroí. Neart ár ngéag. Beart de réir ár mbriathar.*

"May yer heart remain pure, yer limbs remain strong, and yer actions always be true to yer word."

Auburn Tempest

1

EMMET

"Emmet Cumhaill, descendant of the great Fionn mac Cumhaill, our hearts are full with the warmth of your welcome." Thrain Ironfist raises his tankard. "To live within the enchanted city is an honor as grand as the deepest mines and as precious as the rarest gem."

I grip the handle of my stein and reach across the table to clank cups with the portly dwarf and his young gnome girlfriend. "Isilon opens its gates to those who need a safe place to live in peace. I'm sure you'll find everything you need to thrive here."

Thrain throws back his head, glugging his ale. When he's drained it dry, he straightens and wipes the foam from his beard with the back of his sleeve. "All I'll ever need is my sweet Oda girl."

Oda sips her drink as her round cheeks flush pink. "Simply being able to live and love in peace is a blessing. Our thanks to you and your family."

I swallow another mouthful of Guinness. "We believe in love —wherever you find it. Our da always says, 'Deep down we're all the same. The subtle differences are the spices that make the stew of life rich with flavor.'"

Thrain grins. "Your da is a wise man."

"He definitely is."

"Does he live on the island as well?"

"No, only my siblings, their families, and a few of our friends. Our father lives in the human realm so he and his second wife can watch over their aging parents."

Thrain gestures across the pub at where my siblings and friends are getting wild around the mechanical bull. "Still, it seems you have quite a clan here."

"I do."

"All of you are druids?"

"Almost all. My brother Brendan, who helps me run the city, hasn't found his druid roots yet, but the rest of us have all been trained."

"But it's your sister who Fionn named his successor to the Fianna, correct?" Oda asks.

"That's right, Fiona." I sit straighter and point to my younger sister. "She's the pregnant redhead sitting at the tall table laughing."

Oda looks over and grins. "I love that she's the one he chose to lead the druid warriors. In my culture, the males think so highly of themselves a female can rarely rise to her potential."

"You won't find that here. Introduce yourself to Fi and tell her about your aspirations. She'll make sure you get what you need to build toward your dreams."

Oda's blush deepens. "All I want is a binding ceremony and a little workshop to tinker in while my babies sleep."

"I can make that happen." Thrain grins.

"How many kids are you hoping for?" I ask.

Oda shrugs. "However many the All-Father blesses us with. How many are in your family?"

I take another drink and swallow. "I'm the fifth boy, and Fiona is the sixth born. Mam and Da gave up after that."

Thrain grunts and leans back. "They likely couldn't keep you straight. I'm terrible with names. I can't imagine having six and remembering them all."

Oda tugs on his beard. "You'll remember."

The teasing look he flashes her is too funny.

"To make it easier, you can always take a page out of my Mam's book," I offer. "She named us alphabetically. Aiden, Brendan, Calum, Dillan, Emmet, and Fiona."

"That's brilliant." Oda giggles. "I'll start lining up my names right away. Although gnomes and dwarves have different alphabets."

"I'm sure you'll figure it out."

The two talk more about names, then Thrain bangs the table with his fist and shuffles out of the booth. "We've taken enough of your time, friend. We're off to pick ourselves a forever home."

I stand as they get ready to leave. "Have you got the map from when you arrived?"

Oda pulls it from the front pocket of her overalls. "We've narrowed it down to three."

"Well, happy house hunting, then. Let me know where you settle, and we'll mark it off as claimed on the master list."

"Blessings, Emmet." Oda bows her head.

"To you as well."

Thrain extends a beefy arm toward me, and I clasp his forearm as he clasps mine. "Fare thee well, friend."

They shuffle out of the pub, and I reclaim my spot in the corner booth against the front window. Over the past eighteen months, this has become my unofficial office and the place where residents can usually find me when they have a problem.

I try to be available to the people of Isilon.

I'm the island's guardian, and Mother Nature chose me to watch over the sentient city as it comes out of hibernation.

It's a lot, but I knew this was where I needed to be from the moment I stepped foot on this island. The power that runs in my veins belongs here.

Whatever I became that day resonates in harmony with the magic here.

A flashback that blurs the lines between memory and fantasy ensnares my consciousness. It drags me into a familiar loop of horror—the most terrifying moment of my life.

Part of me knows it's over, but it doesn't make it any less awful or stop the panic from taking hold. I see and feel everything as if it's happening for the first time.

A vengeful witch blasts me through a gaping hole in a broken wall. Pain explodes in my chest at the same time the hit throws me backward into the flowing channel of a fae ley line.

Raw power swallows me. Magic invades my cells, and I'm dragged into the current of the prana river.

I flail, desperate to grab hold of something to pull myself out, but there's nothing.

It sucks me under.

Tumbling with no idea what direction is up or down, my lungs burn with the need for oxygen.

I'm about to die.

I'm not ready.

When I breach the surface, I reach for anything to pull myself out of the deadly water. I can't see. I'm terrified to breathe, to open my mouth, or to call for help in case I ingest even a drop of the power encasing me.

There is a fine line between dead and immortal and I'm not willing to chance it.

The memory is so intense, so real, I feel the fae energy as if it's still a tactile presence enveloping me like a second skin.

It seeps into my pores with an eager insistence.

Every nerve and every cell in my body tingles with an electric charge, a sensation akin to the crackle in the air that precedes a thunderstorm.

Being exposed to such a transformative power reshaped me

from within, and even trapped in the dreamscape, I sense the profound changes taking hold.

It's the same feeling I'm swamped with when I stand next to the prana currents of the fuchsia river of Emhain Abhlach. The fae power thrums within me, intertwining with the forces that sustain the mystical island.

In this place between memory and reality, I sense the metamorphosis unfolding, an alchemy of spirit and energy that promises to wake within me…

Laughter bellows, a rich chorus of mirth that yanks me from the fluid grasp of my nightmare. I jolt back to the present, my blood pounding with a wild rhythm.

For a heartbeat, the world skews at an impossible angle, the lingering embrace of the prana's magic clashing with the raucous scene unfolding around me.

My brothers roar as Dionysus, the god of revelry, wrestles with the jerking bucks of the mechanical bull. Across the pub dining floor, his antics send waves of amusement through the crowd.

I blink hard, once, twice, and press my hands flat against the table I tucked myself away behind. The world swims in a dizzying dance, images blurring, then snapping into sharp focus.

I draw a deep breath, the air heavy with the scent of dark ale, the smoky whisper of food sizzling on the grill, and the undeniable tang of magic.

It's familiar and grounding.

Even before we moved to this island and opened this pub, Shenanigans was our family pub in Toronto.

I guess old habits die hard.

When we moved here, it seemed only natural to open Shenanigans II and create that same sense of fond belonging for the people moving to our city.

I draw another steadying breath and find my equilibrium.

Around me, the pub's walls pulse with life and laughter rebounding off the aged wood like a living thing. I swallow, hoping my momentary disorientation went unnoticed in the chaos of cheers and claps.

Dionysus dismounts with a flourish only he could pull off. Waving his hands, he bows, hamming it up for his admirers. He pulls Jonah into a dramatic kiss, spinning his boyfriend in a Hollywood-style dip before setting him back on his feet.

The crowd goes wild, and Dillan hands his beer to Fiona so he can take his turn.

There, amid the revelry, I find my anchor in the now. With Fi in my sights, I rein in my panic.

I'm safe.

I survived my dip in the ultimate magical energy bath, and I'm still around to talk about it.

I slip out of the booth, my grin wide enough to mask the remnants of a restless dream. The laughter of my family and friends blends with the Celtic rhythm, both filling the air, and it's a welcome soundtrack that drowns out the echoes of my subconscious.

It's like old times…only on the other side of the world…and with magic.

That Aiden, Calum, Dillan, and Fi moved their families to join Brendan and me has meant the world to us.

It might sound stupid to those who aren't close with their siblings, but when I became the island's champion and Mother Nature brought Brendan back from the dead and said he could only live here, the thing we both missed most was the connection to our family.

While Toronto will always live in our hearts, home is where my family is—and right now, my family is having some mighty craic at Shenanigans II.

"Hey, what did I miss?" I sidle in beside my sister and her hubby, Sloan.

"The boys are trying to out-rodeo one another."

I laugh. "What are the stakes?"

"The loser has to abstain from sex and alcohol for forty-eight hours."

"Wow, this is serious."

Fiona grins. "Go big or go home. What Dillan and Dionysus don't know is that Kevin took Bizzy to his parents for a few days, so sex is already off the table for Calum."

"Well played, Calum."

"Right?"

I laugh as Dillan strokes a hand over the mechanical bull's leather body and leans down to whisper something. "Bro, you're supposed to ride the bull, not seduce it!"

The group bursts into another round of laughter. Dillan flashes me a middle-finger salute, his eyes sparkling with the same playful energy that fuels our banter. "I've got this, angel. Never fear."

Dillan's wife Eva laughs where she's standing with Dionysus' boyfriend and honestly, neither one looks worried. "Ride that beast, studly man."

Before I can lob another jibe at Dillan's expense, I feel Fiona's attention on me. When I turn and meet her gaze, her eyes lock with mine, and I feel exposed.

"You okay, Em? You seem off."

"No, I'm good. Just tired."

"Still having the nightmare?"

Nightmare implies sleeping. I'm sucked into that moment whether I'm sleeping or not. The weight of her gaze slices through my jovial façade to the uncertainty beneath. She has always had a knack for seeing through me, no matter how thick the veneer I put up. "Now and then. But really, Fi. I'm fine."

She doesn't look convinced but nods. "Let me know when you're not fine. Sloan's good with healing, but he's also good with cognitive stuff. Maybe he can help."

Sloan is standing behind Fi with his arms around her waist

and his hands resting on the roundness of her baby bump. He glances over at the mention of his name. "Aye, whatever I can do, Em."

I shake off the feeling of being defective with a chuckle, turning back to the group. "I'm good. Really, guys. Let's have some fun tonight, yeah?"

A chorus of laughter greets my request, accompanied by a medley of good-natured scoffs and jibes from my siblings. Slinging shit and razzing one another is part of our love language.

This is us.

The pub's ambience is alive with kinship, the air thrumming with the clink of raised glasses and the comforting hum of conversation. Laughter bubbles up like a wellspring, mingling with the occasional curse and the soft thud of tankards on wooden tables.

It's taken a lot to get here.

When I first gained stewardship of the city, it was only me and my familiar, Doc. Then, because Fiona pretty much saved the balance of the world, Mother Nature gave us Brenny back for a second chance at life.

The two of us spent a long and lonely period while we worked to reinhabit the island but look at what we created.

Isilon is growing into a genuine community, and now that the fam jam is all in one place, all is right in my world. Well, except for having no idea what I'm doing or what I'm supposed to become.

Meh, why sweat it? Take life as it comes, amirite?

With that in mind, I lean over to chat with Fi and Sloan over the din. "Hey, let's say we take to the skies tomorrow. We can give the dragons a workout and run the city's boundaries."

Fiona flashes me a wide grin. "That's an awesome idea. I'm babysitting Han for the morning, so after lunch?"

"Sounds good."

Sloan nods. "Aye, it does."

A chorus of hearty assents and whoops of joy greet Dillan as he dismounts the bull. "And the crowd goes wild!" He tosses a playful jibe toward Dionysus and shares a conspiratorial wink with Eva. I'm not sure what they're up to, but honestly, who can keep up?

"Emmet! You're up, little brother!" Calum calls, waving me in.

I hand Fi my beer and raise my hands to the jeers and the cheers. From the outside looking in, we might look a bit crazy, but the unconditional acceptance and light-hearted goofing around have always been the soothing balm on any wounds the world can wield.

Really...it doesn't get any better than that.

This is the Cumhaill way.

Brendan

Perched on a stool with my elbows propped on the bar's worn wooden surface, I watch my brothers living it up in the mirror's reflection. The mechanical bull bucks and spins, eliciting a chorus of hoots and hollers from the crowd. It's a good time all the way around.

My fingers curl loosely around a glass of Redbreast Irish whiskey, the amber liquid barely disturbed.

It's not the raucous energy of the pub that has me in its grip. It's the relentless tide of my thoughts.

Outside, the city of Isilon pulses with life.

The faint laughter of children playing echoes up the cobblestone streets. The fleeting shadows of dragons gliding overhead darken the windows as they pass. The pink sky, while pretty, doesn't feel natural.

The symphony of everyday magic here stands in stark contrast to the original Shenanigans—the *real* Shenanigans.

Outside *that* Irish pub stretches the buildings and streets of Toronto.

My city. *My* home.

It seems stupid to mourn the loss of a building, but the family pub we all grew up in back in Toronto was our touchstone. It set the course of our lives as our safe space, where we made memories, where friends knew to drop in for a pint, and where my life made sense.

Even during all the stints I spent working undercover with Guns and Gangs, I could drive by and feel less alone. When things got rough, if I got a coffee across the road, I could always glimpse Liam, one of my siblings, or a friend from the neighborhood coming or going, and I knew everything would be all right.

Here, everything is different.

We live in a city of dragons, feline folk, and rivers of raw magic. Our friends teleport anywhere in the world in a blink, and they're gods, angels, and immortals.

My baby sister—who was sixteen and nervous about getting her driver's license when I left home—is the leader of the Fianna Warriors, the savior of the human realm, and totally the shit in the magical world.

I find Fiona's reflection in the mirror. My baby sister is not sixteen anymore.

Fi thrives in this world.

She's married to the smartest guy I've ever known. She's best friends with Dionysus, the god of drunken debauchery and a Greek immortal. She's bonded to a badass battle bear that bursts out of her at a moment's notice and a freaking dragon that would raze the world for her. And she's pregnant.

It's a lot to adjust to.

The pub thrives with vibrancy, my brothers cheering on the next brave soul mounting the mechanical beast. Their voices blend into the collective celebration, yet to me, they sound as if they're at the far end of a tunnel, their encouragement distant and muffled.

I meet my glassy gaze in the mirror, my ebony hair and emerald eyes a carbon copy of Calum, Dillan, and Emmet. How can we look so similar and yet I feel so different?

Fiona and Aiden both got Da's russet hair and bright blue eyes, but even so, you couldn't look at any of the six of us and not know we're siblings.

We all share the same upbringing, code of honor, and sense of duty—so why am I the only one struggling?

The *clinking* of glasses and the *thud* of boots stomping in time to the Celtic rhythm fail to pull me in. You'd think after being dead for two years and given a second chance, I'd be tearing up this new life, so what is wrong with me?

In my mind's eye, the laughter of the children outside twists into the crackle of a police radio...the flap of dragon wings becomes the distant wail of sirens.

As a cop in Toronto, I had everything mapped out. I knew my purpose and my trajectory in the world.

Now, the world has changed.

I take a slow sip of whiskey, the smooth burn of it grounding me for a moment. It's not enough to anchor me fully to the now, not when the undercurrent of my past pulls so strongly.

The Celtic song ends, and the next song brings the chirping of crickets, followed by the wailful cry of a wolf howling in the distance.

I blink back to the present as Shakira's *She Wolf* plays over the sound system.

Liam stands behind the bar and sets a shot glass between us. As he tips the bottle of whiskey to pour himself a drink, I ready myself for what's coming.

His father and Da were partners from the beginning, and when his dad was killed on the job, he grew up as part of our family.

Liam reads me like an open book and vice versa.

He tosses back the shot and raps his fingers on the bar. His gaze is fixed on me with concern and silent inquiry.

I draw a deep breath and sigh. All right, so not everything is different here. I down my drink and push my empty glass forward for a top-up. "Thanks for the song."

Liam chuckles and pours us both a refill. "You've stewed long enough. Time to spill."

My lips twitch into a half-smile. "You'll think I'm a selfish idiot."

Liam's laugh is a soft rumble. "I *know* you're a selfish idiot, B. I've known that since you boffed Stacey Greene in the coat check room when you knew I was into her."

I laugh, raise my glass, and take another drink. "You got me back with Victoria Scain."

Liam waggles his brows. "Fair's fair."

Damn. Those were the days.

I swallow another mouthful of liquid courage and exhale a silent acknowledgment of defeat. Liam knows me too damned well to let me get mired in my mind. "I had it all lined up, you know? A job I loved. Living on the edge of a knife. Wild women. An amazing city. It was real…and it was fucking awesome."

Liam nods. "Yeah, right until you stepped in front of a spray of bullets and died."

Yeah, well, all good things come to an end.

"No regrets on that one. I'd do it again in a heartbeat, but it cost me, you know?"

Liam nods, but years of bartending have taught him when to speak and when to let someone unload.

I draw a deep breath, hoping it will steady the storm within. "Then Fi—my baby sister—becomes the world's hero and saves the damn world. Next thing I know, I'm back from the dead with a second chance."

A sandy blond brow arches. "Are you bitching because Fi

outdid you? 'Cause if that's what this is, yeah, selfish idiot isn't the half of it."

I wave off his ire. "No. It's not about Fi. She's amazing, and I'm so fucking proud of her for finding her lane I could burst."

Liam dials back his hostility meter a few notches. "Well, good, because we both know I can beat the shit out of you if I have to."

I laugh. "Not since we were twelve."

"Try me."

Yeah, well, I haven't had nearly enough to drink to take him up on that. "So, here we are. Em and I standing guard over Isilon, this mystical, magical city. I'm grateful for this second shot at life —I am—but it's like I'm a ship with no anchor, adrift in a current between the shores of what I wanted and what I've been given instead."

Liam frowns. "You're not the only person who had to adjust, dude. Fiona, Dillan, Aiden, and Calum moved here to support you and Emmet."

"Think about Kevin and Kinu and me. We don't have magic. This isn't our world. But we're here because we're family and the band is better together than separated by two realms."

"Yeah, sorry. I warned you I would sound selfish."

"You forgot idiotic." A lopsided grin tugs at the corner of his mouth. "This brooding isn't about being given a second chance or Fiona growing up while you were undercover."

I lean back on my stool and cross my arms. "No? Then, by all means, go ahead and tell me what I'm feeling."

Liam leans over the bar. "You're an adrenaline junkie who thrives on conflict, fast women, and the thrill of danger knocking at your door. This isn't Toronto. You don't have scumbags to take down, or your motorcycle to tear up the streets, or an endless string of leather-clad women to nail in the pub washroom."

I snort. "Is that what my life breaks down to in your eyes?"

"In yours too—don't pretend I'm wrong."

I'd like to tell him he's way off base, but hearing it out loud… yeah, I miss that stuff.

Liam leans in, his hair catching the dim light behind the bar. It casts a warm glow around his face as he claps a hand on my shoulder, the weight of it as familiar as the countless nights we've shared over pints and tales of misadventure.

His smile is one part mischief and two parts wisdom—a cocktail he's perfected over the years of our friendship.

"It'll come, B." The corners of his eyes crinkle with his smile. "You've got a whole new crew to call family. They're not half bad if you ask me."

A chuckle escapes as I turn to watch the chaos of their group unfold. "Fi has always been a collector of souls, hasn't she?"

"Yeah. Just think, if you hadn't been brought back, you never would have met Carragh, Ireland, or little Han. Give them another couple of years, and I'm betting they'll think their Uncle B is the bomb."

Leave it to Liam to pull me out of my pity party and set me straight. Yeah, my path might have veered off the expected course, but at least I'm not dead.

There's still time to turn this around.

A knock on the glass of the front window crashes the party like a rogue wave. I twist around to see the six-foot black panther warrior, Kidok, wave me out, the look on his face grave.

When Kidok points at Emmet, too, I know there's a real problem. "Thanks for the chat, man. Looks like I'm being summoned."

"Always. I hope everything's all right."

"Yeah, me too." I drop off my stool and stride through the pub toward the front door. As the chief of security for the city, Kidok knows he can always call Emmet and me out for help.

It rarely happens.

The guy can handle any bumps along the road to us repopulating this city. The look on his face tells me whatever he's going to say isn't good.

2

EMMET

I leave the raucous merriment of my family getting their groove on, the sarcastic jeering and belly laughter gradually giving way to the hush of the evening outside. The night air is a soothing balm against my skin, the island's magic so much stronger outdoors.

Brendan is ahead of me as we exit and by the tension in his shoulders and how he's tapping his pant leg with his thumb, he's anxious about what's happening too.

Before we have time to ask Kidok what this is about, a tide of fae citizens surging around our security chief sweeps us up.

Kidok, an imposing feline figure at the best of times, is practically vibrating with tension, his white whiskers noticeably twitchy against the deep ebony of his fur.

"What's going on?" I ask. "What's wrong?"

Kidok shakes his head. "They led me to a dead tree nymph in the grove by the city's center. I can't understand a thing they're saying and hoped you could do one of your spells to help me find out what happened."

There's a flutter of wings and a whimper of sorrow ripples

through the crowd. They're all talking at once and yeah—I see why he's having trouble.

"Okay, you two, bring it in." I extend my hands, and Brendan and Kidok set their palms on mine.

"Ancient tongues of pasts long gone, Fill the air like Babylon. Charm my ears and bless my words, To sing their tune like sweet song birds."

The overlapping nonsense chatter straightens out the moment I speak the words and becomes understandable.

"All right. Who here found the body?" Brenny asks.

When a faerie with blue, sparkly wings flutters over, Brendan raises his palm for her to land on.

"Perfect. Now, tell us what happened, and we'll help as best we can."

The wee thing tells us about finding her friend but doesn't know anything beyond that. Brendan lets her fly back to the others, and I see the questions rising to the fore in his eyes.

They're the same questions I have. Except, with the circle of a dozen upset citizens, now isn't the best time to get into the nitty-gritty of insensitive inquiries.

"Show us," I tell Kidok, gesturing for him to lead the way.

The three of us take the lead, and our long strides put some distance between us and our upset followers.

Once we've got a buffer of space, I cast a quick spell to keep our conversation to ourselves. "You can speak freely now. We're in a privacy bubble."

Brendan nods. "Thanks, Em. Okay, so, dead how? Age? Did she fall from a tree? Was she attacked? What are your first thoughts? Are we looking at natural causes, an accident, or something more?"

Kidok lets out a long growl. "Something more."

I have a hard time wrapping my head around that.

In the year and a half since we first came to the island to safeguard access to the prana river during the Culling, then remove the Light Weaver spell hiding the city and repopulate it to rebuild Isilon's strength, there has never been an overtly criminal act.

We've had some emotional conflicts and drunk and disorderly moments, but no one has been outwardly aggressive or hostile.

I sigh. "I suppose it was too much to hope that the city could remain a sanctuary of peace and goodwill in the long term."

Brendan grunts. "Maybe, but it was a nice thought."

It was. "All right, tell us what you know, Kidok."

Kidok glances over his shoulder sash to check where the others are and frowns. "From what I've been told, Randa was in good health as of yesterday, and her tree is also strong and in good health."

"You think she was killed?" The words slip from my lips, barely audible.

Kidok's dark eyes narrow, and he nods. "The body is in a strange state. You'll have to see for yourself."

My guts knot tighter. *Strange state?*

What the hell does that mean?

"The thought that someone could snuff out a life in our mystical refuge is unsettling, to say the least." Brenny mirrors my thoughts.

As we walk side by side, our boots scuff over the cobblestone paths that cover the maze of Isilon's streets. Even under the veil of dusk, the city is a patchwork tapestry of colors and chaos of architectural influences collected as beautiful bric-a-brac.

Buildings painted in hues that only fae artists could dream up line the streets, their whimsy betrayed by the somber mood that clings to us like the luminescent moss draping the edges of the rooftops.

The glowing green carpet acts as a natural streetlamp guiding our way, but tonight, its beauty is lost in the taking of a life on our watch.

Brendan is quieter than usual, and as we get closer to the

grove, I watch his transformation. Like Da and Aiden, Brendan was born to be a cop.

It gave him his life's purpose more than it did me.

I became a cop because I wanted to help people, and in our family, it was kinda what the men did.

Brenny did it because he bled blue.

He lived and died one of the most devoted cops in the Toronto Police Department. Isilon is lucky to have him.

We're all lucky to have him.

"I feel like an asshole," he confesses in a hushed tone for only my ears. "I was wishing for a bit of action, you know? A crime to solve. And now…"

I clap his shoulder. "Not your fault, B. Not even a little."

"Maybe, but Da always told us wishing for trouble in our line of work was akin to tempting fate."

"Don't care. This is still not on you."

The grove Kidok leads us to is in a less populated area of Isilon beyond a cluster of larger homes. If I were to guess about the people who lived in this neighborhood a thousand years ago, I'd say this is where the high priestesses and elven royalty might be.

"Fancy digs." I point at some of the stone mansions across from the gathering of trees.

Brendan grins. "We live in the penthouse of the palace. Doesn't get any fancier than that."

I hadn't thought about it like that, but honestly, our place is more like an epic bachelor apartment with a view of the city. It's not fancy or pretentious.

Our family doesn't do highbrow.

We step into the grove, and the world hushes around us. Brendan is all business now, his jaw set and his gaze scanning the surroundings with the precision of a hawk.

The fae citizens are a solemn bunch as they arrive behind us. Their whispers drift to us in quiet echoes that barely disturb the air.

I feel their grief like a weight on my chest.

Isilon is the place people come to escape violence and persecution. It's supposed to be a haven.

My boots press into the forest floor, cushioned by the spongy grass and cool soil. As a druid, nature is the balm to my soul. As the caretaker of this island, my connection to nature here is so much more.

The dead nymph is lying on her back at the base of the tree, but we don't approach yet, taking in the scene as a whole.

Brendan catches my eye, and without a word, we're in sync. He's the one with the seasoned eye for detail, and I'm the one to make sure we do right by the nymph who's lost her life.

"Look at the branches," Brendan murmurs, pointing up at the oak that towers over us. This home tree is a witness to what happened, its leaves rustling with secrets we itch to uncover.

Brendan crouches, his movements methodical and practiced. He's in his element, and I'm taking mental notes. We never got to work together—he was undercover when I graduated from the police academy, then was shot on the job.

Maybe I'm a sappy little brother, but there's something special about us getting the opportunity to work together. I'm sure he'd rather work with Da, Aiden, or maybe Calum, but I like that we get this chance.

When we move closer to the body, I can almost taste the wrongness of the energy in the air. It's acrid and foul and makes the hair on my arms stand on end.

It sets off something squirrely in my system, and I fight not to freak out and start turning into random zoo animals because been there, done that—it's a thing.

"Em? What is it?"

I meet Brenny's concerned stare and shake my hands. "The magic here is wrong. It's giving me the heebie-jeebies."

His jaw flexes as he scans our surroundings again and nods.

"Okay, let me know if anything sets off your magical alarm bells to a new level of heeb."

"Will do." I scan the grove, noting the movement in the trees and the shadows in the street beyond, searching for the one clue that could lead us to answers.

Policing is a dance of sorts, the cop and the answers we seek moving around the scene in tandem.

As we work, I scan the faces of the fae gathered by Kidok, then the buildings and the trees surrounding us. Is the forest watching us? Are the trees standing guard over their fallen kin?

A shiver runs the length of my spine, and my hands tingle with the magic fighting to be put to use. I'm not only a cop anymore. I'm a protector of a world few know about and most couldn't imagine.

While Brendan does his thing, I kneel beside the lifeless fae and brush the back of my finger against her pale green skin. The chill of the grove at night has completely taken her over, poor thing.

"We'll figure this out, Randa," I vow. "We'll find the one who did this and bring them to justice."

I pull my phone out and tap to light my flashlight so I can take a closer look. Tree nymphs—or dryads as they're also known—are born with an interesting veining pattern on their skin. It grows more pronounced with age and can vary from silver to brown to forest green.

Randa has a thin, pale brown line that etches over her features. The patterning looks a lot like bark and is immediately identifiable as the markings of her kind.

One of Fiona's closest friends, Myra, is a dryad whose home tree grows through the center of her bookstore in Toronto. Her skin is accented by a beautiful silver veining that she accentuates by dying her hair electric blue.

Knowing what Myra's skin looks like makes it easy to see that whatever killed Randa has caused an unnatural withering of her vibrance.

"I've seen death similar to this before." I lean in to get a closer look. "In Ireland, a few years ago, there was a group of necromancers siphoning fae energy for a power boost."

Brendan meets my gaze. "Similar or the same?"

I consider that. "This is similar, but still different."

This peculiar desiccation tugs at the edges of my understanding, leaving me with more questions than answers. Flicking open my phone, I thumb a quick message to Sloan.

Need your eyes on a situation. Keep it quiet. No Fiona. Lower grove past the city square toward the river.

Brendan is watching me and lifts his chin in inquiry.

"I asked Sloan to join us."

The fact that we can still use our phones here to contact our friends and families beyond the island's wards is one of the greatest gifts of magic.

When I first moved here, Merlin and Dionysus worked together to give me the tools I needed most.

Communication was at the top of that list.

While the golden palace isn't exactly a cell tower, with the magical intervention of a demi-god and a god among magicians, it acts as one.

No sooner do I speak the words than Sloan pops into existence with that soft *whoosh* of displaced air that accompanies his arrivals when he uses his wayfarer gift.

"Hey, thanks for coming," I say.

Sloan strides over to join us and frowns. "I see why ye didn't want me mentionin' it to Fi."

"I thought it might hit too close to home for her."

"Aye, it would. The pregnancy is wreakin' havoc on her protective instincts. She's already havin' nightmares about her friends in Toronto sufferin' because she's not there to help them."

I grunt. "An hour ago, she lectured me on *my* bad dreams."

Sloan chuckles and lifts one shoulder. "She's better at puttin' out other people's fires than dealin' with her own."

True story. I gesture at the body. "Can you have a look and tell me what you think? It reminds me of what the Barghest did when they attacked the fae in the Doyles' sacred grove a few years ago."

Sloan crouches beside me, and I give him space to examine the nymph. Brendan, ever the stoic one, stands a few paces away, his gaze sweeping the gathered crowd like a searchlight cutting through fog.

I follow his gaze and watch as the onlookers murmur and shift, a mosaic of fae faces painted with loss, concern, and curiosity.

Brendan moves off to speak with them. "Why don't you all go back to your homes? There won't be any answers tonight, but I swear we'll figure this out and take good care of Randa."

"What about her tree?" one asks.

Brendan shrugs. "I don't have any connection with trees, but maybe we can ask one of the other dryads to check on Randa's home tree."

"That's not how it works," one of the fae snaps.

I tune out the rest of his conversation and focus on Sloan and his assessment of Randa. Brenny's been in the thick of things a lot more chaotic than this and has good instincts about how to deal with people.

A strong sense of community is a trait Da instilled in all of us.

While he talks to them about Randa and her tree, I share a glance with Sloan. "It's similar, right? To the energy desiccation of the Barghest?"

"Aye, it is. Although not exactly. There are signs of desiccation, but it's not so severe that I'm certain it's the cause of death."

The air holds a tang of unease, and I can't shake the feeling that something's off with the magic around here. The fae around us are a jittery bunch, their gazes flitting to the darkened alleys like they expect something to jump out at us.

"Do you feel it? The magic here has spoiled."

Sloan meets my gaze and nods. "Aye, the air is rife with toxic energy."

"Any idea who or what might cause that?"

Sloan shakes his head. "Not offhand, no. The dark magic of the Barghest had a smell to it, but it didn't feel like this."

"Didn't feel like what?" Brendan asks, back with us. "Describe it to me."

I think about that and come up with the closest description I can manage. "You know when you walk through an unseen spiderweb, and it clings to you? It's creepy and freaks you out, and you want to jump around and wipe it off your skin. It's like that."

Sloan nods. "At the same time, it curdles the contents of yer stomach."

Brendan frowns, scanning the streets. "I can't say I'm sorry not to be feeling that. Looks like being the odd man out on the magic front has advantages at times."

It's bizarre, this tingling across my skin, a sensation that's foreign and familiar. Magic has been a constant in my life even before my dip into the prana river, but this...this is a different beast.

It's like the city itself is whispering warnings, and I'm straining to make out the words. Since Fi discovered we come from a family of druids, we've faced down some pretty wild stuff, but nothing that made the air feel thick with bad mojo.

I catch the eye of a trembling pixie and leave Sloan and Brenny to go talk to her. Her wings twitch more than flutter as I draw closer. "Hey, talk to me. What's got you all spooked? What is it we feel in the air?"

She glances around, her voice a hushed rush. "The last few

nights, it's like the shadows have teeth, biting the edges of the light."

Uh-huh. All righty then.

That's just what we need, carnivorous shadows.

As I stare into the darkness of the night taking hold of the city, the weight of what that could mean settles on my shoulders like a yoke. Mother Nature made me the champion of this island, and it's on me to keep these people safe.

Am I cut out for this?

I have some solid druid tricks up my sleeve, but facing down an unknown magical menace is leagues away from anything I've done before.

As a sidekick for Fi, sure, but not on my own.

Hey, if Mother Nature believes in me, I guess it's a question of fake it 'til I make it, right?

I draw in a deep breath and let it out slowly. It's time to step up and prove to myself that I'm the protector Isilon needs.

All right. Let's do this.

3

BRENDAN

Da taught me years ago that the best way to assess what happened at a crime scene is to stand back and watch. Study the physical evidence. Pay close attention to the gawkers who come out to rubberneck. Always consider the scene as a stage set for an investigator to use for context.

That advice has never steered me wrong.

Everyone complaining that the energy here feels dark and sickening and the air is thick with the weight of something gone wrong is a new one, but I'm sure the same principles apply.

I circle the body, my boots barely whispering against the grass as I crouch. The nymph has an otherworldly grace even in the grip of death.

Her skin stands as a sad testament to the type of death she might have suffered, but unlike Emmet and Sloan, I've never seen anything like it.

No blood, no bruises, no sign of a struggle. Nothing to show for what snuffed out her light. Only the weird withering, like her life was sucked out of her.

"Emmet mentioned you might have seen something like this before?" I ask Sloan.

He straightens and brushes his hands together. "Aye, similar but not the same. There's no way to be sure unless we conduct a proper examination."

"Is that something your father does at his clinic?"

Sloan tilts his head from side to side. "He has the ability and the equipment to do it, although he usually deals with the livin' and not the dead."

"Unfortunately, that's not where we are."

Emmet returns from his chat with the onlookers. "Anything?"

I turn my back to the crowd and shrug. "The grove appears undisturbed. The surrounding flora and fauna seem unaffected. The body's position is unremarkable. There are sightlines to the buildings across the street, but the deep shadows cast by the structures or trees could provide cover for any manner of assailant while the moon falls behind the clouds."

Emmet makes a face. "This will sound weird, but when I asked the faeries why they are so jumpy, one of them told me the shadows have teeth and are biting the edge of the light."

I blink. "Do you have an extra decoder ring for that statement?"

"Not on me. No."

"Any idea what that means?"

"Not even a little."

"Okay then. We'll take that literally for now because this is a magical realm, and I don't know shit. Maybe the shadows *do* have teeth, or maybe the faeries have been into the magic mushrooms."

Sloan scrubs a hand over his jaw. "Weel, I know a great deal about the magical world, and while species such as phantoms, ghouls, and wraiths can slip in and out of the shadows without detection, I've never heard of shadows themselves being able to devour people."

I shrug. "It's early in the investigation, so we won't discount anything off the top. For now, we'll consider all possibilities."

The crowd gives up their sorrowful vigil for the night, and as the last of our faery fan club heads off, Kidok makes his way over. When he stares down at the dead girl, he sighs. "It's a horror."

Emmet rubs his nape. "Yeah, it is. This isn't our usual alley brawl or misplaced magic—this is something else, something that has its claws in deep."

"Do we know anything?" Kidok asks.

"Nothing for sure, no."

"Do ye want me to take the girl to Stonecrest Castle and have my father examine her?"

"Well, we can't stand here looking pretty." I feel more useless on this scene than I have since my rookie year. "Yeah, see what your father can find out. Thanks."

"Of course." Sloan gently picks up the girl before portaling out.

When he's gone, I look around the scene again. "I say we head to the security office and come back here when there's daylight, and we can see what we're doing."

"I'll meet you there," Kidok replies. "If you don't mind, I'd like to check on HaiLe and the cubs first and let her know what's happened."

"Good idea," Emmet agrees. "Maybe tell her to keep the kids inside tomorrow instead of letting them play in the streets. Just to be safe."

Kidok thinks that's a decent idea and strides off. With only the two of us, Emmet and I make tracks and head back toward the city's center.

"I can't believe this is happening." Em rubs his chest. "That poor girl."

I smile in the darkness and set a hand on his shoulder. "You've always been the heart of the family, Em. It's nice that even after everything else has changed, that's still a constant."

Emmet shakes his head. "Fiona's always been our heart."

"Nah. Fiona's our glue. She's the touchstone that keeps us grounded when the world's axis spins, but you're our heart. I'm sorry I wasn't around more while you were in high school. I would've told you that working a beat probably wasn't your thing."

Emmet shrugs. "I did okay."

"I'm sure you did. It's just you were always meant for more than being a badge in the sea of blue."

"And here we are."

"Yep. Here we are."

We stride through the city's streets, our pace brisk, my gaze scanning the depths of the shadows every step of the way.

Shadows have teeth, biting the edges of the light.

No iteration of that description is good.

The security office is a shiny bronze building with engraving across the roofline like the Elgin Marbles. When Emmet and Sarah were first here to help Isilon with its reawakening, the doors were locked, and entrance was denied.

Then, during the weekend of Fiona's wedding—when the city took her guests hostage—Isilon allowed us inside to access the portal gate.

The city still has a will of its own as it comes out of hibernation.

Inside, Emmet and I are greeted by a myriad of screens staring blankly at us from the half a dozen monitoring stations and the hologram mapping system dancing over the war table in the center of the room.

A meshwork of pulsing lines and shifting images sprawl before us. Emmet leans over the console, his fingers flying across the surface to call up any imaging data gathered over the past twenty-four hours.

"Anything unusual?" I ask.

"In the thirty seconds since we got here? No."

Oh yeah, right. "These are the moments I wish I still smoked. There's something to be said for doing something soothing with your hands."

Emmet snorts. "That's what she said."

I roll my eyes. "I wish. Who is she and when can I soothe her things?"

Emmet waggles his brows. "Talk to Dionysus, man. Tell him what you need, and I bet there will be a pair of raunchy females waiting for you when you get back to the apartment tonight."

I make a face. "First, I don't need a pimp. I'm completely capable of connecting with a woman and finding my calisthenics partners. Second, why raunchy? Maybe I want a nice, wholesome girl to spend time with."

Emmet tips his head back and busts a gut. "Oh, gods, sometimes you slay me."

Rude.

"Did I hear my name?"

I jump and turn as Dionysus appears beside me in a burst of golden mist. "Holy shit! Don't do that."

The guy's brow pinches. "Do what?"

"Just appear beside me. Do you ever use a door?"

"I can if that makes you feel better." A doorframe appears beside me, and Dionysus opens it from behind and steps through. "Better?"

I let out a long breath to release my annoyance and remember that aside from being one of the most powerful Greek demi-gods in the pantheon, he's also Fiona's bestie. "Thank you."

He nods, and his brown curls bounce playfully against his bare shoulders. With him wearing only some kind of ancient, pleated skirt, there is a shit ton too much skin showing in front of me right now.

"Dude, do you wear shirts?"

His eyes widen as he grins. "Yes. Shirts, tunics, sashes, chitons, himations, and after a few kegs of wine, I've even been known to put on a peplos or two."

I stare at the guy chuckling at his own joke and have no idea what he's giggling about.

Scrubbing a hand over my stubbled jaw, I fight to keep this civil. "Is there something we can do for you?"

Dionysus smiles blankly and shrugs. "I don't think so. I thought I heard Emmet say there was something I could do for you."

Something Emmet is doing affects the holographic table and the images flicker like an uncoordinated firefly on PCP at a rave. The city's all there, sparkling and spinning, and it throws out this ghostly light that makes everything look like we're underwater.

"Brenny's cranky because he misses his motorcycle and getting laid to let off steam." Emmet is barely paying attention to us. "I told him you were the man to talk to if his life is lacking in the finery of females, fornication, and macho moments."

Dionysus curls his fingers into a heart and presses them against his bare chest. "You get me, Em. Mad love."

Emmet winks. "Right back atcha, Greek."

I'm not sure what kind of player's handbook I missed out on in the years before my second chance, but there's so much I don't understand about my family's relationship with this man.

I mean…why does he hang around here when he's a freaking god of the Greek pantheon?

"Because I'm a Cumhaill." Dionysus frowns. "Da welcomed me into the family. I'm going to be the demi-god-father to Fiona's baby. And Gran is teaching me how to can preserves. That's why."

Energy snaps in the air, and Dionysus is gone.

Emmet stops typing and frowns at me. "Dude, what did you say to him?"

"Nothing."

My kid brother gives me the stink eye. "Well, I've known Dionysus for years now. He doesn't storm off, and he doesn't get offended easily. You said something that hurt his feelings."

"I was wondering why he's always here. He's a god of Olympus, yet he's always hanging around at the pub drinking or shadowing Fi. He does understand that *Sloan* is her husband and father of her kid and not him, right?"

Emmet goes back to typing. "You fucked up just now, bro, and I'm calling you on it. Dionysus is one of the sweetest beings of all the realms, and he loves us, and we love him. He's here because he belongs here. I'm not sure what thistle is stuck up your ass, but you need to work it out."

I roll my eyes. "I didn't say a fucking word."

"But you thought it, and like you said, Dionysus is a god of Olympus. He hears your thoughts, and you hurt his feelings."

I press at the tension headache taking root over my eyes. "We're not in junior high, Em. He's a grown-ass adult."

"In some ways, yes. In other ways, he needs reassurance and nurturing. He's good people and has had our backs every time we've ever needed him, no matter what it cost him. If you know what's good for you, you'll apologize."

"Why? Do you think he'll come after me?"

Emmet gives me a droll stare. "No, dumbass. It'll be Fiona who comes after you, and with her emotions all muddied up in baby-making, your ass will be grass."

Emmet

I focus on my work and leave Brenny to chew on that. As much as I'd like to see Fiona kick some sense into him, I get that he's struggling. He's out of sync with us. He missed a huge chunk of time as part of the family, and we all changed and moved on while he was gone.

Sucks to be him.

He chose undercover. He got shot. He needs to figure out how that looks now that he's back.

An energy feedback snaps between my fingers and the table

controls, and I yank back my hands. Every sensor hums, buzzing with the fae juice arcing off me.

Okay, so maybe Brenny isn't the only one feeling hostile. The bad juju from the grove is sticking with me.

I shake my arms and work on ridding myself of the wrongness that has sunk its claws deep into the edge of my consciousness.

It's like dark magic has taken up residence in my skin.

I glance at Brendan and consider that maybe his mood has been affected too. I almost offer that to him as an explanation, but bite my tongue.

There's a chasm between him and the rest of us, and it's been the elephant in the room since he got back.

Maybe it's about his death and getting left out of the magic gift doling that followed.

Maybe he's missed too much and hasn't caught up.

Maybe dying did a number on him and he needs time and understanding.

Before I can come up with any answers on that, the security feed blinks across multiple screens on multiple consoles. My gaze darts from one screen to another, searching for anomalies or anything out of place.

Nothing.

Isilon is a labyrinth, and I don't know what I'm searching for. There are no cameras in the grove and if our culprit is a shadow, how will I find it?

I scan the screens, hunting for anything that doesn't belong.

Nothing. Zip. Nada.

"This is dumb," I mutter, stepping back from the table before my fluctuating energy shorts the thing out. "Astrid, can you join us, please?"

With my request comes the arrival of Astrid. The magically generated guide to the city materializes out of thin air. She takes on a different persona depending on the person who calls her.

For Brendan and me, she always appears as Lara Croft from *Tomb Raider*, right down to those tight little shorts and the weapons strapped to those gorgeous thighs.

That I might have a thing for a hologram is sad. I get that. The sources for sexual inspiration are few and far between on an almost uninhabited island with only a few fae races and my family living here.

So, yeah, I might occasionally lose myself in Netflix and video games and let reality drift into the background.

Tonight is straight to business. "One of our members was killed tonight. I need you to check the portal gates. Make sure our seals are holding tight, and the enchantments haven't been tampered with."

Her head cants to one side and her long braid swings freely beside her arm. By the distant look in her eyes, she's already scanning through layers of magic and data.

While she does that, I pivot back to the holographic map of the city and study its web of streets, courtyards, and green spaces. There are huge sections of the city that haven't awoken yet and other areas we haven't begun to explore.

Our bad guy could be anywhere.

Minutes tick by before Astrid's voice slices through the silence. "The security protocols are intact. No breaches detected."

I should feel relieved, but her words don't sit right. We have a dead nymph, and if her killer didn't come from outside our community, the danger is here, within our walls.

Whoever or whatever took that nymph's life is hiding among us. That's a whole different kind of scary.

There's a heavy bang on the door, and Brenny jogs over to see who's calling. "Hey, fellas."

He steps back and opens the door as wide as it will go to let in Bruin, Fiona's Kodiak bear companion, with my pine marten animal companion Doc riding atop his broad shoulders.

As Bruin lumbers into the space, Doc springs onto the holographic table, his little claws clicking against the surface. "What's the craic? Why did the two of you leave the pub so early?"

I exchange a look with Brendan. "No craic tonight, I'm afraid, buddy. There's been a death. A nymph's body was found in the grove a few hours ago."

"What kind of death?" Bruin asks. "Natural or intentional?"

"Looks like intentional, Bear." I hold my hand out for Doc to climb my arm and settle across my shoulders. When he's perched on my shoulder, I run my fingers through his soft brown and white fur while I think.

"At first glance, it looks like her essence was drained somehow. Sloan took the body to Wallace's clinic. We should know more soon."

"Do we have any idea who might be responsible?" Doc asks.

I relay the question.

"Not really." Brenny steps up to the opposite side of the table. "The only thing we could get out of the fae who found her was that the shadows are alive and possibly dangerous."

"The shadows?" Bruin asks.

I nod. "Yes, the shadows. Listen. I want the two of you to patrol the Cumhaill-de-sac at night. Until we know more, I want you on alert to keep the family safe."

"Do you think I'll need my battle armor?" Doc asks.

I try not to chuckle. "Oh, yeah, dude. Definitely your battle armor."

Doc calls forward the battle armor Dionysus gifted him when Bruin calls his forward. Then he scampers across the table and jumps onto his back. "On it. Manx will want to come too. We should swing by and get him first."

Bruin smiles. "Aye, consider the family under our watch. And know this, not even the gods will be able to help anyone who tries to harm them. I will shred them into tiny confetti bits."

Doc chitters his agreement, and the two trot off.

"Well then." Brenny arches a brow. "I didn't catch those last bits, but I guess we don't have to worry about the home front and can focus on the problems at hand."

Even so, it's time to raise the alarm. Pulling out my phone, I text the family WhatsApp chat room.

On your toes, people. A nymph was found dead in the grove tonight, and there are rumors of something wicked lurking in the shadows. Buddy system until further notice.

The replies start cascading almost instantly, each one a buzz against the palm of my hand. It's a symphony of concern and readiness from the fam jam.

Do you need us? Dillan asks.

Nothing to do yet, I text back.

Do you want me to check the wards on the portal gate? Nikon asks.

Astrid assures me they're secure, but if you want to, take someone with you.

Pick me up, Greek. I'll go, Dillan offers.

Is that where Sloan disappeared to? Fiona asks.

Yeah, I asked him to take the body to Wallace's clinic to determine cause of death. Bruin, Doc, and Manx will patrol your street. Fi, can you ask the dragons to keep watch over the city through the night?

Will do. Let us know if you need us.

Thanks. We'll know more when Sloan gets back.

Morning meeting? Calum asks.

Great room breakfast buffet? Dillan suggests.

Got you covered, Dionysus adds.

K. Watch your six, boys, Calum warns.

You too, I text.

With the warning dispatched and acknowledged, I refocus on the task. Somewhere out there, someone is responsible for that nymph's death…and I aim to find them.

4

BRENDAN

I leave Emmet to his screens and texts and decide to take another look at the scene. Yes, I know he told everyone to buddy up, but something about the grove calls me. Besides, working undercover, you get used to relying on yourself and your instincts.

My gut tells me that whoever killed the nymph is long gone. They preyed upon a delicate female alone in the grove because they could overpower her and steal her magical essence.

Ha! Good luck trying that with me.

As it happens, I'm one of the few people here with no magical essence. Ergo, I shouldn't be in danger.

I thread through Isilon's muted avenues and feel more at home in this moment of uncertainty and danger than I have since I arrived here.

This I understand.

This gets my adrenaline flowing and makes me truly feel alive and not just living. Is it totally whacked that I'm at my best when the world around me is at its worst?

I'm sure the department shrink might have something to say about that, but hey, I don't have to go there anymore.

Maybe that's why my reality is a little warped.

Maybe all those years living undercover broke my "normal" meter.

Boots to cobblestone beats out a quiet resolve as I close the distance to the scene. Whether the *shadows* attacked Randa or something hiding *within* them did, I'll get to the bottom of it.

I'm not excited there's been a death and now there's a mystery to solve, but it's given me a purpose I've lacked.

I take in the scene when I get to the edge of the green space. The quaint little grove is more than silent. There's an absence of noise that almost feels like the trees are holding their breath.

Does the nymph's oak know what happened? Do nymphs communicate with trees the way humans communicate? Could another tree nymph talk to Randa's tree and get its account of things?

The fae said that's not how things work, but how exactly *do* things work?

I make a note on my phone to ask Emmet about that. He mentioned that Fiona's friend Myra is a tree nymph. If I could talk to her, I might be able to get some answers on how things work.

Would she come here and talk to the oak?

I kneel and brush my fingers over the dark, cool grass. Moisture seeps through the knees of my jeans as I shake off the tension of the past few hours. Drawing a deep breath, I rest my hands against my thighs, close my eyes, and listen.

Is the energy here still toxic? If the energy clears, does that mean the unsub has been gone long enough that their dark energy dissipated or was the dark magic residue attached to Randa's body?

Focused as I am on my senses, I notice when the air drops a few degrees.

Opening my eyes, I search the shadows.

Am I still alone?

I rise. My steps are deliberate as I patrol the boundary of the tree line. The moon above is a silent witness, bathing the trees in a ghostly light that stretches their shadows into grasping fingers on the forest floor.

When the skin at the back of my neck tingles with an irritating burn, I scratch the itch.

It feels like someone is watching me.

A flicker in my peripheral vision yanks my focus, and I spin on my heel, every muscle tensing. My hand snaps to my side, grasping for a weapon that's not there anymore.

My gaze narrows, slicing through the darkness, hunting for the wisp of movement that ghosted out of sight. Did I see it, or are the shadows playing tricks on me? I wait, ready for anything, or so I tell myself.

The shadows might be playing tricks, but I've learned to trust the niggling in my gut. It has saved my hide more times than I can count. It's also what got me killed. I didn't hesitate to step between the shooter and that woman and her little girl.

I wouldn't hesitate even if I was back in that moment and knew how it would turn out.

Come on, show yourself.

Stepping silently, I creep deeper into the enchanted grove. I've been in the family's sacred grove enough with Fiona and my brothers to know about flying rabbits, brownies, and pixies, but my instincts tell me what's out there is bigger than that.

And more dangerous.

Maybe this—whatever *this* is—is why everything is so quiet. Step by step, I ease forward, wishing I had my Glock in my hand instead of a stick I picked up off the ground.

I'm not about to jump at shadows like some rookie, but I have to admit the suspense is killing me. There's something here. I can feel its presence.

Stretching my neck from side to side does nothing to ease the tension. The feeling of someone watching me is back. I scan the darkness. Dammit. If there was one magical advantage I would pick in life, it would be night vision because this sucks.

Dividing my attention between my surroundings and the placement of my next step, I navigate deeper into the shadows. Adrenaline pumps hard in my veins, and I strain to hear past the rush of blood flowing in my ears.

The hit comes from above, and I'm taken off-guard, knocked backward by a blur of fur and little hands wrapping around my head.

I drop the stick and grab the little beast, but damn, the thing has suckerfished onto my face.

"Ow, stop pulling my hair."

The maniacal giggle I get for that is maddening.

Twisting as I stagger, the heel of my boot catches on a root, and I fall backward into a bramble bush. The fall knocks my furry face mask to the side, and with one wide eye, I glimpse the bush I'm lying on come to life.

Thorny vines whip out with startling ferocity. I roll to the side, narrowly avoiding getting tangled in the flailing ropes.

"It's a guardian bramble," a female voice calls from somewhere in the canopy. "Get away from the Strix nest it's protecting."

"Where's the nest?" I mumble against the belly of whatever asshole furball is teabagging me. "I can't fucking see."

"Roll to your right. Once you get out of the proximity, it'll stop attacking."

Ignoring the indignity of it all, I roll.

I roll like a motherfucker.

I roll until I crack into the trunk of another tree, then scramble onto my hands and knees and crawl.

The female laughter that follows me is degrading, but honestly, I'm sure I look like a total tool.

When the bush stops trying to kill me, I drop onto my ass and work on removing my furry facemask. The thing has its leathery fingers woven into my hair and holds on with a vice grip.

"Dude, get off my face. Seriously. What's your damage?" Nothing I do works no matter how hard I try, so I take another tack and go the niece and nephew route, tickling the thing.

A peal of cackling laughter rings through the grove, and I know I'm onto something. With a big breath, I raspberry the belly against my face, and it releases its hold and falls backward into my hands.

A knot of frustration twists in my gut.

As much as I want to throttle the little bugger, it's cute AF and has a big, stupid grin on its face and wide, joy-filled eyes.

Finally able to breathe again after all of that, I lean back against the tree trunk and bring up my knees to cradle him in my lap. "Seriously, dude. That was not cool. You nearly got me shredded by a feral shrub."

Bigger than a Mogwai but smaller than an Ewok, he looks like a blue and gold spotted teddy bear love child.

"What the hell are you? Do you speak? Do you understand what I'm saying to you?"

The smile on his little face grows wider, and he reaches up and taps a finger on my nose. "Boop."

I blink. Did this little Yub Nub boop me after the drop-down drag-out of him dry-humping my face for five minutes?

I scan the darkness of the grove to see if anyone witnessed my humiliation. At least one person did. The female who warned me away from that possessed protector plant had a front-row seat to my moment of shame.

I don't see her, though.

I don't see anyone.

Right, because it's the middle of the fucking night, and anyone with any sense has turned in and locked down until morning.

"It's late, little dude. Head home and tuck in for the night. And be careful. I hear dangerous things are lurking in the shadows around here."

After setting the fuzzy little fool down, I brush the detritus and debris off my black jeans and T-shirt, and head back the way I came.

Note to self: Not all noises need to be investigated.

As I break free from the line of trees near the street, I stare at the palace up the hill where Em and I live. It's a softly glowing golden tower with a domed roof, and ever since Fiona coined it the golden dildo, I can't look at it and not see how phallic it is.

I try not to think about it because it's my home.

Striding out of the green space and back toward the more heavily populated part of the city, I rub the tingle on the back of my neck for the second time tonight. I glance up at the buildings as I pass.

Are there people living up there? Could they have seen something when the nymph was attacked?

I need to check the settlement map tomorrow. Ninety-nine percent of the city has yet to be repopulated, but someone might be living in this area.

Unlike Yub Nub, the woman who warned me off the nesting site spoke perfect English and might be able to answer some questions about the grove and what the others sense in the shadows.

"Looks like I'll be back again at the crack of dawn."

Yeah, maybe fresh eyes and daylight will give Em and me something more to work with.

For tonight, I'm done.

5

EMMET

The great room pulses with a symphony of familial chatter and the tantalizing scents of a Dionysian feast. I step inside the long, rectangular space and take a moment to absorb the dynamics of our crew.

Calum and Aiden are out on the stone terrace, shooting the shit with Dionysus and his boyfriend Jonah.

Nikon and Dillan are sprawled out on the floor with their young ones.

Fiona is hanging out with Kinu at the buffet.

Aiden's four kids, Jackson, Meg, Caragh, and Ireland, are running around in a game of "follow the swooping purple pseudo dragon" as Dillan's familiar leads them on a jaunty chase.

These are the moments I live for.

While I would prefer if the fam jam had gathered because of a holiday or a birthday and not a murder update, living here alone for so long taught me to be thankful for *all* the moments.

"Uncle Emmet!" Meg breaks away from the dragon chase to run across the room and throw herself at me. "Will you turn into a panda so I can rub your belly?"

I chuckle and tug the ends of her two braids. "Not this morning, Meg, sorry. I've got island stuff to take care of. Why don't you rub Bruin's belly? He has lots of fur and lots to rub."

Meg follows my gesture to the mountain of chestnut brown fur in the corner. The mound of bear rises and falls in concert with the loud, resonant snore of a deep sleep.

"We can't bug Bruin. Auntie Fi said he was up all night with Doc and Manxy. She said he's cranky pants when he doesn't get sleep, so we need to leave him alone."

"Well, Auntie Fi knows best," I agree loud enough so my sister hears me and chuckles.

Jackson gives up on chasing the dragon with the twins and joins us. "Hey, Uncle Em. Are you still going dragon riding later?"

"As much as I'd love to say yes, there's an island issue that needs my attention today, buddy."

He lifts his chin, inviting me to say more, and I tilt my head toward his six-year-old sister. He's old enough to understand that we don't get into things in front of the little ones. "Maybe once you get that sorted?"

"Count on it. In the meantime, if you're playing with Binx or any of his brothers or sisters, I want you inside either HaiLe's house or one of ours, okay?"

He nods. "Da said that too."

"Okay, good." I ruffle his hair and point at a smorgasbord that could make Olympus envious. "I'm going to make a plate. Have you eaten?"

"Yeah, I'm good."

As my nephew trots off to join his dad and the others on the balcony, I say good morning to Fi and Kinu by the buffet. "Wow, nice spread."

Fruits jostle for space around pastries, while robust platters of meats and cheeses flank hot serving bins of omelets, back bacon, hash browns, and pancakes.

"Dionysus, you never cease to amaze me. Thanks for this, dude."

Even with him standing outside and talking to the others, he nods in response. The guy is a marvel and has been a welcome addition to our family.

After heaping my plate full, I turn to stand with Fi, who eyes my selection like a sailor who's been too long at sea.

"There's plenty here, sista. You don't have to look so longingly and not grab yourself a plate."

She groans. "I was waiting for Sloan. He went to Stonecrest Castle this morning to find out what Wallace learned about the body. I figured we'd eat together when he got back."

I snort and shovel a forkful of cheesy hash browns into my mouth. "Who are you kidding, Fi? You could eat a plate now and another plate when Irish gets back in ten minutes. No need to abstain. If my baby niece is hungry, feed her."

"That's what I said," Kinu agrees. "When I was pregnant with Jackson, I tried to eat sensibly and stay within the weight ranges on the pregnancy charts. With Meg, I was more relaxed. With the twins, Aiden had a dozen food delivery sites on speed dial and kept his babies fed."

"Smart man." Nikon strides over to us, cradling his six-month-old baby girl Melina in his arms. "I've still got my money on Baby Mac being a boy."

Fiona rubs her growing belly and shrugs. "I guess we'll see in a few months."

"Eighteen weeks and two days!" Dionysus calls from the balcony.

Fiona rolls her eyes and laughs. "Best demi-godfather evah!"

"Damn straight."

I scoop another forkful of breakfast into my mouth and laugh at the two of them. Dionysus and Fi are great for one another and have been since the day they met.

It makes what Brendan said last night even more annoying.

"What's with the face, Em?" Fi asks.

I chew longer than I need to while I think about the ramifications of telling her the truth. "Nothing. This is my normal face."

She chuckles. "No, that's your disappointed face. What's up?"

I shrug. "Something Brenny said last night is bugging me. Not to worry. I'm sure he'll get his head out of his ass and fix it."

Fi's gaze narrows. "What did he say?"

I *sooo* don't want to be the one to rat out Brendan and set Fiona on the warpath. "Switzerland."

Her eyebrows arch. "You're calling neutral territory? Now I'm even more interested. What did he say?"

I shake my head. "That's the whole point of calling Switzerland, Fi. I don't have to answer that."

Fiona crosses her arms and scowls, but she knows the rules and knows I'm right.

Nikon doesn't have the same conflict of interest since he tilts his head toward the balcony. "Brendan questioned why Dionysus is here when he has another life in the Greek pantheon."

"He didn't," Fi snaps.

I tilt my head back and forth. "Well, not really. He thought it and Dionysus picked up on it."

Fi frowns. "Picked up on it?"

"Brenny's been a little pissy about life here, right?"

Everyone nods.

"He mentioned a few things were lacking in his life and I said he should bring it up with Dionysus because the Greek's good like that. He'll help a brother out."

"He *is* good like that," Fiona agrees.

"Yeah, I know." I take a bite of my bacon. "So, Dionysus pops in and is all, 'Did I hear someone call my name?' I explained the sitch, and I guess Brenny had a burr up his ass from a day of death because he missed the whole point of what being family means to Dionysus and called him out on it."

Fiona frowns. "Tarzan didn't say a thing to me."

"He wouldn't," Nikon interjects. "Guys handle guy stuff. We don't let it spill over to our girl stuff."

"Where is Brenny?" Fi asks.

Danger. Danger. I shove another forkful of food into my mouth to give myself time to think of the best answer. "He went straight to the security building this morning to get a jump on the day. When is Sloan supposed to arrive?" I ask, blatantly changing the subject.

My sister brushes an auburn curl from her brow, her blue eyes narrowing on me like she knows exactly what I'm doing. Who are we kidding? Fi has always been able to read me. "I'm sure he'll be here soon."

"In the meantime, you should get some food into you, Red," Nikon encourages. "You look hungry. Baby-making is the toughest job there is."

She meets Nikon's comment with a roll of her eyes. "Having battled Unseelie princes, trolls, and angry sasquatches, I'll have to disagree on that, Greek. Try again."

Nikon chuckles. "Baby-making is one of the most rewarding and important jobs, so you need to keep fuel in the furnace."

She reaches over to put Melina's soother back into her mouth and relents. "Okay, I'll accept that."

The sunlight streaming through the arched openings to the balcony paints Nikon's ancient Greek features in a warm glow. Baby Melina looks more like her mommy, her hair chestnut versus his blond, her eyes brown versus his hazel.

"What's Kallista up to this morning?" I ask.

He beams at me, shifting Melina to his other arm. "She's elbow-deep in the kitchen, prepping food for my grandfather's visit in a few days."

Dionysus joins us. "Papu's coming to the island this week?"

"Yeah. He and I thought it would be nice for Kallista to have someone who knew her back when we were first married. They can speak in the ancient dialect and talk old times, and she can spoil him with traditional Rhodes cuisine."

Dionysus' grin widens. "May I remind you I also check the box in all those categories?"

Nikon nods. "She asked me this morning to make sure I invited you."

Dionysus beams. "Score!"

I chuckle, watching as Fiona eats her fill. "That puts you on babysitter duty for the day, does it?"

Nikon scoffs. "It's not babysitting when it's my child, Em. But yes, I'm on Daddy duty all day." His gaze softens as he glances down at Melina. "We have a full schedule—hanging out with Fi and Han."

"Kinu's bringing the twins over too," Fi adds, stacking bacon, hash browns, and syrup into a pancake, then rolling it into a tube and eating it like a wrap. "After their morning nap."

"Let the baby fest begin!" Dionysus cheers.

"As soon as Baby Mac's done eating and Sloan's back with the news." Fi pats her belly with a contented smile.

While Fi and Nikon go to Dillan to work out their morning plans, I take Dionysus aside. "Hey, about last night and what Brendan was thinking. Don't take it to heart. You *are* family. You are part of us. It's *him* that's struggling to figure out how he fits."

Dionysus nods. "I know. It just hurt to think that he doesn't get me. I have dozens of siblings who don't get me, but never here. This is my safe place, you know?"

I pull the guy into a hug and clap him on the back. "I know, Greek. Give him time. He misses his life in Toronto and is mourning its loss. People who are hurting sometimes hurt the people around them."

Dionysus eases back and smiles. "Thanks, Em. You know what? Instead of being sad and making this about me, let's make it about him. I have an idea."

Before I get a chance to ask what that might be, Sloan *poofs* into the room. "Good mornin', all."

"Hey, hotness," Fiona replies while refilling her plate. "Do you want to get it while it's hot or talk first?"

In truth, Dionysus' feasts always remain fresh, hot, and delicious. It's a good thing because there isn't enough room in any fridge for the amount of food he lays out in one of his spreads.

"Go ahead and make yerself a plate, *a ghra*. I'll help myself in a bit."

Fiona digs in, and I laugh. "He doesn't have to tell you twice, does he?"

"Hells no." Fi slides a mushroom omelet onto her plate. "What did Wallace figure out, hotness?"

Sloan looks around the room and points at Jackson. "Would ye mind takin' yer sisters onto the balcony to look at the big dragons fer a bit, buddy?"

"Island business?" he asks.

I nod. "Yeah, and we don't want the little kids to get upset or hear too much. Make sense?"

Jackson nods. "I'm not a little kid. I'm nine."

"No. Of course you aren't. We'll fill you in later."

He considers that and nods. "Okay, monkeys, let's go see the big dragons flying over the houses."

Jackson herds his three younger sisters onto the balcony and Aiden strides in to join us. "Okay, Irish, what do you know?"

Sloan checks that the kids are out of earshot and frowns. "The wee nymph was drained of her fae essence, as we suspected."

"Could your father tell who did the draining?"

Sloan shakes his head. "The desiccation hid any possible point of siphonin'."

"What types of creatures and beings siphon magical energy?" Calum looks at Sloan and Dionysus.

"Too many," Dionysus replies.

Sloan counters, "Aye, but if the wards truly haven't been

breached, our list narrows. It would have to be somethin' or someone here in the city."

"If the city is awakening after a thousand years of dormancy, is it possible that other beings could be coming out of hibernation, too?" Fi asks.

Sloan regards Dionysus and nods. "Aye, that's a possibility, *a ghra*."

Those words hang in the air, heavy like a fog rolling off the moors. We have no idea how many people died here when the Light Weavers hid the city, and Isilon went dormant.

"Was there a manifest of citizens?" Fi asks.

"Is that something Astrid could find after all these centuries?" I wonder.

A sense of unease crawls up my spine as I meet the worried gazes of my family. We've come up against empowered monsters before but what makes this hit home even harder is that this isn't happening in Montreal or San Francisco. It's happening here— where our family lives.

"Okay, the first thing we need to do is figure out who and what can drain magical essence," I direct. "Also, if any of those species were present during the downfall of Isilon."

"I'm not the only one seeing a giant neon Dark Weavers sign flashing in the sky, am I?" Calum asks.

Sloan scrubs a hand over his jaw. "Obviously that's a consideration, but we don't know enough about them to know if the kind of desiccation Randa suffered applies."

Dillan frowns. "So, we need to know what races could do this and if any of them were—or are—here."

"And possibly how a Dark Weaver might be involved," Calum adds.

I draw a deep breath and meet Dillan's gaze. "Can Eva help us with this? She must've seen every kind of death possible in her years as a reaper. She might be able to tell us who our culprit is."

Dillan brushes a finger over the downy feathers of his baby boy. "She left last night for her next guardian assignment."

"When do you think she'll be home?"

"Not for a few days unless I call her back sooner."

Damn. As much as I'd love to ask the angel what she knows about species desiccation, reanimation, and hibernation, we can't wait a couple of days. We also can't call a guardian angel back from her duties to answer questions.

"All right. Sloan, are you willing to spend a day hitting the books with me?"

Fiona snorts. "You slay me, Em."

Sloan flashes a smile. "I'm at yer service, Em. Whatever ye need." His words are casual, but his eyes are all business. Being the scholar of the group and a historian to boot, Sloan's exactly the man I need for this part of the investigation.

"Who else is around today?" I ask.

Aiden and Calum shake their heads. "Sorry. We're helping Garnet with a vampire issue in Toronto."

Dillan shrugs. "I'm on Daddy duty, but if Fi's good for more than a play date, I can help."

Fiona nods. "Of course. Han and I will be fine. We'll move the play date to your house, so we have everything for however long you're busy."

As Sloan heads off to fuel up for the impending research marathon, I return my attention to Dillan and the storm cloud he's projecting. "What's up? Why do you look so constipated?"

"Fuck you. You're constipated. I'm fabulous."

Okeedokee. "Can you and Dionysus hit the streets and find out what the citizens meant by the shadows having teeth and biting the night?"

He scoffs. "It means nothing. That's stupid."

"Right, but let's pretend it *isn't* stupid and the scared people living in my city were telling me something they couldn't quite describe."

"We can do it," Dionysus agrees.

"Thanks, Greek."

Dillan hands Fi his angel baby. Han's fluffy white wings flutter as he stirs in his sleep. "I'm getting my Cloak of Knowledge. Maybe it can make sense of that, even though it *is* stupid."

"Cool. Maybe take another run at the grove now that we have daylight."

Divide and conquer.

It's a strategy that has served us well on many occasions. "Everyone, be careful. We don't know what we're dealing with yet."

6

BRENDAN

The morning sun casts a colorful pink hue over Randa's giant oak and the scene of her death. Despite how the warmth of the summer day has taken hold, it does nothing to ease the icy chill that settled deep in my bones last night.

An innocent girl is dead, and from what we've surmised, it was a torturous, agonizing end to a young life.

The locals are afraid of what's in the shadows.

Even I felt the unnerving burn of unseen eyes watching me while I was here.

As much as I brushed that sensation off to it being Yub Nub, the female I never truly got to see, or possibly another fae inhabitant of the grove, the more I stew over it, the less I think so.

Bright and early, I give the area another once-over, my cop instincts screaming that I missed something in the dark.

There's nothing.

The grove by night is the same grove by day. The light swallows the secrets that seemed shrouded by shadows last night. As I wander between the trees and the wild overgrowth of a magical grove, I keep one eye on the branches and canopy above.

Being dive-bombed and booped by a fuzzy blue beastie is a

"once is enough" experience. No need for a repeat performance from the little bugger.

I finish my scan of the crime scene and return to the perimeter of the tree line, turning my attention to the row of abandoned buildings along the street.

This city area holds a fancy-schmancy air, and I could see the governor of Emhain Abhlach living here with the magical Grand Poobah and the local celebrities.

According to our master list of what houses have been claimed by the new arrivals, nothing along this street has been assigned.

There are several buildings tall enough and with enough windows looking down here that anyone playing Peeping Tom could've gotten an eyeful.

Enough to witness what happened to the nymph.

Or possibly enough to plot their attack on the girl.

If so, I'll either find them or at least where they hid in the shadows doing their creepy peepy thang.

I stride off and head toward the nearest building first. It's a long-forgotten three-story brick home with arched entrances and leaded-glass windows. A twist of the ornate knob and a long, creaking moan of the hinges brings me into the foyer.

I half expect the building to protest my intrusion, but it seems I'm welcome enough. Inside, dust motes dance in the slanting beams of morning light, and the air smells of must and old memories.

Room by room, I search for any sign of life—or afterlife even. A perch, a hideout, anything.

There's nothing.

I get into a rhythm as I exit and move from building to building. It's fascinating to walk through the private spaces of beings from other cultures and races whose existence ended over a thousand years ago.

It reminds me of Pompeii.

I've never been to the historic site, but I've watched documentaries where people walk through the homes that have been unearthed. The fossilized loaves of bread and bowls and cutlery were still on the tables. The artistic mosaics still lined the floors. The murals and artwork still adorned the walls of homes buried under twenty feet of ash and pumice stone.

Incredible.

The silence hangs heavy as my steps echo in the empty spaces. This side of the city feels like a ghost town, and it's not lost on me how eerie it is…especially with the comments about the malevolent shadows.

If someone was watching from any of these buildings, they were damn good at covering their tracks.

I exit yet another home and look at the next one along the cobbled street. Sunlight bounces off its domed tower, catching my eye and glinting like a beacon of promise.

"That one has got to offer a better view." I quicken my pace, the rubber soles of my boots tapping a steady rhythm on the ancient stones as I jog up the front steps and try the door.

Strangely enough, it's locked.

I'm not sure if it's an Isilon thing or the fact that the city died under the attack of Dark Weavers, but the only doors we found locked were the doors the sentient city itself wanted to keep sealed.

This feels different.

"Okay, Plan B." With a glance up to figure out my path, I scale the brick retaining wall bordering the empty flower beds. The poor dirt boxes are aching for a gardener's touch, but it suits me fine.

From the stone cap on the flower bed, I jump and reach for the railing of the second-story balcony. When my fingers grip the cold iron rail, I haul myself up with a grunt.

I try to get in through the balcony door, but it won't budge either. My choices are up, over to the next balcony, or give up and go back down.

Ha! Da didn't raise no quitters.

Neither going up nor over holds any obvious advantage, so I go with the one that will cause the least damage if I fail and fall.

Over to the next balcony, it is.

Balancing on the balls of my feet, I climb onto the far edge of the railing and grip the brickwork. The rough jags of brick and mortar meet the fleshy pads of my fingers, and I swing my boot to the side, searching for a toehold big enough to take my weight.

The neglect of a thousand years didn't translate to the city's architecture. The place didn't age so much as sleep. Still, I find a little masonry ledge that seems strong enough, so I test it.

When it holds, I step back to the rail to figure out where my second step will be. Once I've mapped out the path where I think I can make it across, I throw caution to the wind and give it a go.

It takes sweat and a few choice words, but I get to the next balcony without breaking my neck.

I consider that a win.

The door here doesn't open either, but an open window beckons me from beyond.

By the time I make it over to the window and grip the frame, I feel more myself than I have in the eighteen months since I was re-alived.

Once I swing a leg and roll over the windowsill, I'm pretty damned psyched.

Yay me!

That's when an eerie feeling crawls over me like spiders skittering down my spine. My breath mists in the air, a ghostly exhalation in the room's stillness.

I shouldn't be here.

Every instinct within me screams for me to get out.

I look out the window and consider leaving, but it doesn't

make sense. There's work to do, and I'll be damned if I let a little chill and a case of the creeps get in the way.

Stepping deeper into the elegant mansion, I'm gobsmacked. I've entered a realm that defies the ordinary, where the arcane pulses through the walls.

The interior stands as a tapestry of grandeur and gloom. I entered at the end of the hall, so I explore the second story as I head toward the staircase.

There are the mundane rooms one would expect to find—a sitting room, a powder room, and a spare bedroom.

I also find what looks like a magician's laboratory, a place of alchemical experimentation and magical research. Flasks, beakers, and arcane instruments clutter the tables, alongside scattered notes written in a cryptic script and Celtic symbols.

There are symbols on the walls and floors as well. They're painted over the door frames and inlaid in circles using the floor's mosaic tiling.

I'm careful not to step within those circles.

The city has been asleep for over a thousand years, but it's waking up, and there is no telling what else might wake up at the same time. There is also no telling what kind of magic the inhabitants once practiced here.

The air is thick with the scent of stillness. It's a smell that sticks to the back of your throat and makes you think of long-forgotten legends.

The truth is, I'm not here to admire the building's history. The domed tower that rises three stories above my head offers the greatest potential for viewing the grove and possibly watching me while I examined the scene last night.

I leave the alchemist's love nest as I found it—sleeping—and hope it stays that way.

If we're lucky, the city is all that's waking. I scan the workroom of a high-level magic user and ignore the itch between my shoulder blades.

It's warning me there are more than old memories floating around in this place.

Magic is a tricky beast, especially the kind that's been brewing in silence and building unchecked for a thousand years.

It's like a sleeping dragon—you poke it, you better be ready for the fire and fury when it wakes.

On the opposite side of the house, I confirm my theory about the owner and step into an impressive library. The black wooden shelves rise from floor to ceiling, accessible by ladders that slide along long, horizontal rails. The collection of books is amazing but with no English in sight, I don't know what they say.

It's a multi-level chamber with a spiraling iron staircase against the back wall that might lead up to the domed tower above.

I head that way, hoping I've found my way to get up to the top floor.

Ascending the iron staircase has me winding up to the next floor. Across from the landing is a black wall covered with thick gold gilded frames. They feature the aged portraits of the man I assume is the magical master of the house.

The portraits range from him being a dark-haired rake in his twenties all the way along until he's a hard-looking man in his fifties.

Tall and commanding, with sunken ice-blue eyes and a cascade of silver hair that falls to his shoulders, he wears flowing robes adorned with sigils embroidered into the lapels.

Definitely a wizard of some kind.

Staring at the image of the building's former inhabitant makes me uncomfortable, so I skip this floor and continue up the iron stairs to the top.

When I step off the top landing, the dome's apex draws my gaze. It's stunning. A celestial map of stars and constellations is painted in painstaking detail among a midnight sky frozen in time.

The stars must be glass because each celestial point lets in the morning sun, lighting them up as if they were distant points of fire.

Super cool.

Taking in the sanctum, respect for whoever this guy was floods me again. Even without a connection to magic like my siblings, I feel how the air in the room thrums with unseen energy.

For a moment, I wonder what it would feel like if I possessed my druid spark. When I first came back after the Culling, Fiona still had so much on her plate. The veil between realms was down, and there was always someone trying to kill her.

She offered to give me the druid spark that would connect me with our shared heritage, but I didn't want to take anything away from her.

She needed every bit of power she could get.

Now...

Maybe after she has the baby, I'll ask her about it. I don't want to mess with her system while she's making Baby Mac, but perhaps after...

I snort at the thought of me with druid magic.

Do I want to grow flowers at a touch and talk to the trees in the sacred grove of our family? It's lovely to see Gran do it, but no.

Do I want to be able to understand when Daisy, Doc, Manx, and Bruin speak? Yeah, that would help.

Would it be cool to throw up shields and command vines to grab people or ride a dragon and have no fear that I would fall off?

Okay, yeah, that would be cool.

For now, I'm a human cop in a realm where cops hold no advantage. My fellow officers back in Toronto are fighting the fight. My friends are in a position to make a difference. Here I am, useless and stuck in a magical world with nothing to contribute.

A visceral swell of nausea twists in my gut, and I rub the ache in my chest.

I'm lonely. I want more out of life.

But what more is there?

Here, like this, nothing.

The despair that fills me is tangible, wrapping me in a shroud. I walk over to the grand window, the view below offering a vista of the grove and cobblestoned streets.

There's a haunting beauty to this city, but it's not *my* city. Being here won't ease the weight on my soul.

Five stories…

Would jumping end the suffering?

I stare at the cobbled street below, my hand moving to test the window's mobility. My fingertips brush against the cold metal lock, the stiffness of years yielding under my touch.

I push, the lock *clinks*, and the window obliges. It tilts open with an eager creak. The rush of fresh air is a comfort. I lean forward, half out of the window, my mind grappling with the gravity of my contemplation.

The idea of ending the aching in my soul is appealing—compelling, even.

To turn off the loss and sorrow.

To end it all and to be at peace.

I open the window wider, ready to climb out.

It's better this way.

"Brendan? What the fuck are you doing?" Dillan is on the street below, glaring up at me.

What *am* I doing?

I fight against the fog of despair gripping me and step back. A glint of something in the window glass catches my eye—a reflection—but not mine.

Silver hair frames a spectral man standing directly behind me. I tense and pivot as the ghostly apparition surges forward and thrusts both hands into my chest.

My world upends as I tumble backward out the open window.

7

EMMET

The library of the Light Weavers is a sanctuary of knowledge and ancient wisdom found behind the public area of their temple. The stone walls of their temple pulse with ancient magic, alive and breathing, as though the powerful sisters who used to guard this island are still here somehow.

As we arrive, the stone walls shimmer and shift with magic and the images of five oddly tall women push forward out of the flat surface.

These are the carvings of the original Light Weavers.

Kyna, Syma, Lyri, Tany, and Jaya are the women who first recognized my connection with spatial magic and my bond with the island.

These women trained me to be a Light Weaver, although I don't know even a fraction of what they did about light manipulation magic.

I can do one spell and its reversal—hide and unhide physical things from this world.

As Sloan strides across the mosaic circle, I silently nod at my mentors.

Irish releases the security spell on the back wall. A little

"Clickety Click—Barba Trick" and a section of stone switches from fixed to moveable. The wall swings out of our way, and we enter the hidden sanctum.

"I've learned to love the smell of old parchment," I remark as we step inside.

"Aye. In my mind, it's the essence of bygone eras and untold knowledge waitin' to be rediscovered."

I like that.

"Where should we start?" I move before one of the many floor-to-ceiling shelves, daunted by the hundreds of tomes.

"Can ye read the spines of the books?"

"No. Good point." This entire search will go better if I can read the fae languages.

"Ancient spirits of wood and glen, Lend me the wisdom of ages then. Fae tongue unknown, to me reveal, Your hidden words, to me unseal.

By elder bark and mistletoe, Let this foreign script be shown. As I speak, so mote it be, Set my knowledge and understanding free."

In the moments that follow, the spell takes hold and the unknown script and runes on the page before us shimmer until something subtle clicks in my mind and I can read them.

"Done. Now what?"

"Search fer books on species, races, and creatures that feed on magical essence. As well, we should include those who use energy drainin' and desiccation as an offensive or defensive skill."

I snort. "You think that dainty wee nymph was an aggressor, and something defended itself against her?"

Irish strides over to the side wall and starts pulling books. "Och, no. But details matter, and we mustn't overlook possibilities simply because we've made assumptions about what might've happened."

"Even so, I'll start with the beings we know. Dark Weavers, necromancers, incubi, etcetera."

"Fair enough. Grab books on species lore, too. Ye never know what we might find."

"On it."

It takes us half an hour to go through the shelves and select all the books we think will help, and by the time we're sitting and sifting through pages, the massive oak table in the center of the room is heaped with textbooks, parchment rolls, and tomes.

The gentle rustling of pages creates a soft, rhythmic sound that bounces lightly off the cold stone walls. Sloan is the picture of concentration, his eyes dancing over the delicate script with a trained precision that speaks of his scholarly leanings.

I'm more haphazard in my approach, scanning through sections at random, hoping to stumble upon a hidden gem in this sea of text.

I'm on the hunt for anything—a mere mention, a whisper of a tale—that might lead us to understand the nature of the creatures that drain the life force from others. We need to figure out who did this and stop them before they do it again.

The silence between us is one of mutual understanding, broken only by the occasional thump of a book being set down in frustration.

That would be me.

Sloan is in his glory and never gets frustrated when books surround him.

I pluck another tome from the pile, its cover worn and the title barely legible. Flipping it open, I scan the pages. The words blur as I sift through the irrelevant to find that crucial piece of information we desperately need.

It's like looking for a needle in a haystack, but the needle is the key to saving lives, and the haystack is a multi-realm universe of magical creatures that may or may not be known to us.

Easy-peasy.

Frustrated with the book part, I focus on our growing list of thaumavores—beings known to feed on magic.

"So far we have wraiths that feast on spiritual energy, mana leeches that can siphon arcane power, and djinns that absorb magic to increase theirs. Succubi and incubi consume life force or magical essence through seduction. Liches can drain life. Magical siphons can be created using enchanted objects. Then there are ley line predators, some iterations of banshees, and Dementors."

Sloan arches a brow. "I don't put much stock in yer Harry Potter theory, Em."

I shrug. "There's a bit of reality in all fiction. You're the one who said we don't want to overlook things because of assumptions."

Sloan chuckles. "Aye, I did. Yer right. Dementors make the list."

"We've considered the ones that feed to sustain their life, to strengthen their magical output, or to satisfy a hunger for power. Are we missing anything?"

"Unfortunately, we are. Dark Weavers are one of the most obvious possibilities, and from what we know, they consume to annihilate other races."

"I don't get that." I circle Dark Weavers on the list. "If they consume fae energy, it makes no sense to kill off everyone they find. Eventually, they'll have no one to feed from."

"There's a Chinese proverb that says, 'To learn what is good, a thousand days are not sufficient; to learn what is evil, an hour is too long.' I'd say the fact that we can't understand the motives of the Dark Weavers is a good thing, Em. Fer now, we need to focus on stoppin' the attacker from takin' another victim."

True story.

The two of us go back to our search but before long, Sloan pauses, propping a book up in his palm to read aloud. "And lo, the essence was drawn forth, leaving naught but a husk…"

The passage brings a prickle to the nape of my neck and chills up my arms. Sloan's brogue, usually so warm, feels like the harbinger of a storm. "Yeah, that could be something. What creature is being described?"

"The Dark Weavers."

Dammit. That's a page from history I never wanted to revisit. "Astrid? Can you join us, please?"

When she arrives, I sort through what I want to ask her. "Astrid, did the condition of Randa's body bear any similarity to the damage done by the Dark Weavers a thousand years ago?"

Her digital eyes meet mine. "Yes."

The calmness of her voice slices through my hopes to the contrary like a blade. "You're sure the wards are secure, and there's been no one in or out other than our family or the immigration of Thrain and Oda last week?"

"I am certain, yes."

Relief should flood my veins, but it doesn't. Instead, a knot of anxiety tightens around my cheesy hash browns.

If they didn't *get* in, they already *were* in.

I catch Sloan's gaze, and he's thinking it too.

"Is it possible that when Isilon went dormant, he didn't kill the Dark Weavers but somehow trapped them within his hibernation?" The words taste like ash in my mouth.

Sloan's gaze hardens. "Aye, I suppose it's certainly possible. If we knew more about the race and their ways, we could say for sure, but in all these books, I've found almost nothing about them."

I think about that for a moment, and it comes to me. "I know where we might find more answers."

Sloan's brow arches. "Where is that?"

"In my apartment. Syma kept a journal. We found it when Brenny and I asked Dionysus to do the reno to make it ours. I glanced through it, but it was pretty grim stuff, so I set it aside."

"Grim how?"

"She was keeping a death tally of the end of days. It was a lot about how she and her sisters had failed the citizens and Isilon. The Dark Weaver raid was in full swing, and they were trapped.

The enemy had commandeered the portal gate and the wards and were slaughtering the entire population."

Sloan frowns. "Perhaps Syma left us details we could use for a different outcome."

I draw a deep breath. "Maybe. I didn't read it to the end. It seemed morbid. She was my friend."

"I know, sham. Maybe, with her help, we'll be able to get her and her sisters some justice in the end."

Yeah. I like that idea—I like it a lot.

Brendan

Falling....

I crack the top of my head on the window frame as I tip out of the open portal. The black spots that explode behind my eyes block my vision as I flail to get a hold of anything that might stop me from plummeting to my death.

Quick reflexes have always been my friend, but as I somersault backward and thrust my hands through the air, I realize I've grown slow and complacent over the years of my death and beyond.

With my heart jackhammering and cold sweat slick on my palms, I catch the windowsill. I'm hanging on by the tips of my fingers, but there's no way I can lift myself up and back inside.

Dangling five stories up, I worry about my mortality.

It seems crazy to worry about it now when I was contemplating a swan dive a moment ago.

Yeah no, I'm not sure what that was.

I don't think it was me.

At least I hope it wasn't.

That's a problem for later. Right now, I'm worried this will be the ultimate test of Mother Nature's resurrection. Whether or not it ends me, it will suck ass because the stone street is a fucking long way down.

My fingers are burning, bleeding from their frantic grip. It's no use. I'm going to fall.

A rush of wind hits me from below and lifts me enough for me to adjust my grip. I reach over the edge of the windowsill and thank whatever miracle of nature gave me a push in the right direction.

Then it dawns on me.

"Again, Dillan! Give me another push."

"I got you, B. Three…two…one…"

As he calls out the one, I yank upward, and Dillan's buffeting gale force launches me back inside. I hit the floor with a grunt and flop onto my back, my muscles screaming.

Panting hard, I scramble to get to my feet and look for the ghostly motherfucker that sucker-punched me into a nearly fatal freefall.

The air crackles around me, charged with magic, and there he is—the silver-haired specter, looking like he stepped out of his portrait and into my worst nightmare.

"Not cool, asshole. What the fuck did I ever do to you?" I square my shoulders, facing him head-on.

I've dealt with some shady characters in my time, but a phantom? That's new.

The ghost before me ripples with a creepy black rush and comes at me again. "Get out!"

I widen my stance and brace for impact. Clenching my fist, I swing hard. My right hook has clout, and I've laid out more than a few troublemakers in my day.

My fist sails through the ghost, and my shoulder screams in hot displeasure. Yeah, I seriously pulled something there, and it leaves me off-balance and pissed.

I shove my hands through the shimmering image of the mage. It's like trying to punch smoke and about as effective.

The smug specter laughs. It's a sound that doesn't belong on this side of the grave, all eerie echoes and mocking tones. He floats closer, and his hands pass through my jacket and into my chest.

I gasp as the chill hits me.

It's like being dunked in a frozen lake, the cold sinking deep into my bones and stealing the breath from my lungs. I stagger back, my body trembling with hypothermic shivers.

Fuck. My first case in almost four years and I'm getting my ass handed to me. Why couldn't he be a normal fucking low-life bank robber or something?

I hate to take the defensive, but I need to think.

Dodging left and right, I keep my boots moving despite the Arctic chill turning my blood into sludge. There has to be an angle, some way for me to hit back.

No matter how fast I move, I can't land a blow.

The dickwad is enjoying this way too much. His ghostly form darts in and out with a grace that's infuriating. Another pass and his touch leaves frost on my skin, a stinging reminder of how outclassed I am in a fight against a magical being.

I grit my teeth and keep moving.

Giving up is not in my nature, but man, this is one hell of a rough one.

I'm backed into a corner. The ghost's chilling whispers curl around my mind like tendrils of ice. Despair hits me hard, and my gut twists with everything I've lost. My chest tightens, and my breaths come in ragged gasps.

I'm lost, lonely, and useless in this world.

I should've let go of the windowsill and ended my suffering. If I stop fighting back, it will be over soon.

The thought of an end to this existence is seductive.

Battered and breathless, I dig my heels in, my jaw clenching as a wild fury ignites deep within my core.

I'm Brendan fucking Cumhaill, damn it!

I refuse to be a territorial spirit's punching bag.

With a surge of rage and desperation, I reach deep inside myself, refusing to be coerced again. I focus on where he has hold of me and will him away with everything I've got.

Something within me shifts, a door flung open in my soul, and suddenly the world changes.

My vision is awash with new colors, and I can see the ghost more clearly now. It's not a haunting presence but a nexus of spiritual energy—a swirling vortex of spiritual power.

"Fuckety-fuck," Dillan mutters, coming into the room and sliding across the floor as he tries to stop. "Is that a ghost?"

"Yeah. You wouldn't happen to know how to beat its ethereal ass, would you? It's taking me to town."

My younger brother searches the room, grabs a wooden staff, and tosses it my way. "Use that. I'll find something too."

Good enough.

I twist away from the mage's next assault and grip the nifty staff with iron vines snaking around its shaft. Propelled by a newfound determination, I swing it wide, cutting through the air, and for the first time since I climbed through the window, it backs off.

"Oh, there we go," I goad, feeling more myself now that it's not touching me. "Not so tough when I even up the odds, eh?"

"Be gone!" he shouts, pointing at the door.

"You first, asshole!" I raise the staff, swing back, and line-drive the ghost through the middle.

A shockwave erupts from the staff, and the ghost's form shatters like frozen glass. Its essence scatters into a shower of sparkling particles that dance in the air before dissipating into nothingness.

"Wow. That worked?"

Dillan blinks. "Why do you look so surprised?"

I'm not sure. I guess I didn't realize he'd know how to take on a ghost. Now, so do I.

Feeling a little punch drunk after my win, I crack the staff's blunt end against the floor and throw up my free arm. "Go back to the shadow."

Dillan snorts. "Did you quote Gandalf the Gray?"

I take a couple of sloppy steps back and prop my ass against the edge of the table behind me. "You didn't like it? I thought it was fitting."

"No. It was great. It's been a while since we've seen that side of you."

His words hold no censure but hit a sore spot within me anyway. Here I thought I'd been keeping up the happy-happy-nice-nice façade like a champ.

"While we're on the subject," he continues, his brows pulling tight. "What the fuck were you thinking?"

I blink. "More words. What are we talking about?"

He points at the window, and his scowl grows even darker. "I've answered enough calls to know a jumper when I see one. You were about to take a fucking header into the street when I got here."

"No, I wasn't."

Dillan strides forward and pushes his Peter pointer into my chest. "Don't even bother to deny it, asshole. You've been moody AF for months, and if I hadn't caught you and called you out, you would've been a plasma puddle on the street."

I twist out of his gaze and put a bit of distance between us. "You're seeing things, D. That was the ghost's doing. I wouldn't do that, no matter how lost I got."

"I wouldn't have thought so either until I saw you."

I run my fingers through my hair and think back to what was going through my head before the ghost of wizards past tried to shove me out the window.

While rubbing the ache in my chest, I take a deep breath. "My mind is a muddle, but I swear it wasn't my doing...at least I'm pretty sure it wasn't."

Dillan lowers his chin. "That's not what it looked like from where I stood."

I exhale and shake it off. "Well, I'm not sure what happened, but I'm good. Besides, is it possible for me to die? Mother Nature said I would live on this island with you until I decided to pass to the next plane. Doesn't that sorta mean I'm immortal?"

Dillan is still watching me…reading me. "How about we don't try to find out anytime soon?"

"Done deal."

"FYI, dispersing a vengeful spirit doesn't last forever, so how about we take our leave before Sir Robes-a-lot comes back."

"Even better."

We head for the door, and Dillan points at the staff still in my hand. "You claiming that as your new look?"

"Accessorizing is everything, man. Besides, if Mad Mage comes at us again, I want to be ready to knock him out of the park."

"Fair enough."

Aching from the fight and confused about almost everything that happened, Dillan and I beat feet. We get gone as fast as our boots can get us down four flights of stairs, out the window, and jump off the second-story balcony.

Fresh air helps to wipe the cobwebs from my mind, and the world shifts back to normal—the weight of dark intentions dissipating like the magician inside. Maybe that's all it was.

Maybe the mage's dark mojo whammied me.

Staring up at the August sun, I let the heat and brilliance of the new day wash over me. It's grounding and good. I'm still lightheaded from the adrenaline rush of being attacked by a ghost and specifically of being pinned and whatever mental fracture that caused.

With a deep breath, I return to the now and nod at Dillan. "All right. Let's get to the security office and see what news Emmet has. Did Sloan get back from his father's clinic?"

As Dillan fills me in on what went down in the family breakfast meeting, I focus on putting one foot in front of the other and resetting.

I'm fine. Everything is fine.

I lift my gaze to the street ahead and groan. Nope, I take that back.

Everything is definitely *not* fine.

8

EMMET

Sloan *poofs* the two of us from the Light Weavers' temple to the sanctuary of my palace home. We materialize in the living room, the rest of the open-concept suite sprawling before us.

I jog over to the tree habitat by the window and check on Doc. He, Manx, and Bruin were up all night on patrol, and the little guy is tuckered out.

Leaving him to his slumber, I point at one of the spare rooms and stride across the space. This place is my dream home, from the colossal entertainment center to the stocked bar, to the panoramic view of Isilon beyond the glass wall.

Well, except for not having someone to share it with.

Not for the first time, I wonder how Ciara is doing in Toronto. The woman I fell in love with and took to Toronto to share my world with chose my city over me.

Ironic, right?

She lives on the street I grew up on, reports to my old boss, and sits as the druid representative for the city I introduced her to.

All right, so it's a little less ironic and just plain sad.

I reach the spare room, round the bed, and kneel by the wall. I trace my fingers over the silky finish of the hardwood floor, feeling for my predecessor's magical signature.

This used to be Syma's private space, and she hid things beneath these beautiful old wood planks.

Because she was wise and a Light Weaver, she didn't lift the floorboards and create a hidey-hole. She phased the wood and created a magical pocket undetectable to those without her power.

I have her power. So…

I press my hands to the floor, stretch my neck from side to side, and connect with the magic humming in my veins. It takes me only a moment and a thought to phase the floorboards out of existence and reach into the void Syma created a millennium ago.

I move a couple of crystals, an amulet, and a few other magical baubles to the side and lift the leather-bound journal from the bottom.

"Thank you, Syma. If the Dark Weavers have returned, maybe we can stop them with your help."

"Aye, that's a good thought," Sloan agrees behind me.

We walk out to the kitchen table and I set Syma's journal out for us both to see. I'm not the scholar or master of subtleties of ancient tomes like Sloan, but I do all right.

I have nothing but respect for the sisters and what they tried to do to keep Isilon safe and its people alive. If we can carry on their efforts and reach a different outcome, that would make me damn proud.

With its faded script and discolored pages, Syma's journal could be the key to understanding the dark forces that might become a problem here again. More so, a source to help us stop them.

I let Sloan take the lead in the page-turning. He's the man in all things bibliophile. He skims through the pages, his finger tracing the delicate swoop and swirl of Syma's writing.

As it dances before my eyes, faded but fierce, I wonder about the battles she and her sisters fought and the fates they eventually met.

When we traveled back in time with Fiona to learn from them, we told them they were no longer here by our time and the city was abandoned.

Did that help them prepare for a contingency?

Deep inside, I hope so.

In a perfect world, us giving them a heads-up about trouble on the horizon could've given them the chance to make plans.

"It's sad, isn't it?" I sigh and straighten, leaving Sloan to do the lion's share of the reading. Mam always used to say my strength was my empathy for others.

I'm not sure that's true in this case.

There are times when feeling the pain of other people gets to be too much. That's why I joke around a lot.

Laughing is better than crying any day of the week.

"Och, aye. It's a tale of tragedy for sure." Sloan turns the pages, frowning. "Syma's account speaks of a time when the Dark Weavers brought Emhain Abhlach to its knees. It details the last stand of the city's defenders, their sacrifices, and the eventual realization that Isilon couldn't take the despair."

The impact of that hits me hard. I know enough about the downfall of the island and the Light Weaver sisters to play that scenario out in my mind, and it hurts my heart.

Our friends were invaded—set upon by a race of murderous predators that consumed the people of this once thriving and vital city.

"Em? Did ye see this when ye looked through the journal before?"

Sloan hands me a folded sheet of parchment with my name

written on the outside, directly beneath an oxblood wax seal—
Emmet mac Cumhaill.

I blink and hold my hand out to accept the ancient missive. "No. I, uh, didn't read this far into the accounts of what they suffered. There's a lot in there about Syma's thoughts and fears. It felt too personal."

"Aye, it is, but it seems she had somethin' to tell ye and knew ye'd be here one day to hear it."

"I'm not sure what to say to that."

"Ye don't need to say a word, Em. Open the letter and see what Syma wanted ye to know."

With trembling fingers, I crack the wax seal and open the two ends of the parchment to reveal the same swirly script dancing across the belly of the page.

My dearest Emmet,

If this letter finds its way into your hands, it is because the threads of fate have woven it so and because you, our most cherished pupil, have risen to meet the destiny that has long been etched in the stone of Emhain Abhlach.

I write to you across the expanse of time with a heavy and hopeful heart, for the task I lay before you is one of great peril and profound importance.

You have grown, I trust, into the formidable Light Weaver my sisters and I foresaw you becoming, adept in the spatial magics that are the lifeblood of our kind. If you are reading this, the city of Isilon, our sacred haven, is waking, and with it, whispers of unrest will awaken once more.

As the shadows lengthen, we fear the Dark Weavers we fought so valiantly against might not be as vanquished as we hope. This is, I believe, the true reason you came back in time to meet us. You are destined to carry on our work and safeguard Isilon for those who live there and cannot protect themselves.

In the heart of our city lies the Corestone, the nexus of Isilon's life force, where the energies of the living converge with the ancestral spirits of our realm. Should the Dark Weavers seek to corrupt this wellspring of power, the consequences would be dire. We would see our beloved city fall into decay and ruin, its light extinguished forevermore.

Emmet, you must journey to the Corestone and reignite Isilon's Embers of Existence that we, the Light Weavers, once tended. These sacred flames are the antithesis of the darkness that encroaches and feed the soul of the city. Their light can dispel the shadows that seek to consume our world.

In my time, we created a key—a vessel of our combined powers—that alone can unlock the Corestone's sanctum. This key was split into three fragments, safeguarded by the elements of air, water, and fire to prevent it from falling into malevolent hands. You must retrieve these fragments and make the key whole once more. Only then can you access the Corestone and perform the Rite of Existence.

Trust in your training, Emmet. Remember the patterns of the ley lines we traced together, the ebb and flow of the world's hidden currents of power. These skills will be your compass as you navigate the challenges that lie ahead.

Know that the love and faith of your teachers, the sisters who once stood as guardians of Isilon, remain with you. Although we are gone from the sacred island, our spirits endure, entwined with the magic that courses through your veins.

Gather your allies and kin for this burden is not yours to bear alone. In unity, there is strength, and in love, there is indomitable power. Stand tall, be brave, and let the light of your soul shine forth.

With eternal hope and boundless trust, carry on.

Syma

My mind is numb, and I have to read the letter again before I begin to grasp the scope of what Syma is tasking me with.

"She thinks I'm the guy."

Sloan grips my shoulders and lowers his head to meet my gaze. "She's right, Em. Yer the guy and yer the only one who doesn't see it yet. Once ye see what we all see, ye'll rock this island like a boss."

I search Sloan's pale green eyes, looking for any sign that he's giving me a pep talk, knowing that I got assigned the quest of my lifetime.

He seems genuine. Wow…all right. Heat flushes my cheeks, and I bob my head. "Okay, Irish. I'll take your word for it."

"If that's what ye have to do until ye believe it, that's fine. Now, how do ye want to handle it?"

I consider that. Usually, it's Fi who rallies the troops and readies the party for the quest. This is going to take some getting used to. "I guess we need to get everyone together and figure out where the Corestone is, what 'challenges' Syma thought we'd come up against, and then what the Ritual of Existence is."

Sloan nods. "Do ye mind if I keep this journal with me fer a bit? I'd like to read it to the end and see if there's any mention about holding the Dark Weavers at bay."

I swallow against my reservations and agree. "Please be very careful with it. It's Syma's intimate thoughts and memories. I'd like to put it back safely when you're done to preserve that for her."

Sloan squeezes my arm. "Aye, of course. I'll protect it with my life and bring it back tonight to set back fer safekeepin'."

"Cool. Thanks for understanding, Irish."

Sloan winks. "Not a problem. Whatever ye need, and whenever ye need it, I'm here fer ye, Em."

I draw a deep breath and fold the letter to put it in my pocket. "Thanks, man. I have a feeling I'll be taking you up on that offer sooner than you think."

My phone *pings* in my pocket, and the sharp sound cuts through the solitude of our shared discovery, making me jump. I pull it out and read the message. "Okay, new plan. It's Dillan. He's in the street across from the grove and Brenny's lost his marbles. We need to get there."

Sloan grabs my arm, and the tingling of his wayfarer energy

rushes over me. From one moment to another, he's transported us.

Gone is the room where Syma changed the course of my life, and we stand in the street staring at Brendan looking ghostly pale.

9

BRENDON

Emmet and Sloan appear before me, their expressions a mix of concern and confusion. "What's up, B?" A brotherly tease tinges Emmet's voice, but his emerald eyes betray his worry. "Shit, man. You look like you've seen a ghost."

I snort. "I have, little brother."

The odd tingle of energy I first felt when I was certain the mage's ghost would kill me buzzes in my veins and makes the hair on my arms stand on end.

My gaze drifts up the street, locking onto another half-dozen shimmering figures that populate our path back to the center square.

"Now that I see them, I can't unsee them. They're freaking everywhere."

Sloan's brow pinches and he casts an appraising glance around us. "Are ye sayin' ye see ghosts, sham?"

I steal another glance at the silent gathering of the departed, their ethereal forms flickering like candle flames in the wind. "Sure do. And after the spectral donnybrook I had with the one in that house, I'm not keen to take on six more."

"Six?" Emmet swings around to look. "Where are they?"

I groan and grab Emmet's arm, pulling him back around to face me. "Be cool, Em. I think they attack when they know you can see them."

"Is that what happened?" Sloan asks.

"Yeah. I was in that brick house, checking sightlines to the grove and searching for evidence of someone lying in wait, watching the nymph. That house there, the five-story with the dome, was the home of a wizard."

Emmet follows my pointed finger. "That's one sweet-looking house."

Yeah, it is. "I was staring out the window, and I saw his reflection in the pane of glass behind me. Then he went homicidal and shoved me out the window."

Sloan turns and frowns at the house.

"The domed part of the top floor is some kind of wizard sanctum. He had a laboratory, a killer library, and all kinds of high-level magic shit. And even dead, the bastard doesn't like visitors."

"Aye, all right. It sounds like a vengeful spirit anchored to his home. We should release him."

I chuff. "Have at it, Irish. I'll pass."

Emmet frowns. "Were you there, Dillan? Did you see him too?"

Dillan flashes me a look and shrugs. "I was on the road when Brenny flew out the window. Once I helped him back inside, I ran up to help him. Yeah, I saw him. A silver-fox kinda guy with over-the-top Dumbledore wizard robes."

"Do ye see ghosts out here?" Sloan asks.

Dillan looks around and shakes his head. "No. That's all Brenny. I've got nothing out here."

Sloan finishes looking at my brothers and stares at the empty street—or at least empty to us. "The question is whether the ghosts have always been here and we're becoming aware of them or are they beginning to manifest for some reason."

"Because the city is waking up?" Dillan suggests.

"Possibly."

Emmet scoffs and shakes his head. "The real question is whether Dionysus can set us up with an Ectomobile and some proton packs so we can get to ghostbusting."

Sloan chuckles. "I wish that would work, Em, but ghosts are nasty business. Depending on what kind of ghost and why they're here, they can have some nasty powers, too."

"Could they be the shadows people are afraid of?" Dillan asks.

Sloan nods. "It's possible."

"Is there any scenario where the asshole in the robes could be the one who killed the nymph?" I sit on the edge of a low stone wall that lines the grove's green space.

My legs are rubbery, and if I don't sit, I'll likely fall and embarrass myself. I touch the back of my head, and my hand comes away slick with blood. "Oh, shit. That could be why I'm so dizzy."

There's a round of cursing, then Sloan's standing beside me, pressing his fingers to the back of my head. "What part of yer battle led to this?"

I close my eyes when the warmth of his healing tingles at the back of my throbbing skull. "When he shoved me out the window, I cracked my head pretty good."

"Maybe that's why you're seeing ghosts," Em remarks.

"If that's all it took, we'd all be seeing ghosts, Em," Dillan counters. "We've all had more than our fair share of noggin bonks."

"True story."

The magical mending of my head goes a long way to getting me back on my feet. Within a couple of minutes, the spinning has passed, and the throbbing has faded into the background.

"Thanks, Irish."

"My pleasure." He pulls an honest-to-goodness handkerchief from his pocket and wipes his fingers.

"Back to Brenny's question," Emmet continues. "Could the

ghost in that house be responsible for consuming the tree nymph's essence?"

Sloan crosses his arms and looks from the house to the grove. "Could a ghost consume fae energy? Yes, it's possible. It would depend on what kind of apparition he is and how powerful he was before he died."

"You don't sound convinced," I observe, reading him.

He tilts his head from side to side. "I'd have to get a look at him. From what you described, it sounds more like he's a vengeful spirit haunting his home."

Emmet sighs. "I'd much rather it be an infestation of ghosts than Dark Weavers. At least with ghosts, we know their weaknesses and how to fight back."

I frown as the ghosts up the street turn and move toward us. "Uh, guys?"

Dillan pauses what he's about to say as I hold up a finger. The surrounding air grows denser, charged with the unseen. I feel the weight of countless gazes, the city's spirits drawn to our conversation like moths to a flame.

"Maybe we shouldn't discuss this here," I add.

"They're coming, aren't they?" Emmet asks.

"Uh-huh." A shiver runs down my spine, and I rub my arms, trying to shake off the chill. "Before, when I didn't see them, they didn't attack. Is the trick to ignore them and pretend they're not here?"

"They're not here for us," Emmet replies. "This is all you, bro."

Dillan nods. "Pretend you don't see them. At least until we figure this out."

"I've got a better idea, boys." Sloan extends his hand in front of us.

The four of us each pile a hand on and Sloan *poofs* us away. A moment later, we're in Shenanigans II, and I beeline it to the bar.

It's only mid-morning, so the place is empty, but Liam

straightens from stocking up for the lunch crowd, takes one look at me, and frowns. "Been that kind of day already, has it?"

"You have no idea."

He pours me a three-finger salute, and I toss it back fast. The sweet burn of the whiskey leaves a trail down the back of my throat and warms the ice in the pit of my belly.

Closing my eyes, I allow the scent of malt and wood polish to ground me in the familiarity of my sanctuary.

I'm fine. Everything is fine. S'all good.

Liam is checking out the wizard's staff when I open my eyes. "This is a new direction for you. I always pictured you more as a leather vest and daggers assassin type, but hey, fly your freak flag."

Ignoring him, I spin the seat of my chair and scan the pub's interior for any sign of trouble. No phantoms lurk in the shadows, and I let out a long breath.

Man, when did I get this jumpy?

Oh, right—when a wizard's ghost decided I'd make a good sparring partner.

"Dude. Seriously. Are you all right?" Liam's concern breaks through my thoughts.

I sit straighter and give myself an inward shake. "Yeah, sorry. I guess it was only a matter of time before something magical took a shot at me. I feel like a wuss. On the job, I was right and tight. I was killer calm when the shit hit. It's how I made Guns and Gangs."

Sloan sits on the stool next to me and chuffs. "No one is judgin' ye, Brenny. Ask yer sister sometime about how much I hate ghosts. I can square off against nearly anything and not flinch, but ghosts…well, they're my panic button if ever there was one."

Well, that's nice to know. "I see why you're not a fan. Man, if I could've taken it down with a baton or my gun, it wouldn't have freaked me out so much. Nothing I did affected it. I don't know how Fiona got thrown into all this and took it on without losing her mind."

The soft smile that curves his mouth speaks to how crazy he is about my little sister. "Fiona is one in a million, that's fer sure. She amazes me every day."

"Who needs a baton or a gun when you've got Skeletor's staff?" Liam laughs at the scepter lying across the top of the bar.

"Hey, this staff saved my life today." I open my hand and frown. "It also gave me a splinter. Do you think you can sand a wizard's staff?"

Emmet scoffs. "No, dude, but you happen to be sitting with three highly qualified druids. We can smooth out the wood for you."

Sloan leans in, dragging his fingers over the iron branches adorning its length. The scuffed part of the wood where I got the splinter is gone with one pass. "It's one impressive staff."

"That's what *she* said." Emmet laughs.

I chuckle, and it feels good. "I tried everything else within reach, but this was the only thing that worked against that asshole."

"You only used it because your smarter and handsomer brother tossed it to you in the clutch." Dillan waggles his brows.

Sloan traces the intricate vines of the fretwork. "Aye, these iron vines would dissipate a ghost fer sure."

Emmet sweeps a hand in front of me, his grin infectious. "So, spill it. Give us the whole play-by-play."

I recount the tale between sips of liquid courage, soon realizing that I skipped breakfast this morning. Emmet and Dillan provide the comic relief, ribbing me about being a magic noob every chance they get.

It feels good to laugh it off, to transform fear into a story we can share over drinks. Even in a world laced with magic, some things never change.

A drink at Shenanigans with my family and friends is still the best cure for what ails me.

My frayed nerves begin to stitch back together, and by the bottom of my third tumbler, I've got all the hatches battened down. "I knew that from the observation dome on the fifth floor, someone could watch the grove, so I went up to check it out."

Emmet frowns. "Remember last night when I texted everyone that we were on the buddy system? What made you think you were exempt?"

I shrug and deflect. "Did I mention that Dillan was alone when he came to find me?"

Dillan flips me the bird. "And this after I saved your ass, too."

Emmet moves his attention to Dillan. "Where did Dionysus go, D? He was supposed to be your buddy this morning."

"Jonah called him and said Garnet's vampire issue spilled over into headquarters. The moment he heard they were under attack, Dionysus was gone."

Emmet's frown eases. "Well, no fault there. I hope everything is all right. Since you got to Brendan and saved his butt, you're off the hook, and Brendan is still in the hot seat."

"Ha!" Dillan laughs, pointing at Brendan. "Right back atcha, dude."

I roll my eyes. "The next thing I know, I'm getting shoved out the window by something that wasn't really there. That's when Dillan saved my butt."

Dillan's gaze narrows, and I know what he's thinking. He saved my butt thirty seconds before that by calling my name and breaking whatever trance I'd fallen under that made me want to swan dive out the window.

"Yeah, but me being the hero is no shocker to anyone."

Emmet snorts. "Please."

"Dillan gives me a boost of wind to thrust me back into the window and the mad mage tears into me. I fought, but nothing fazed him. I was getting my ass handed to me, and it got bad. I was pinned and thought I was about to get my ticket punched. I think that's when it happened."

"When what happened?" Sloan asks.

I wave my hand in a circle, gesturing at myself. "When my ghost vision kicked in. It felt like the lid of a box unhinged inside me. Then I could see this magical glow and the ghost came into focus, clear as a bell."

"Did you try to hit it after that?" Sloan asks. "Did it lock any physical connection with the ghost?"

My mind is a whirl as I try to remember.

"Dillan came in then, and when he saw I was getting a beat down, he tossed me the staff. I took a few swings, and when I finally connected, the ghost shattered like a vase hitting a concrete floor."

"Do you think the ghost whisperer effect is a one-time thing?" Emmet asks. "Or when you grabbed the staff you got whammied by a spell, and that's why you can see the ghosts. Or the flip of the switch could've been your survival instinct kicking in."

I like that idea a lot. "I *was* in a wizard's lair, after all. Anything in there could've been booby-trapped to affect me. Thanks, Em."

Emmet raises his glass of Coke in salute.

Sloan remains the picture of skepticism.

Dammit, why couldn't everyone get on board with Emmet's version of things? "You don't buy that, Irish?"

Sloan offers a noncommittal shrug, his expression unreadable. He moves his hand and brushes his fingers over the aged wood and the iron vines again. "Emmet could be right, but I don't feel anything magical when I touch the staff."

I catch the unintentional innuendo and chuckle as Emmet bites his lip, fighting the urge to crack a joke. It's a Herculean effort for my kid brother, who's more at home with levity than gravity.

Yet, there he is, committed to adulting.

"If not the staff, what do you think happened?" I ask.

Sloan's response is a soft murmur, his words carrying the weight of consideration. "Ye were dead for two years, Brendan. Ye might well have developed a connection to the spirit world, and the stress of being attacked opened that conduit."

A chill skitters down my spine, the implications of Sloan's words spreading through my system like icy branches. Could death have indelibly marked me? Could my brush with the afterlife have bestowed me with an unexpected byproduct of my experience?

A gift—or a curse?

This newfound sight, this eerie connection to the spectral realm, is disturbing. I don't want to be altered by any kind of magical influence.

Then again, isn't everyone in my family altered in one way or another? Maybe my destiny was always slated to be different. If Fiona were here, she'd say everything happens for a reason.

As daunting and unnerving as the prospect is, being able to see ghosts when Isilon is lousy with them might be a good thing.

At least that's what I tell myself.

"What do we do about the ghosts?" The thought of facing them makes my mouth dry, so I drink again. "If they're all as deranged as the wizard, we can't leave them there. When a new round of settlers arrives, they might pick that house or another that's haunted, and we'll have more dead on our hands."

"Aye, that's true," Sloan agrees. "Although vengeful spirits are relatively uncommon. From what I read in Syma's journal, the people living here during the end of days were trapped, being hunted by Dark Weavers, and Isilon shut down to end it all. There could be a great many souls who feel unjustly dead."

Emmet frowns. "Do you think Isilon knowingly went dormant while there were still citizens here fighting for their survival?"

Sloan nods. "Isilon is a sentient city. Don't frame its existence with human morals. I expect that by its logical assessment, the

Dark Weavers were torturing its citizens and there was no chance of winning that battle. Given the choice, it might have thought it better to shut down than have the innocent tortured and the assailants free to move on to torture others."

Dillan curses. "That's cold."

"Possibly. But it makes logical sense and is effective."

I take another long drink. "I can only imagine how angry and scared those people would've felt. Now that the city is waking, the streets are full of angry souls ready to beat the shit out of us— or worse, suck a nymph dry of her life essence."

Sloan rubs his chin, considering. "It's possible. Depending on how powerful the wizard was in life, his spirit might possess the means to siphon magical essence. It's definitely grounds for us dispatching him."

"If only to keep the next guy who wanders into his house from getting a beat down," Emmet adds.

"How does one dispatch a vengeful spirit?" I ask.

Sloan takes that one. "In most cases, ye need to find the skeleton of the deceased to salt and burn the bones to release the spirit from this plane."

"And in other cases?"

"Spirits can also be tethered to an object of considerable meaning—something precious to them or imbued with a piece of their soul."

"Like a Horcrux," Emmet points out.

Sloan offers Em a patient smile. "Aye, Em. Exactly like a Horcrux."

"Eva could help too," Dillan interjects.

I set my tumbler on the bar. "With the number of spirits I saw, Eva might be a better option. When does she come home from her assignment?"

Dillan frowns. "I was telling these guys at breakfast. She still has a few days, but I could call her back if we need her."

Emmet looks at me. "What do you think?"

I wave off the offer. "Don't pull her away from her duties for the Choir of Angels to make life easier for us. We'll handle the psycho wizard ourselves. As long as the other spirits behave, we'll plan on releasing them once Eva gets home."

Em nods. "What's our plan for the wizard?"

"Find his bones," Sloan answers.

I roll my eyes. "Please don't tell me we're going to stalk a graveyard."

Sloan shakes his head. "No. Fae don't bury their dead in organized plots. That's a human thing."

"Where do we look?" Emmet asks.

"In his home. Odds are he's hauntin' the manse because he's tethered. Dillan, we'll need yer cloak, and I'll pull together a scrying spell. Everyone grab yerself an iron weapon, and we'll meet back here in an hour. Och, and don't mention it to Fi. Ye know how she gets."

Emmet snorts. "You mean her insane adrenaline FOMO? Yeah, we're aware."

10

EMMET

Sloan portals the four of us back to the street opposite the five-story brick home. The place is awesome, and somewhere I would love to live, minus the homicidal horror haunting its halls.

"Discreetly, Brendan, can ye confirm yer still able to see ghosts?"

Brenny doesn't turn but scans the area. "There aren't as many as there were earlier, but yeah, definitely. I see them."

Sloan nods. "The rest of us are at a disadvantage."

"I saw the ghost up in the workroom," Dillan counters.

"Aye, it might be that the amount of energy it emitted during the battle with yer brother made it visible. Still, I'd rather cast *Spectral Sight* so we don't get taken by surprise."

Dillan nods. "Good plan. I'd rather not get jumped by a ghost, thanks."

Sloan straightens before us and holds out his hands. Dillan and I join hands and complete the circuit so we're all touching. Once we are, Sloan begins the spell.

"In the realm where spirits dwell,
Grant us sight beyond the veil.

Eyes of flesh now pierce the night,
Spectral forms come into light.
Whispers silent, shadows cast,
Reveal to us the ghostly past.
Druid's power, now alight,
Bestow upon us spectral sight."

Sloan's incantation hums in my ears as the spectral sight spell mimics putting on a pair of ghost glasses. My vision sharpens to the unseen—the apparitions of our city taking on an eerie vibrancy.

Dillan looks around and arches his brows. "Well, then. Giddy-up. Let's get this party started."

The electric tingle of arcane energy makes the hairs on the back of my neck stand on end. "Are we doing the second-story window thing?"

Dillan scoffs. "Please. This dickwad is no match for Team Trouble. We're going in the front door."

I snort. "You expect Sloan to break the privacy spell and let us in, don't you?"

Dillan pegs me with a look. "Maybe."

"How about we split the difference?" Sloan suggests. "I'll portal us through that open window. That way we'll get in with no fuss, but we also won't tip off the ghost that we've broken through his wards and are in his home."

Brendan chuckles. "Yeah, I vote for that plan."

The floorboards groan under our weight as we move through the darkened hallways, our steps quiet but purposeful. I can feel the remnants of power woven into the fabric of the place. It's like walking through a morning fog—every air droplet is heavy with a hint of magical energy.

Brendan holds up his hand, signaling us to split off. We arrived on the second floor, and when Brendan was attacked, he was on the fifth.

That's a lot of house to cover.

In every shadowy corner, I half expect a specter to emerge, gnashing its ethereal teeth, but nothing stirs. The groan of the stairs makes me wince as I ascend the main staircase. It's probably not as loud as it sounds in my head, but it's deafening in the hushed silence of the haunted house.

I grip the banister to displace some of my weight, and the wooden rail is as cold as ice. Each room I check on the third floor mirrors the last.

They're all elegant, expensive, and empty.

The wizard's spirit is elusive, but the sense of foreboding grows stronger with every step I take.

Where would the guy's bones be? Where he died, or where he hid them after his death?

If I were rocking the spirit world and knew someone could dispatch me for good, I'd hide my bones somewhere sneaky. Being a wizard, he might have hidden them behind an intricate network of spells so no one could find them.

Sloan walks by the doorway, focused on the golden pendulum dangling from the chain pinched between his fingers. I've watched him, Fiona, and Merlin scry before—they're good.

That he looks so annoyed while the pendulum hangs straight down isn't a good sign.

I push open a door at the end of the hallway, and the scene inside makes me pause. The room is untouched by time, like all the others. A desk sits in the center, papers in place and quills ready as if the man of the house stepped away.

I move deeper into the space, reaching out with my powers, seeking that which might be hidden.

A shiver runs down my spine when the air turns sharp with a cold that bites at the edges of my senses. I straighten, turning to ensure I'm not about to be jumped by the wizard's ghost, and admonish myself for being so jumpy.

I need to tighten up. People are counting on me to be the leader this city needs. I think about how commanding men like

Garnet Grant and Da are, and my heart aches. They are great men with a strength that draws people to follow them.

I'm just me. Emmet.

The youngest Cumhaill boy. The goofball. The clown.

The image of Randa lying dead in the grass fills my mind, and the encroaching shadow of panic takes hold of my heart with icy fingers. She deserves so much more than me trying to find her justice. I didn't even suspect there was a danger.

What about the other citizens? Do I have what it takes to keep them safe?

I don't think I do.

I slump into the office chair behind the desk and swipe my hand under my eyes. I'm drowning in a sea of lackluster, knowing I will either crumble under the weight of expectations or let down everyone who ever believed in me.

Brendan steps into the room and stops mid-stride. "Em? What's wrong? What's going on?"

I shake my head, lost to the despair. "I can't do it. I can't be the champion of this island because I'm not champion material—I never have been."

"What are you talking about, buddy? You're rocking the island thing. With your connection to the raw fae essence of this place, you're practically Luke Skywalker at one with the Force."

There's a thunderous crash in the hallway and Brendan curses and rushes off. He comes back a moment later, grappling Dillan and wrestling him into the room. "Dillan. What the fuck, man?"

Dillan is throwing fists and spouting off that the Choir of Angels could take Han if they don't think he's the right father for him.

Then Sloan comes in and looks like he might be sick. "At least yer workin' with a solid knowledge of what it is to be a good father. Niall was amazin' and who have I got to take from? My parents were so emotionally detached and self-interested that I grew up hating them. I don't want my child to hate me."

"What the fuck is happening right now?" Brendan runs his fingers through his hair. "Guys, seriously…snap out of it!"

Our collective despair hangs heavy in the air, and I struggle to breathe under the weight of it. Seconds, minutes, hours—time loses all meaning as the void swallows me.

"Fuck this." Brendan pulls out his phone.

Dionysus appears in a sudden burst of golden mist and a faint scent of vineyards in summer. The despair is banished as quickly as it came.

Relief is a palpable force, washing over me in waves, cleansing my heart and soul from the darkness that had me in its grip.

"What the hell was that?" Dillan snaps, scowling at the rest of us.

"Whispering shadows," Dionysus replies while checking on Sloan. "They are formless, sinister entities that amplify fear and feed on the despair they cause. Once they've got you in their hold, they can drive even the most well-adjusted person mad."

Sloan straightens and squeezes Dionysus' shoulder. "Thanks fer comin', Greek. Is everything okay with Jonah and the Batcave?"

"Fine. They're dealing with the aftermath now. Speaking of aftermath, why are you all here?"

"There's a nasty wizard ghost here that—" My words mist in a white cloud as the temperature plummets.

I scan the room as a dozen grayed-out phantoms pour out from every crack and crevice in the walls. "We've got company!"

Brendan whirls and raises the wizard's staff as I position myself to stand back-to-back with Dionysus. "You'll need an iron weapon, Greek."

"I'm more of a bronze man, myself."

The air crackles with a charge as the first wave of specters lunges. A hollow-eyed shade comes at me, and even though I'm prepared, it's still creepy as hell. They aren't gross like zombies.

They look like pale, luminescent people stuck in the most murderous moment of their lives.

The clamor of battle fills the room. The clash of iron weapons shattering ghosts becomes a discordant symphony against the angry wails of the dead. Brendan grunts behind me, and I glimpse a blur of motion as he targets a half-troll, maybe, with unerring precision.

The number of ghosts seems endless, and a malice that is hard to comprehend drives them. Yes, it was tragic that they died, but is this natural?

I twist and drive my fireplace poker through the chest of a specter bearing down on me with outstretched, clawing hands. His arms are freakishly long. Although my hit shatters him into a bazillion bits, it's not fast enough.

Sharp talons tear through my shirt, slashing my collarbone and chest. Blood spurts out of the wound in an alarming arc.

Shit. That can't be good.

I'm not as skilled a healer as Sloan, but as I brace myself for the next attacker, I split my attention and push some of my energy toward closing the channels of gouged flesh and staunching the blood.

There's no time to focus, but hopefully it'll help.

The next ghost shrieks, rushing me like a shark drawn to the blood. Beside me, Brendan grunts and swings like a major leaguer, the staff in his hands singing a bitter song.

The ghost doesn't see him coming and shatters.

We knew the spirits were riled up, but this is a whole new level of fury. The air crackles with malevolent energy as the ghosts of Isilon's past take their grievances out on the new management.

It's a good thing iron is ghost kryptonite because each strike sends a spirit soul reeling, their ethereal forms exploding into a cloud of gray dust.

The next one moves in, and I duck and make a half-assed

swing. Luckily, my poker cracks my spectral assailant, disrupting his form.

The hand I'm holding over the hole in my flesh is slick with blood and steaming in the air as it hits the frigid atmosphere the ghosts have brought with them.

"Emmet, that's one helluva leak, brother," Dillan warns, his gaze fixed on the mess I've become. "Sloan! Emmet needs a hole plugged fast."

I want to protest, but my swings are getting sloppy, and the cold of our attackers is seeping deeper into my veins by the minute.

Sloan materializes beside me in an instant and hands Dillan his iron rebar. "Back in two." The signature of Sloan's wayfarer gift swamps us. We materialize in the kitchen of my bachelor suite, and Sloan shoves my hand out of his way. "A quick patch and I'll fix ye up proper when the battle's won."

"Sounds good." I tip my head away, giving him maximum access to my injury.

Sloan's healing power is like drinking the smoothest hot chocolate with Baileys and a bit of whipped cream froth. It's decadent, and I have to make a concerted effort not to moan in pleasure and make it weird.

"There ye go." He grabs my dish towel and rips it lengthwise down the middle. "A stylish scarf for you and a wipe of the hands for me so I don't lose hold of my weapon."

I wrap my neck with the black-and-white checkered cloth, then take the tip about drying my hands and do the same.

All in all, we couldn't have been gone for over two or three minutes. Still, fights don't last nearly as long as people think they do.

Sloan portals us back and rushes to reclaim his iron bar from Dillan. I jog out of the office to check on Brendan and Dionysus.

Brenny is in the upstairs hall, taking on a cheetah female

against the banister. I rush to help him. If Kidok is an example of the fighting prowess of the feline folk, he'll need backup.

A few running strides puts me into striking distance. At the same moment, a ghost with hair flowing like a field of the deepest violets blows through the wall like a storm. Purple hair flies out from her face like Medusa's snakes, and I'm caught in her haunting lavender gaze.

My moment of hesitation lasts only a split second, but it's a mistake she takes advantage of. I have no time to raise or thrust my weapon before she slams into me like a tempest.

I'm struck by the whirlwind of her sorrow and rage and fly backward over the banister. The world tilts as I flip into the open air and fall.

"Diminish Descent!" I shout, the words barely a breath as I focus my druidic power to slow my fall. *"Feline Finesse!"*

The air around me thickens, catching me like a net. I use the drag of the wind to right myself in the air, and as my descent slows, I get my feet under me so I don't break my neck.

When I land, I pick up my iron bar from where it fell and take the stairs two at a time to get back up to help my brother.

Only there's no need.

The battle is over by the time I race up the flights back to the fight.

Brendan is doubled over, his hands braced on his knees, and Sloan and Dillan seem mostly unscathed. Dionysus grins ear to ear, spinning in a Prussian blue robe with silver embroidery. He throws his hands out with dramatic flair.

"When did you have time to raid the wizard's closet?" I pant, placing a hand against my chest as I catch my breath.

Dionysus settles and brushes his hands down the robe's lapels. "My last opponent rushed through the closet to hide. I merely followed to be diligent. Then I found this beauty."

I laugh as I look over the others. "Is everyone all right?"

Brendan chuckles. "At least we kept our feet on solid ground. Nice trip, brother. How was your vacation?"

I grin. "Hey, you gotta check gravity every once in a while to make sure it still works. It does, by the way. No problems there."

He laughs. "Good to know."

"Did anyone see the damned wizard through all of that?" Dillan asks.

By the shaking heads, that's a no.

"So, what?" He's still breathing heavily. "He guessed we'd come back and had some friends ambush us while he slipped out the back door?"

"How did he do that if he's stuck in this house? And where is he now?" I counter.

Sloan brushes off the leg of his pants. "I don't know enough about whispering shadows to say. Perhaps the wizard isn't tethered here."

"Or the wizard *is* the tether," Dionysus suggests.

"I don't follow, Greek," Dillan replies.

"Agreed. More words," I add.

Dionysus looks us over and shrugs. "Whispering shadows are a nasty, angry manifestation of the undead. For there to be dozens here and united against a foe suggests this isn't a natural occurrence."

"That's not how they normally behave?" Sloan asks.

"Not at all. Whispering shadows are uncommon. For there to be so many of them, my guess would be that they are being tethered and controlled by a necromancer, a lich, or someone with powers over the dead."

Well, that doesn't sound good at all.

Brendan gives up fiddling with a piece of his shirt that got ripped in the battle. "If the wizard was a necromancer before he died, can he still be a necromancer who can control ghosts now that he's dead?"

Sloan nods. "If he were powerful enough, it's certainly possible."

"Let me get this straight." I go over the highlights in my head. "The wizard we came to dispatch isn't here. His bones aren't here. He's not tethered to his home and likely not haunting this place. Instead, he could be a necromancer who is transforming the ghosts of the citizens trapped here into whispering shadows to instill fear and beat the snot out of us."

Dillan blinks. "Well, shit, Em. That got dark fast."

"Aye, but he's not wrong," Sloan points out. "I think that's a fair description of where we are."

I sigh. "How do we figure out if the wizard is a necromancer, a lich, or some other demented fuck?"

"Check his library," Brendan offers. "When I first came through here this morning, I searched room by room. There were a hundred books in the library. Maybe they could tell us more."

Sloan gestures at the stairs. "Lead the way."

11

BRENDAN

The five of us descend to the wizard's library and I show Sloan what I meant about the ancient tomes. "If you can read these, they might tell you what kind of magic the wizard is into, right?"

Sloan's fingers trail along the spines of the books, his gaze scanning titles as a knowing smile curves his lips. "I think we can safely say yer mad wizard is a necromancer."

"Good," Dionysus grouses. "I hate liches."

Everyone in the room offers him a sympathetic smile, and for the millionth time, I feel like everyone knows something I don't.

Emmet recognizes my frustration and fills in the gaps. "Last year, Dionysus was part of Fi's team that went to New Orleans. They had a nasty run-in with a lich who got his claws in Dionysus and drained his magical energy to the point where he almost died."

"He's an immortal god. How could that happen?"

Dionysus shrugs. "I was on an immortality time-out."

"Because he saved my life," Sloan adds.

"I wasn't going to let you die. That would've destroyed my family."

Sloan nods. Although he doesn't speak, it's obvious by the way they've locked gazes that my brother-in-law is saying something privately to our demi-god plus one.

When that's over, Dionysus presses a hand to his heart. Man, Emmet was right. I really *don't* know or understand Dionysus.

I'm sorry, man, I think at him. *I shouldn't have questioned your motives. You are part of this family. My bad. Whatever you get in return is your business.*

Dionysus looks at me and smiles. *I get lurve, dummy. Unconditional, irreverent, awkward, silly, and often chaotic lurve.*

Yeah, there's no arguing with that.

"Can we talk about the hottie elf ghost?" Emmet grins. "All the other ghosts were almost completely grayed out, but she was lusciously purple."

The others look at him blankly.

"Seriously? You didn't see her? She was the one who straight-armed me over the railing and knocked me down the stairs."

Dillan snorts. "And what? Now you have a crush on her? You've been alone too long, dude. Attempted murder is not a meet cute."

"You didn't *see* her," Emmet says. "Brenny did. Tell them, B. She was worth a near-death experience, wasn't she?"

"Yeah, she was something." I'm unsure what else to say because my mind is still spinning. After she burst through the wall and shoved Emmet, she came after me. With no time to crack her with the wizard's staff, I raised my arm to push her away.

The moment we touched, she was no longer ethereal. I grabbed her shoulder, and she was solid and warm. Shocked, she backed away and ghosted off.

Is Sloan right? Has my time in the afterlife given me a connection with those tethered to the spirit world? If so, why did touching her give her physical form?

"Does the fact that her hair was so vibrantly purple instead of being grayed out mean something?" Emmet continues, oblivious to my mental spin. "Could she still be hanging onto her soul? Could her being an elf have something to do with it?"

As Emmet shoots questions in rapid fire, I rein in my racing heart. Why does his enthusiasm about her annoy me so much? I clench my fingers into fists and wander off to put some distance between us.

It must be the adrenaline from the fight, right?

I couldn't be jealous of my brother over a woman—no, a ghost —we both saw for only a few seconds.

That would be crazy.

"You sound like you've got a hard-on for the female who tried to end you, Em," Dillan ribs.

"Nah, I like my women sassy but soft and sweet. I'm just saying she had a wow factor."

She definitely did.

My anxiety eases with Emmet's admission, my mind replaying the encounter with the ghostly figure. Glancing down, I study my hand, my fingers still tingling with the feel of her solid within my hold.

Her long violet hair was a vivid flash in the darkness of my life lately. Emmet is right. There's something different about her.

Something important.

"What do you think, Irish?" Dillan asks. "Is our necromancer wizard a victim like the rest or the man behind the chaos?"

Sloan shelves the book in his hand and turns to answer. "I'd say there's a better than fair chance the wizard isn't one of the whisperin' shadows' victims, but instead, channelin' a power he possessed in life and transformin' the ghosts trapped here."

"How do we stop him?" Dillan asks.

"How do we release the souls he's turned into whispering shadows?" Emmet asks.

I circle back to the conversation. "More importantly, how do we safeguard the city's citizens against the despair and despondency the whispering shadows create?"

Emmet nods. "Yeah, that was awful. I was ready to curl up in a fetal position and bawl like a baby."

Dillan grunts. "I was ready to kill anything or anyone who came near me."

Sloan frowns. "They create a dangerous state for those caught in their spell, fer sure."

"Maybe tackling my quest would help," Emmet suggests.

That draws my full attention to my kid brother. "What quest is that, Em? Did I miss something?"

Emmet pulls a folded piece of parchment from the back pocket of his khakis and hands it to me. It's old…like, really old. When I open it, I stare at a page of elegant script I can't read. "What is it?"

"It's the quest Syma and the sisters left for me. Sloan and I found it today while searching for information about the Dark Weavers."

"Do you have any idea what it says?"

I hand it back to him, and he reads it aloud. "My Dearest Emmet, if this letter finds its way into your hands, it is because the threads of fate have woven it so…"

He continues reciting the words of his Light Weaver mentor. When he finishes, we're all pretty much gobsmacked.

"That's unbelievable, Em," Dillan marvels.

"It is." Dionysus leans in and high-fives Emmet. "You won over the trust of those powerful ladies. They left this for you, knowing you'd make it back here and be part of Isilon's future. It's a testament to how much they believed in you."

"You think so, Greek?"

"Absolutely. They saw your destiny was bright and left this quest for you, knowing you're the one to pick up where they left off."

I love how Dionysus' words light the kid up. "Yeah, Em. Good on ya, little brother."

Emmet has greatness in him that everyone recognizes except him. Once he realizes his power and strength, the kid will be unstoppable.

"I was thinking." He tucks the letter back into his pocket. "If the citizens are afraid of the shadows and we now know anxiety-inducing ghosts have infested the city, maybe empowering the city with goodness and light while we work to stop the darkness is a two-pronged attack."

Dillan grins. "You think an active ghost shutdown and a passive reinforcement of all things sunshine and rainbows is the way to go?"

"Yeah. Syma says it's important that when the darkness encroaches, we shift the balance to bring the city back to the light."

"Well, I'm always up for a quest," Dionysus remarks.

"Hells yeah," Dillan agrees.

Emmet looks at me. "What do you think? Are you up to try reigniting Isilon's pilot light?"

I hold my palms up. "I'm all for keeping the dark crap at bay, but we can't ignore the ghosts. Who will safeguard the citizens from the whispering shadows if everyone focuses on your quest? We still need to find those bones and release any ghosts as quickly as possible."

"Aye, that's fair," Sloan agrees.

"As much as it freaked me out at first, Sloan's right," I continue, working through my thoughts. "I have a magical connection to the spirits the same way you have a magical connection to the island. I think we both have our parts to play in this, even though we're on slightly different paths."

Emmet straightens, his grin widening. "Okay, you're in charge of the active plan of ghostbusting, and I'll head up our passive plan of igniting the Embers of Existence."

"Yeah, I think that's where we're headed."

Everyone is on board with that plan, but I have one detail to add.

"Since Syma tasked your quest to you as a Light Weaver, and Dionysus and Nikon are trained in the spatial magic of the Light Weavers, you three should work on that. I'll take Sloan, Dillan, Calum, and hopefully Eva when she gets back to work on freeing the ghosts."

Emmet nods. "That makes sense. Do you think you could talk to them? Maybe if you can explain that you're going to work to free them from their limbo of anger, they might help you find the wizard."

I cross my arms and grin. Emmet's optimism never ceases to amaze me. "They travel in groups and have a pack violence mentality. It might be possible if I could get one alone."

"Try the sexy elf ghost," Em suggests. "She seemed less 'We are Borg mind collective' than the others."

The idea of seeing the violet-haired ghost again is intriguing on many levels, but not all of them are helpful in this scenario. "How do I get her attention and not the others? Maybe a Ouija board?"

All four of them flinch and wince.

"Hells no." Dillan frowns. "That shit is dangerous."

I laugh. "I was kidding. We used to play Ouija as drunk teenagers. It's not real."

Sloan leaves his mission of studying the books to join the conversation. "Oh, it can be very real. But Dillan's right. It's a dangerous practice because yer willfully invitin' an entity from the other side to communicate, yet ye do not know who or what they really are. It could be a demon pretendin' to be yer mother, and there's no way to know until yer in serious trouble."

I hold up my hands. "Okay, no Ouija. Got it. Give me a better idea."

"Cast a spell?" Emmet suggests.

Sloan frowns as he scrubs a hand over his mouth. "There's the *Summon Undead* spell, but that only brings ghosts forth. Without something personal of the elf ghost, there's no way to guide the spell to bring her specifically."

I wave that suggestion away. "Pass. With my luck lately, I'd end up face to face with a berserker ghost."

"There's also *Soul Cage*," Sloan continues. "But a captured soul only knows what it knew in life and nothing beyond that, so it's not worth tormenting a spirit."

"Yeah, that sounds macabre," Dillan agrees.

"What about *Spirit of the Dead*?" Dionysus asks.

I roll my eyes. "This all sounds very complicated. Why don't we focus on finding the bones, and I'll see if I can pull a ghost to the side and have a chat? We've seen dozens of them today. I'm sure it won't be a problem finding one I could talk to."

"Okay, so on the topic of finding the bones, can I make a suggestion?" Dillan asks, and we all turn to give him the floor. "Instead of searching building by building and poking the bear—so to speak—why not bring the bones to us with a summoning spell?"

I raise an eyebrow, intrigued. "And eliminate weeks and possibly months of laborious leg work scouring the city? I'll try that for a dollar."

"To blanket the city with one spell would take a shit ton of power," Dillan points out.

Sloan nods. "Aye, it would. Fer shits and giggles, let's imagine that Dionysus and I bind our powers to cast it, and Emmet acts as our buffer to boost our juice to cover as much of the city as we can."

Emmet nods. "I'm game to try."

As they discuss how to proceed with summoning the bones of the island's dead, a weird hum buzzes in my blood. I shake my head to clear it, but nothing changes. I roll my shoulders, working out some of the battle's tension, but the buzz is getting more insistent.

"Brenny? Are you all right?" Emmet asks.

Sloan's ring draws my gaze.

On his left hand, he wears a platinum Claddagh wedding band that matches my sister's, but on his right hand, he wears a wide, bone ring. It's rough and asymmetrical. I've seen it a hundred times, but today is different. Something about that ring is calling to me.

"Sloan? Can I ask you a strange question?"

He ends his conversation with my brothers and gives me his full attention. "Of course. What is it?"

"It's your ring. It's giving off a weird vibration that's buzzing in my head. Can I ask where you got it?"

He glances down, following my gaze to the ring on his right hand. "It was part of Fionn's cache we rescued from the Fianna fortress before it was bulldozed. Fiona took a crack at it but said it seemed to fancy me."

I focus on it, and yeah, I'm sure the hum in my body is coming from that ring. "Would you mind if I hold it or maybe put it on? If I believed in that kind of thing, I'd swear it's calling to me."

Sloan chuckles. "Since I *do* believe in that kind of thing, I think ye should see what it's tryin' to tell ye."

Sloan slips the ring off his finger and hands it over. The moment I slide it over my knuckles and nestle it against my palm, the world tilts on its axis. A surge of power hits me, and in a racing heartbeat, I'm yanked from the wizard's library and spat out into a vast green plane of land.

Standing before me is the blond, weathered warrior of my ancestry. The ends of Fionn's braids brush his leather sash as he bows to me. His thick cloak drapes forward with the motion, and I stare at the Fianna crest on his two bronze shoulder brooches.

I recognize my great-great-however many greats-grandfather

from the brief time he manifested at Fiona's and Sloan's wedding last summer.

It's trippy, that's for sure.

Then he clasps my wrist and pulls me chest-to-chest with an ease that speaks of his muscled strength. "Brendan, lad. What's the craic?"

His Irish is laden with a heavy accent, the consonants and vowels clashing together with an ancient rhythm.

What's the craic?

"Why am I here, Fionn? Wait. *Am* I here?"

He chuckles, his skin heavily lined with his smile. "Yer wee sister asked me the same question when I first spoke to her, so I'll give ye the same answer. Yer here, and yer not."

"Did you call me here? Was that the humming and the ring?"

He places a scarred hand against the wide leather belt around his middle and grins. "Aye, this oul man still has a few tricks. Ye know I watch over yer lot, but it's not so easy when I want to spend time with ye."

"Why did you want to spend time with me?"

The legendary warrior has a mischievous twinkle in his eyes as he throws an arm across my shoulders like we're old battle comrades. "Come, lad. Let's take a walk, the two of us. There is much to discuss."

1 2

EMMET

The bone ring slips onto Brendan's finger, an heirloom from the legacy of Fionn mac Cumhaill, and Brendan's knees buckle. He crumples to the floor of the wizard's library like a fallen tree.

We're at his side in an instant, my brothers and I reaching out to assess what's happened. The panic that seized us all evaporates as my fingers brush against his skin. The thrum of power pulsing against my palm is familiar. "It's Fionn's energy signature."

Sloan is next to sit back and exhale. "Aye, I've felt it enough times when yer sister collapsed to recognize it. It seems yer great-granda has somethin' he'd like to say to Brendan."

"Why don't we ever get sucked back in time to have an adventure with Fionn?" Dillan gripes.

I chuckle and pat his shoulder. "Always a bridesmaid, brother."

"Do you want me to portal him to his bed, or do you think this will be quick?" Dionysus asks.

I consider that and answer for the group. "Yeah, thanks, Greek. There's no telling how long he'll be out, and we've been hanging around here long enough. Take him to his room and meet us to summon the bones. Where are we doing that, anyway?"

Sloan considers that. "How about the town square? It's centralized and might help disperse the spell."

Sounds good to me. "Yeah, meet us at the town square, Greek. We'll do what we can for as many ghosts as we can help."

Dionysus snaps out with Brenny, and Dillan checks his phone and grins. "Eva's home early."

"Excellent," Sloan replies. "Have her join us at the town square. She'll be a great help with the tethered souls if things get harried."

"Will do." Dillan goes back to texting his wife and nods. "She needs five minutes to change and kiss Han, and she'll be there."

Sloan holds out his hand for Dillan and me, and we complete the connection to be *poofed* to the town square—or at least what we call the town square.

Isilon is a massive city, and we haven't begun to explore it all, but the town square outside the security office is like our Times Square.

There are amazing architectural buildings all the way around, with a huge green space in the middle, walking paths, and a fancy fae fountain in the center.

As excited as I am to begin looking into Syma's quest to reignite the Embers of Existence, first things first. The whispering shadows are an immediate threat to the people of Isilon. With Brendan out of commission for the moment, that moves into the top spot.

It takes Sloan about twenty minutes and two trips of him *poofing* away and back before he's ready.

The first time he returned, he had a spell book and a Costco-sized bag of table salt. By the look of things, he plans to burn a shit ton of bones.

The second time he took a side trip, he returned with a dozen black pillar candles. "Once we have the bones of the dead, we'll burn all but a few. Those we'll use to summon the ghosts to have a conversation and hopefully find out who's doing what and where."

That sounds great in theory, except things don't usually work out like that for us.

Meh, you never know. Our luck could turn around.

"All right, boys, set up the circle of protection while I read over and ready the spell."

Dillan and I pour a thick ring of salt in front of the fountain and set up the candles evenly around the edge. The salt provides a barrier so the souls can't advance on us, and the flames of the black candles should give the ghosts a point of calling to follow to get to us.

Dionysus and Eva arrive while we're finishing our preparations. Dillan takes Eva aside to welcome her home and catch her up on our intentions.

Although she's a guardian angel now, Eva's centuries as a reaper working for Death will serve us well when dealing with ghosts and vengeful spirits.

"All right, let's begin." Sloan holds up the spellbook so he can read aloud. "Em, are ye good?"

"Yeah. Ready when you are."

Dionysus stands beside Sloan, who is by far our best caster next to Merlin, and places a hand on his shoulder. I move in and take Dionysus' other hand, calling on my power to amplify.

When I've tapped into the Sloan-Dionysus energy pool, I lock in and get ready for the ride. "Whenever you're ready, Irish."

Sloan clears his throat and projects his voice.

"From sprawling streets to earthen bed, find hidden bones of silent dread.

Bound by root and stone entwined, heed the call that's now assigned.

Earthly remains, shrouded deep, awaken now from death's long sleep.

By druid's word and nature's plea, bring forth the bones for all to see."

Arcane symbols glow within the circle, and I crank up the volume on our magical endeavor. My druidic powers aren't as active or offensive as the others.

I'm not a pacifist or anything. My powers aren't about attack.

It used to bug me that my brothers got all the cool offensive abilities, but since living here, I've realized that the powers we inherited suit each of our personalities.

Everything happens as it's meant to.

As the spell pushes out farther and farther across the city, the symbols on the ground shimmer. They cast eerie shadows that dance like fireflies in a twilight waltz. I reach out, my power an invisible force.

We're close now. I can feel it.

The air is charged with expectation as if the city is holding its breath, not only the five of us.

Then it happens.

With a rush like the tide washing in to shore, the spell expands to the far reaches of the city's wards and splashes back toward us.

It sweeps through Isilon, a silent tsunami of energy that hunts for the restless souls clinging to our world. I can't see it, but I feel it—every whisper of power, every breath of intention.

We're calling the bones of the dead.

We did it.

It's not hard to buffer a magical intention cast by a druid as gifted as Sloan when assisted by a man as powerful as Dionysus.

Honestly, they make my job easy.

Anticipation builds in the air like a balloon filling until it's ready to burst. We're all pumped and ready for the skeletal deluge.

Any minute.

The spell is doing its thing.

It's coming…

The air above our circle opens a yawning expanse. My heart is racing, waiting for the influx of bones to rain inside the circle. Instead of a torrent, we get a trickle.

A few bones clatter to the ground and make a meager pile. Instead of a mountain, we haven't even got a molehill.

Dillan snorts. "No bones about it, that was bone-chillingly underwhelming."

The corners of my mouth tweak up, even though I'm puzzled as hell. "Tibia-honest. That was a letdown."

"Not remotely humerus," Dionysus adds.

Sloan looks more distraught than amused.

"Don't take it too hard, Irish," Dillan consoles. "You can bone up on the spell and take another crack at it tomorrow."

Sloan shakes his head. "I don't understand it. Fer the number of ghosts we've seen today alone, this circle should be full."

"If the bones didn't come, what does that mean?" Eva is more interested in Sloan and his quandary than the three of us acting like fools. "Could they be behind a magical ward?"

Sloan considers that and crouches to examine the bones we have. "I suppose that's a possibility."

I bend beside him and look at the little pile. "We planned on selecting a few bones to summon a spirit to question. Now we don't have to go through a selection process. Do you think there are enough here to do the next spell?"

"I expect so." He lays out the bones, arranging them with meticulous precision. "Em, pour a cup of salt on here and be ready to torch these if things go south."

I do as he asks and we all take our positions again so Sloan can cast the second spell.

"Spirits of the realm beyond, heed this sacred druid's bond. Through the veil that parts our worlds, I call to where the dead unfurl.

Ancestors of ancient might, step forth from the shadowed night. By these bones and candles' flame, to this circle I call yer name.

Whispers lost in time's embrace, I seek to gaze upon yer face. With focus true and guidance clear, I ask ye now to join us here."

The air shifts and not one, but two ghosts flicker into view—well, two and a half—sort of.

"Is that dog missing a leg because we don't have the bone or because it was missing a leg?" I ask.

The three hazy and indistinct forms look confused, staring out at us. Likely as confused as we look, staring at two men and a three-legged ghostly dog with its tongue lolling out in a spectral pant.

"I fucking love my life." Dillan snorts. "Seriously, our normal is so whacked."

True story.

If the oddity of the dog throws Sloan, he doesn't let on. "We brought ye here to ask a few questions. Then we'll release ye to yer final rest. Eva here will escort ye to wherever yer afterlife awaits, and ye can finally be free of this ghostly existence."

The ghosts blink, their expressions dazed, as if they're not quite sure how they ended up here.

The canine ghost cocks its head, and I swear it's sizing us up. It's a mid-sized mutt with long, floppy hair and a stubby tail.

"What can you tell us about your situation?" I ask.

Their forms flicker as one of the men edges forward. "We remember all."

Well, that will be helpful.

"There are a lot of ghosts in the city streets. Have they always been here or is something happening?"

"As the city wakes, he claims the trapped souls."

"He? Who's claiming the souls?"

"The man in the embroidered robes."

"The silver-haired wizard?" I want to be sure.

"That's him," the spirit confirms.

"How does he control you?"

The ghost shakes his head. "Not us. He didn't find our bones, so he couldn't call us. The others, though. They can't escape him."

"You've managed to remain free from his hold?"

"So far, yes. We've been fortunate to avoid his grasp. He is a powerful but cruel man. What he does to the others is sickening."

"We'll stop him," I assure them. "Do you know where he lives or keeps the bones?"

The men look at one another and shake their heads. "We do not. We stay away."

Ask them what areas are safe. Maybe that will tell us where they are, Dionysus suggests in my mind.

I repeat the question for the ghosts, and they give us a dozen places on this side of the city where they were never bothered.

"Is there anything else you can tell us that could help us find him and stop what he's doing?"

They regard one another but come up with nothing.

I don't know what else to ask them and look at the others to see if they have questions. They don't.

"Okay, we're going to burn your bones so the wizard can't call you back, and Eva will take you to your final resting place. Does that work?"

"There are no words," one replies.

"Thank you," the other comments.

With that, I conjure a ball of blue faerie fire.

"Wait!" Eva holds up her hand. "The dog doesn't want to go. This is his home. He wants to stay."

I blink and look around for any objections. There aren't any, so I drag my toe through the salt line and break the protective barrier.

I would never break the seal in a battle scenario, but these two men aren't going anywhere. We're their chance at salvation, and they're eager to take it.

The three-legged dog trots out of the circle, his back end bouncing as he hops along. When he's clear of the circle, and Eva has collected his bones, I toss the faerie fire over the pile that's left.

Although human bones don't burn, with a bit of magic, the circle is empty in a powerful *whoosh* of blue flame.

"Are they gone?" I twist around, searching the night air, but I no longer see their spectral forms.

Eva's blonde curls bounce around her cherubic face as she grins. "No. They're untethered souls now."

"Take them home, angel." Dillan winks at his wife. "I'll wait up."

Eva steps into the circle with her beautiful golden wings stretching behind her. Her feathers catch the light, casting prisms that paint all of us in a divine glow. She holds her hands out, smiles, and wraps her fingers around unseen hands as she looks from shoulder to shoulder. "Come on, fellas. Things will look much brighter for you tomorrow."

When the angel disappears, I meet Dillan's proud gaze and pat my chest. "Seeing her like that never fails to steal my breath. She's magnificent, D."

He nods. "Don't I know it."

"What she's doing with you is the eighth wonder of the world, but hey, good for you."

Dillan laughs. "She honestly thinks *she's* the lucky one. Can you believe that?"

I snort and point at the massive bag of Morton's fine grain. "It's a shame we didn't get more bones."

Sloan sighs. "Weel, if that's how the wizard holds sway over his ghost army, I'm not surprised he's locked them down. But yer right, Em. It is a shame."

"Even so, you rocked socks tonight, Irish." Dionysus holds his fist up for a bump.

"Yeah, you did," I add.

"It's too bad you won't be able to come out tomorrow and help us more," Dillan adds.

Sloan's brows arch. "Oh? What makes ye say that?"

He laughs. "Because when Fi hears about all the chaos she missed out on today, she'll beat the snot out of you."

I laugh. "You're definitely going to be in the doghouse."

He shrugs. "I have a secret weapon ready for such an occasion. A foolproof plan, guaranteed to get me out of the hot seat at any time."

Oh, this has got to be good. "Care to share?"

He grins. "Seasons twenty-three and twenty-four of *The Voice* on DVD."

Dillan frowns. "How do you think that will sway Fi in your favor?"

"Because Niall Horan is one of the season mentors. It's hours upon hours of her teen heartthrob being his normal charmin' self."

"Nice one, Irish." I hold up my hand for a high-five.

"Yeah, well done," Dillan adds.

"Can I watch it too?" Dionysus asks.

"Of course ye can, Greek. Why don't ye pop home, get into yer onesie, and come over in twenty? That should give me time to get to the grovelin' part of my day. Och, and can ye maybe swing by Italy and snag her a pizza from that place the two of ye go to when ye need cheerin' up? That will help."

Grinning like a fool, Dionysus gives us a double thumbs-up. "Done and done."

When he disappears in a spray of golden mist, I laugh. "You have more than book smarts, Irish. You're the man. You're a good sport too. I know Dionysus takes a lot of Fi's time and attention. You handle it well."

He shrugs. "It's easy. Before we were married, yer sister made it clear that Dionysus was part of the package. I accepted it then and still do. Our family might look odd from the outside, but it works."

Yeah, it does.

The bark of the three-legged dog startles my attention back to the moment at hand. "Well, looks like we have a new mascot. What should we name him?"

"Hopalong Cassidy," Dillan suggests. "Or maybe Trike."

"Hat Trick," I suggest.

Dillan grins and gives me the win.

"All right, then. Welcome to the chaos, Hat Trick."

"Speakin' of chaos, I think ye'll need to call a town meetin', Em. The citizens need to hear what happened to the nymph and be told about the whisperin' shadows. Look what shape we were in after five minutes of their influence. They need to be warned."

I check my watch. It's much too late to raise the alarms tonight. Many of the people who have come to live here have families. "All right. I'll have Astrid notify all citizens there's a meeting at Shenanigans in the morning."

Sloan nods. "I'll mention it to Dionysus. I'm sure he'll take care of the refreshments."

"Do you think Brendan will be back from his field trip by then?"

Sloan shrugs. "There's no way to know. Come now, let's get home. Yer sister's goin' to be annoyed with me as it is. I at least want to explain what happened before Dionysus gets there."

I chuckle. "Can we come watch?"

Sloan arches a brow. "No. And if ye laugh at me again, ye can walk home."

I'm waaay too tired to hoof it back up the hill to the palace. "My apologies. You do you, Irish. I'm happy to go home and have a hot shower."

Dillan chuckles. "Me too. There's only so much fun a guy can have in one day before our quota is maxed."

Agreed.

13

BRENDAN

I keep step beside Fionn, a legend of Celtic myth and my many times over ancestor. His presence in my life is hard to fathom. Not only because he's from a different time, but also because as far as I know, he's only appeared to guide Fiona through her trials or helped the others when they were part of her quests.

"Why me?" I ask. "And why now?"

"Ye have the blood of druids and warriors runnin' through yer veins. The lot of ye do."

I like to think so, but the gravity of his statement weighs on me.

"What do ye know of the term Celtic shaman?" He scuffs the dirt with the toe of his boot.

I consider that and shrug. "Fiona's one, and you too. It's not like the native nations' medicine men. It's more about being able to navigate the spiritual planes."

He nods. "A Celtic shaman is a man or woman who enters an altered state of consciousness—usually at will—to utilize a hidden reality to gain knowledge, power, to help, or to banish others. Additionally, they usually have at least one spirit in their service."

I have a sneaking suspicion I know where this is heading and I'm not sure I'll like getting there. "Right. Fiona can retreat into herself, and Bruin was drawn to her and lives within her. I'm with you so far."

"Celtic lore is flush with examples of heroes travelin' between worlds on quests for magical rewards, knowledge, or power. In Old Irish, it's called *immram*."

Yeah, I'm aware. Our bedtime stories were often tales Da would tell us of Celtic gods or tricksters and their battles to balance good and evil.

"Shamans typically undergo exceptional ordeals in their lives. The very nature of a shaman's trials place him outside the norm of society. Most folks can't fully comprehend the lengths he's willin' to go through to follow his moral compass."

I swallow. "Sure. I've gone through a lot, but my family gets me. It's not like I'm an outcast or anything."

"Och, no. I'm not sayin' ye are. Just that experiences can set us apart from the masses."

"Yeah, okay, that's fair."

Fionn's eyes gleam with ancient wisdom, and with a gesture that bends the world to his will, the serene landscape around us shifts.

The air shimmers like the surface of a lake touched by a gentle breeze, and suddenly, we stand on the precipice of a new reality. The sun is bright and warm on my face. We're standing in the backyard of my childhood home in Toronto.

My heart hammers and I look around, panicking. "I can't be here, Fionn. Mother Nature only gave me a second chance at life if I stay in Isilon and don't influence humanity's timeline."

Fionn smiles and waves a scarred hand between us. "Relax, lad. Yer here but yer not, remember? Yer corporeal self is in

Isilon waitin' fer yer return and yer spiritual self won't alter any timelines or break any bargains with the Divine Lady."

I wrap my head around that. "I can be here?"

"Aye, ye can."

Standing here staring at the old Victorian house where we lived and grew as a family feeds something in my soul. Mam, Da, and the six of us…

"It seems crazy that we all fit in there."

Fionn chuckles. "Ye were a great deal smaller at the time. Made the fittin' a bit easier, I expect."

"Yeah. I suppose that's true."

"Are ye ready to move on, lad?"

My gut reaction is to shout "Hells no" and move away from him so I can stay, but I realize his question isn't so much of a question but a prompt to get me ready for what's next. "Will I be able to come back sometime?"

Fionn nods. "Once I've got ye trained up, Fiona can help ye. Eventually, ye'll be able to navigate the spirit plane on yer own. Then yer heart's desire will take ye wherever ye want to go."

I draw a deep breath. It sucks that I can't interact with my old life, but honestly, being here helps. "Okay. You mentioned training me. Is that what this is?"

"We talked about trials and sufferin'. Ye've had yer share of both. First when yer mam passed when ye were a boy, then when ye lost yer high school sweetheart, the toll yer undercover work took on ye, and finally steppin' in front of the bullets meant fer another."

I swallowed. "Okay, but a lot of people suffer."

"Aye, that's true. But yer a mac Cumhaill. Ye've got my blood in yer veins and, as well, ye spent a good long time in the After durin' yer death. Yer connection with the spirit realm was set and now it's active."

"Is that why you came?"

"Aye, ye've been given a gift that needs to be learned and

understood. Since I know better than most what it is to be a ghost and how that throws a spanner into the works, who better to teach ye?"

It's hard to argue with logic like that.

"How do you want to do this?"

He gestures at the sacred grove behind both houses and walks toward the trees. "I realize ye don't have the family spark in ye when it comes to the druid magic, but yer a druid all the same. And druids always do our best work in nature."

We wander deeper into the trees, and the magic of the grove takes hold. It's more than a stand of trees behind two houses. The magic of it being a druid grove makes it a deep and lush forest.

"Fiona gave her fae friends the option to stay here or move to the island. Most chose to move."

Fionn seems unaffected by that and points at the two rattan swing chairs hanging on either side of the path. "What matters is the intention. Fiona, Sloan, and yer brothers put their love and energy into this grove. The dragons lived here. Fi's battle bear lived here. And no matter if five fae remain or fifty-five, there is magic all around us."

I sit in one of the hanging chairs, surprised at how comfortable they are. They were a gift from Sloan to Fi while they were dating if I remember correctly.

"All right, so my teachings will be grounded in the age-old wisdom of Celtic shamans. We are the masters of the spirit realm who walked a path ye've only begun to tread. It'll take years to grow adept, but this will be a deep dive into how the physical and the spiritual are intertwined, for to navigate one, ye must understand the other."

I rub my sweaty palms against my thighs. Why am I so nervous? Maybe because the knowledge I gain here will be crucial, not only for me, but for the safety of Emhain Abhlach and my family?

No pressure or anything.

"We'll start with meditation. Have ye ever tried it?"

"No."

"In yer life before, what did ye do to clear yer mind and center yerself when the world closed in?"

I blink. "Uh…I had my vices."

Fionn chuckles. "Come now, I'm not a fair maiden. Ye can talk yer truth."

I clear my throat. "Either go to the firing range and shoot the shit out of paper targets, drink myself stupid, or find an aggressive woman and exhaust myself."

"Aye, this will be different than those and sadly, less sexually rewarding. Meditation fer our purpose will be about more than workin' off pressures or problems. It'll be about existin' on another plane."

"I'm game to try, but I'm not very Zen."

"Och, don't worry about that. Ye'll soon see that when yer mind is calm, yer senses will be sharp. It'll open ye up to subtleties, lad, and that's where ye'll find the spirits. Now, lean back."

I adjust my seat in the swing and the chair tips in the open air, swaying gently with my weight shift. "Do I sit and think about nothing?"

Fionn chuckles. "Not quite. I want ye to focus on awareness, presence. Yer not emptying your mind, ye need to focus it, attune it to the whispers of the other side."

I cross my legs, trying to mimic the yoga pose you always see. "Like tuning into a ghostly radio frequency?"

"Exactly. Now, close yer eyes. Breathe. Deep, steady breaths. In…and out."

I do as he says, feeling foolish at first. As the minutes pass, the rhythm of my breathing takes over, and the sounds of the grove fade away.

Fionn's voice is soft and distant, a guidepost in the fog. "Allow yer senses to expand beyond the physical. Spirits are all around. Energy imprints everywhere on the fabric of the human realm."

I'm not sure how long I drift in this state, but slowly, an awareness creeps into my consciousness. A presence, faint yet undeniable, moves closer. My heart rate picks up, excitement mingling with a touch of fear.

A whisper, soft as a lover's sigh, tickles my ear. "Hey, handsome."

My eyes snap open, and I'm back in the grove, staring into Fionn's knowing gaze. "Did you hear that?"

He grins. "Ye've got the gift all right. That was good, and with practice, ye'll see them as clearly as ye see me."

"I see the ones in the streets of Isilon."

He nods. "Aye, in yer moment of survival, ye tapped into yer gift. Now ye need to learn to use it when yer not about to be choked to death."

"Yeah. Good plan. I'd love to avoid that."

"All right. Then let's turn up the volume on yer ghost radio, shall we?"

The world shimmers and my reality shifts again. Fionn and I stand by the old fountain in Isilon's city square. My boots are planted firmly on the cobblestones, but I'm unsure if I'm really here or if this is still part of my Fionn-induced hallucination.

"Now, close yer eyes, relax, and expand yer senses. Connect with the fae magic. Ye should feel it right away. This island is a nexus point for the ley lines."

Feeling it isn't the problem.

Controlling it is.

The island's magic surges around me, the prana river's raw power coursing through the ground, radiating from the buildings and the trees, and filling my lungs with every breath I take.

I try to rein it in…to grab hold of it…to channel it.

It's impossible. It fights me and burns my senses.

"It's like trying to tame a wild stallion."

"Och, ye never want to tame a stallion, lad. Ye want to gain its trust."

Oh. I hadn't thought about it like that.

I close my eyes and try again, letting the city's heartbeat sync with mine. The energy flows into me in a violent rush. Instead of grabbing hold, I let it flow through me this time and allow it to take the path it chooses.

The burning stops and after a few moments more, a breeze of pure energy brushes my skin.

"Now open yer eyes and tell me what ye see."

I do as he says and suck in a breath. "Holy shit."

The Hidden City of Isilon is a kaleidoscope of colors, magic, and mystery, flexing in waves before me like seeing a distant mirage in the desert.

"It's incredible. It's like a living prism."

"Aye, now yer gettin' it. Now stay in that moment and let it take root. Sink into the mindfulness and get familiar with how it feels. The energy in the spirit realm feels different. It's lighter with a bit of a tingle."

I do that, and when I feel like I've got it, I expand my senses like he taught me before. "A tingle, yes, but there's also a bit of a bite...like the barb of a shock."

"Och, that's not the spirit realm, lad. That's yer bad apples. Ye've got a worm in yer orchard, and he's causin' damage. Ye'll need to find him and take care of that right quick."

"That's the plan, but how do I do it?"

"Once ye practice up a bit, ye'll learn to slip through the barrier between planes and will be able to seek out different energy. Fer now, it's impressive that ye feel the difference. Good on ye, lad."

The praise is nice, and while I appreciate it, that doesn't help me right now. I need to learn how to track down the wizard and release the souls stuck as whispering shadows under his control.

Another thought strikes me, and I think of the purple-haired elf. Tracking her down wouldn't be bad either. Something about her speaks to me.

My instincts are usually spot on.

"Practice slippin' in and out of the spirit plane. Find the barrier between the two and give it a go."

"How do I do that?"

"It's different fer everyone. To some, it's a door to open. To others, it's a mist to pass through. Ye'll likely know it when ye see it."

You'll know it when you see it doesn't give me much to go on, but I try anyway. I concentrate, navigating my senses through the surrounding air until I reach a shimmering barrier.

It gleams like a mirror as it undulates, but I see beyond that as it wavers and light reflects along its surface. "I see the souls beyond the barrier."

"Good. Once ye know what it looks and feels like, ye'll be able to find it again."

Yeah, hopefully. I'm getting the hang of it. My understanding of the planes solidifies more with each of his training exercises.

"All right, now I need to teach ye how to put up a psychic shield."

I snort. "That sounds rather sci-fi."

"Och, ye jest, but when ye come up against a dark one, ye'll be glad to defend yerself from it gettin' into yer head. Attacks come in different ways, ye see. Ye need to train mentally and physically, both."

I nod. "Then teach me, Obi-Wan."

14

EMMET

I shove open the doors to Shenanigans, and the clamor of worried chitchat instantly swamps me. The pub's a hive of anxious faces, every nook crammed with Isilon's citizens. They're here for the town hall meeting, and the absence of Brendan, my right-hand man in city decisions, leaves me feeling lopsided.

Sloan, my brothers, and Kidok are already on the scene, working to simmer down the unease.

My entrance cues a shift.

I gaze longingly at the brunch spread along the side wall but forego my cravings for crab quiche and accept my duty as their go-to guy for the city.

With a half-hearted wave, I move through the bodies until I'm at the bar at the back wall. I hop up to sit next to the beer taps so everyone can see me.

"Good morning, everyone. Thank you all for coming. I'm not sure what you've heard or what you might've guessed, but as of the night before last, one of our own, a tree nymph named Randa, was found dead at the base of her home tree."

A collective shudder ripples through the crowd, the echo of

anxious whispers bouncing around the pub. I rub the nape of my neck and focus on what I need to say to put these people at ease.

"If I were you, I'd want the truth, so that's what I'm going to give you. Yesterday, Brendan and I, with the help of my brothers and our team, began our investigation into what happened to Randa. What we uncovered was disturbing, and that's why I called you all here."

I give them a moment to absorb that while I figure out how to frame our grim news in a way that won't send anyone into a panic.

"It turns out we have a surprisingly large number of ghosts in our city." There's another rush of whispers, and I raise my hand to quiet them down. "Several of you mentioned you feared something dark in the shadows. After dealing with our spectral souls yesterday, we believe this is what you feel."

"What kind of ghosts?" someone shouts.

"From what we've learned, the ghost of a wizard who lived in the city when it went dormant haunts the streets. Revived and gaining power, he's harnessing other displaced souls to do his bidding."

"What does that mean?" one of the gnomes near the door asks.

"It means we think the wizard is creating whispering shadows to amplify fears and feed on despair. Before we knew what we were up against, my brothers and I fell victim to it. Having experienced it, we're concerned about your safety."

"Is that where Brendan is?" HaiLe asks at the end of the bar.

I shake my head. "No. Brendan is at the palace. He'll be out and about later. When the ghosts attacked us—"

"Attacked!" someone shouts. "The ghosts are attacking people?"

"Well, Randa didn't just die!" a pixie snaps.

"Okay, hold on!" I clap my hands to get everyone's attention again. "Yes, the ghosts attacked us, but we were actively trying to stop the wizard. No, we're not sure that happened to Randa. We're only one day into the investigation and haven't got any final answers yet."

The crowd settles down.

"Given that there are a great number of ghosts, and they are harnessing a disturbing power, I suggest everyone moves into the palace complex until we find the wizard and end his control. We have plenty of room, and while we can't safeguard the entire city, Dionysus can protect the palace."

The roar of negative feedback tells me how much they dislike that idea.

"Hey, guys, listen. It's not ideal, but it's a good plan. We only want to keep you safe."

"Is this going to be a regular thing?" a woman in the back calls. "Every time you come up against something you can't handle, we'll have to uproot our kids and hide behind your walls?"

I sigh. "It's not a perfect solution, I get that, but we're trying to do what's best with what we've been dealt."

"How long?" a pixie asks.

"I'm thinking two days, maybe three. We'll know more soon. I want to safeguard all of you while we work things out."

"Two or three days won't be that bad." HaiLe places her paw on her oldest cub's shoulder. "We lived there last year during a similar scare, and we got to pretend we were royalty. Didn't we, kids?"

Binx and her other four cubs smile and nod.

"If it keeps my children safe and these aggressive ghosts and their master can't get to us in the palace, I say we play it smart and listen to Emmet. He's never led us astray."

Bless you, HaiLe.

I would kiss that feline if I didn't think Kidok would claw me to death.

Thankfully, the mood has swung my way. "HaiLe's right. Let

us keep you and your families safe. You can be royalty for a couple of days, get to know your fellow citizens, and who knows, it might be fun."

"Like camping," Dillan adds.

"When do we have to go?" a centaur asks.

"I'd love it if you went now so everyone is secured. If you need things from your homes, Sloan, Nikon, and Dionysus can teleport you to get your things, so you won't be alone in the streets."

A murmur ripples through the crowd, a mix of indecision and reluctance. I scan their faces, seeing the stubbornness etched into some. "I know you all have your survival stories and you value your freedom, but sticking together is our best bet."

"We didn't flee to Isilon to be herded like sheep!" the gnome by the door shouts. "You can't make us."

I let out a frustrated sigh and run a hand through my hair. "No, and I wouldn't try. Of course you're free to make your own choices. I'm asking that you trust me and help us help you."

"We can get what we need from home?"

Sloan nods. "Aye, we'll make sure of it."

The crowd shuffles, some still mumbling dissent, but the majority grasp the situation's gravity.

Dionysus grins at me with a swish of his hand. "Leave the details to me, Em. I'll make that palace safer than a dragon's hoard."

"Thanks, Greek. Just, uh, try not to turn it into a nightclub, okay? We're going PG all the way."

He winks, already lost in thoughts of his protective enchantments. As the citizens make their way out the door, Dillan and Calum jog to go with them.

It will be a long couple of days, but this is the best option. I believe that.

As the pub empties, I spot my sister sitting in a back booth with a swarthy male with blue hair. I get a boost of adrenaline from seeing Myra's brother. He's a welcome addition to the chaos of the morning.

I stride over and extend my hand. "Zxata, I didn't expect you to get pulled into our crisis, but I'm grateful you came. The extra help couldn't come at a better time."

"I was happy to come. I was saying to Fi that I'm up for a change and might stick around if you'll have me."

"Even better. Yes. Welcome. Tell me how we can make this your home, and you'll have it."

Like his sister, Zxata shares the species traits of vertically slit eyes, and pale silver skin cracked with darker tones beneath. He's an ash tree nymph if I'm not mistaken, but I'm not sure where the lines are drawn in focus among their kind.

He runs his fingers through his bright blue hair and grins. "Honestly, I'm looking to build a community. Being the representative of tree nymphs in Toronto is an honor, but with only Myra and me there, it's kind of pointless. She can take my seat as a Guild governor and watch over things. I'd like to get more involved."

"Well, I'm sorry that your first act of getting involved is helping us investigate the killing of one of your people."

"It's unfortunate, but perhaps together we can find the girl some justice."

"Yeah, I hope so. Would you like to see the grove and maybe check in with her home tree?"

He nods. "I would."

The three of us walk through the streets together, and I point out a few of the buildings in the city—the security office, and a couple of the inhabited houses. "The entire city is pretty much up for grabs. We have a growing gnome community, nixies, pixies, brownies, elves, and a few dwarves."

I point to our right, over the prana river. "The dragons have their lair beyond the city gates in the cliffs over there."

Then I point into the distance ahead and to the left. "The centaurs mostly keep to themselves and claimed a small cluster of houses at the base of that ridge beyond the city's boundary."

"It's very impressive," Zxata remarks.

I shrug. "I can't take any of the credit for that. This city rose to glory back when the Light Weavers sisters had a plan for it. Brendan and I are simply trying to breathe life back into it."

Fiona clucks her tongue. "He's being too modest. Emmet has done a great job bringing people together and getting this city up and running again."

I chuckle. "Well, it's not taking prisoners anymore. That's one good thing."

Zxata chuckles. "Honestly, even when the city locked us in, there was no hardship. Oh, no, we have to spend a couple of extra days in paradise celebrating Fi's and Sloan's wedding."

Fiona laughs. "I'm glad that's how you felt. I don't think everyone shared that sentiment."

Zxata shrugs. "There are enough things going wrong in the world. We don't need to panic about things like spending an unexpected couple of days with family and friends."

Our conversation comes to a solemn end as we arrive at the clearing outside the grove's tree line.

"That was Randa's oak." I point it out.

Zxata steps forward and places his palms against the rough bark of the tree where Randa was found.

He closes his eyes, and a serene expression washes over his face. There's a palpable energy exchange, a communion between the tree nymph and the arboreal giant before us.

"He misses her," Zxata murmurs, his voice tinged with sorrow. "Randa only arrived a few months ago, but their bond grew quickly. After so many centuries of being alone, Randa filled a void. Now there's an emptiness where she used to be."

Fiona steps closer, her hand brushing the bark. "I'm sorry for your loss, Mr. Tree."

"Does he know anything that could help us find who killed her?" I ask.

Zxata's face contorts with a pang of shared grief. "Trees experience things differently than you or I. He didn't see anything, but he felt her pain deep to his roots. The tree mourns, and with him, the whole grove."

It's so sad.

Nature has borne witness to the tragedy, holding the memory of Randa's agony in a silent vigil.

Zxata withdraws his hands. "If it's all right, I'd like to spend some time alone with the grove."

I'm unsure what to say or do to make things better, but leaving him here alone doesn't feel right. "Fi? Can you leave Bruin with him?"

"Yeah. That's a good idea."

A gust of air swirls around us as Fiona's bonded battle bear releases and takes form beside us.

"Bruin, you stay with Zxata while he tends to the grove. I don't want him to be alone. Emmet will escort me back to our street, and I promise I won't go anywhere without you."

With that settled, we leave Zxata to begin the healing process.

15

EMMET

.

My boots thud against the street, the rhythmic *thunk-thunk-thunk* bouncing off the vibrantly colored buildings of Isilon's main thoroughfare. There's a buzz under my skin, a tingle that starts at my fingertips and thrums through my veins like a live wire.

Usually, I'm laid back enough that the torrent of untapped power pulsing within me remains in check.

Today is different.

With the citizens settling within the palace buildings, I'm free to take on the first challenge Syma tasked me to complete—air.

At first, I wasn't sure where the fragment of the key to the Corestone sanctum could be in the sky, but after speaking to Astrid this morning, I'm certain it's somewhere in the ancient roost of the lightning serpents.

Up I go to retrieve the first fragment.

I crane my neck, peering up at the perfect pink sky. As far as I can see, there's not even the hint of a cloud, and certainly no sky city hanging above us.

Astrid says lightning serpents play among the thunderheads,

their scales flashing like shards of daylight piercing through a storm.

I used to love storms.

When Fiona and I were kids, and the sky was losing its shit, we used to sit in the bay window of her room and watch the lightning jag its way to earth. Then we'd count the beats between lightning and the crack of thunder to track its stormy path.

We used to get wound up when it was getting close.

We were adrenaline junkies even then.

The dog's bark is startling and makes me stop to glance around. In the eighteen months since I've been living here, the normalcy of hearing a dog bark in the neighborhood was lost.

A bear roaring, a bobcat mrowling, even dragons shrieking, but not the simple, soothing sound of man's best friend calling in the distance.

I take a moment to turn and wait for Hat Trick to run-hop his way over to greet me. It seems now that we've met, he'll hang out and say hello.

"Morning, buddy. How's things?"

I lean down to pet him but don't get anywhere with that. We might be able to see him, but he's still a spirit dog, and my hand goes through his ghostly form. It's disturbing.

"I'm going to visit the dragons' lair. Do you want to come along?"

By the tail wagging and him falling into step beside me, I take that as a yes.

"Today is a big day for me, boy. I'm going to try to recover the first fragment of a very important key."

I glance down, smiling at the mutt's tongue lolling out the side of his mouth as he motors along beside me. "Yeah, you're right. As Yoda says, there is no try, only do or do not. Good point. So…today I *will* recover the first fragment. Thanks, buddy."

The dog happily hops along beside me as we exit the city's gate and head toward the prana river. The morning sun glints off the deep fuchsia of the raw fae power, and the tingling in my skin ramps up to a bite.

It's always uncomfortable at first, but soon after, it's like my body recognizes the signature of the ley line power as part of its own and gives me a rush of strength and adrenaline.

It is me, and I am it.

I stop on the top of the bridge's arch and stare into the lazy river of ultimate power. Not a day goes by without me reliving the horror of thinking I would die when I fell into its waters.

Thankfully, that was a ley line leading to the Cistern of The Source in Gobekli Tepe, Turkey, and not the source of power convergence it is here.

I leave Hat Trick at the bridge and climb the grassy slope toward the cliffs where the dragons have made their home.

As I near the lair's mouth, I feel the dragons' eyes upon me, the power they possess greeting mine with fond familiarity. Like me, the dragons have become guardians of Isilon.

Dart and Saxa emerge from the shadowed mouth of the cave, their scales shimmering in the new light. Dart, a majestic panorama of blues, nods his broad head in greeting while Saxa, radiant as the golden sun at dawn, stretches out her wings in a gentle salute.

"Good morning, Emmet," Dart rumbles, the sound resonating within the cliff's hollows.

"You're looking well," Saxa chimes in, her tone lighter yet echoing her mate's warmth.

How fucking cool is it that this is my life?

"Morning, Dart. And you as well, Saxa. I have a favor to ask the two of you."

"What do you need?" Dart asks.

"Well, I've been tasked with retrieving something I believe the Light Weavers placed in hiding in the roost of the lightning serpents. I can transform and try to find it myself but thought having a dragon escort was a wiser plan in case I need my human form. If you're up for it, I'd like a ride into the skies and backup if things go sideways."

Dart's eyes glint with the thrill of a quest, a spark of adventure igniting within. "We are most definitely up for it, aren't we?"

Saxa straightens to her full height and stretches her wingspan out in a vibrant show of scales. "Oh, yes. We certainly are."

I chuckle. "Are you finding life here a little dull?"

Dart tilts his head. "There have been few adventures since moving here and since Fi decided to stop fighting battles, fewer still. We were saying we want to spread our wings and take something on."

"Excellent. Then it's a plan."

Dart lowers his head. "When are you thinking?"

"Right now, unless you need more time."

Saxa grins and shakes out her scales. "No time needed. We're ready when you are."

"Feline Finesse." I call on my druidic power to lend me the agility to mount Dart's massive frame. With a surge of energy, I sprint and leap, my hands finding purchase on Dart's muscular forelimb.

The world spins as I vault upward, flipping over to land astride his broad back. I jog to the first of his back spikes and grip the handle of the leather saddle he wears there. The dragon's powerful muscles coil beneath me as I broaden my stance and settle in.

The moment we're ready to set off, Dionysus pops up out of nowhere, his brow furrowed. "Seriously? You were about to embark on an adventure without me? I'm a Light Weaver trainee too. I should get to go."

I scratch my nape, feeling sheepish. "Oh, hey. Sorry. I didn't know you wanted to come."

Dionysus pegs me with a look like I've told him the wine cask has run dry. "First, when have I ever passed up an adventure?"

"Never."

"Right. Second, I'm a fabulous backup."

"No question."

"Third, of course you're supposed to have help. Syma said, 'Gather your allies and your kin, for this burden is not yours to bear alone. In unity, there is strength, and in love, there is indomitable power.'"

Wow, having the memory of a god must be cool. "You're right, Greek. My bad. You're more than welcome to be my wingman. Do you want to ride with me or Saxa?"

He flashes me a big grin and waggles his chestnut brows. "I've got my own transportation, thanks."

He slips his fingers under his tongue and blows out a long breath. I brace for a piercing whistle, but the silence hangs awkwardly between us.

Dionysus notices my confusion and shrugs. "Not a human frequency."

In the next beat, the sky ripples as Contessa McSparkles—Dionysus' pegasus unicorn—cuts through the veil of wherever she's been, and she joins us in the here and now.

Her white wings are a majestic span of power against the pink expanse. When she descends in a prismatic blur of colors, she lands with a grace that contradicts her size. She is a beautiful impossibility.

Dionysus produces a banana out of nowhere, eliciting a delighted whinny from his girl before he swings himself onto her back with a flourish. "Giddy-up, Em."

I chuckle. "All righty then, let's get this show on the road. Or, I suppose, into the sky is more accurate."

We lift off, and the city recedes quickly, transforming into a mosaic of mossy, bioluminescent rooftops atop colorful buildings and the hot pink river that flows through Isilon like a brilliant ribbon.

I take a few deep breaths to settle my excitement as we climb. I can do this. I've always been an amazing support team member.

Now is my chance to show the realms I belong on the starting line.

The Light Weavers believed in me.

I can knock this out of the park.

The higher we climb, the thinner the air becomes until it's tough to fill my lungs.

"Air Bubble." The spell materializes a bubble of fresh air around my head, and I suck in a lungful of oxygen. It's not every day I soar through the heavens on dragonback on a quest to save an enchanted city, and I'm not about to let something like oxygen deprivation stand in my way.

"Do you know where we're going?" Dionysus sounds casual, like this is another Thursday night.

I squint against the sky, channeling my inner Lando Calrissian, searching for Cloud City.

Nothing.

"Astrid said the first challenge would be to find and gain access to the roost of the lightning serpents. The second will be dodging those slithery beasts long enough to grab the fragment and get out."

I scan the heavens, but it's like staring at an empty canvas—nothing but air and light.

"Maybe this isn't where Syma hid it," Dionysus suggests.

Maybe.

Dionysus' words ring in my head. *Syma hid it.*

On a hunch, I ignore what my eyes tell me and reach out with my senses. All magic has a particular feel. It's not a frequency or an energy. It's more nebulous than that.

Having trained with Syma and her sisters, I know how their magic feels. Instead of searching for a city of lightning serpents I know nothing about, I search for my mentor's magical signature.

I find it.

Almost instantly, I'm drawn to my left, and when Dart hovers in the right place, I pump my fist. "Booyah, baby. It's phased. Syma hid it like she and her sisters hid Isilon to keep it safe."

Dionysus stares at the empty air in front of it and nods. "Then, if it's phased from view, we'll need to phase it back so we can see it."

"Do you still remember how to do it?"

Dionysus flicks his fingers dismissively at me and scoffs. "Try to keep up, Cumhaill."

"I'll do my best."

We tap into our spatial manipulation training and begin to unravel the spell that hides the roost.

Light waves are a mix of electricity and magnetism called electromagnetic waves. We see objects because they give off light or light reflects off the objects and enters our eyes.

The magic used by Light Weavers alters the frequency and speed of the molecules beyond the range that humans and most other races can process. The city is still there, but our eyes can't catch its image.

The trickier part of their work is to couple that with another spell that makes it physically not appear there. It's a boundary spell that ensures that if a person or object touches any part of the phasing spell, it instantly transports them to the opposite side of the city.

To the person, they feel like they passed through the distance of space like normal when in truth, they were portaled to the opposite side.

With our hands outstretched, we weave our fingers through the invisible threads of magic that quilt the air. The concentration it demands is intense, the kind that beads sweat on your forehead and makes your arms tremble with effort.

When we removed the spell hiding Isilon, it took a half-dozen of us. Thankfully, the roost is a fraction of the size.

After a long and exhausting session of manipulating the electromagnetic field keeping the roost invisible, we alter the speed of the atoms until the roost of the lightning serpents materializes before our eyes.

It's a breathtaking sight, a floating archipelago of landmasses tethered together by chains of lightning and surrounded by electrified skies. Each island pulses with energy, the air around it crackling with static charge.

The serpents look like someone shoved a rebounding energy coil into a massive electric eel. They remind me of those snakes you fold into a can as a gag gift to scare the shit out of people when they spring free.

Before us, dozens of serpents the size of power poles zip and zap through the air. They're filled with light and sparks, and their scales shimmer with a kaleidoscope of colors that reflect the sun in dazzling patterns.

Dionysus lets out a low whistle. "Well, now. It's not every day I see something new. See? This is exactly why I needed to come. Yay, me."

"Glad you're being enriched, Greek. Yay, you. Now comes the part when we have to get that fragment without becoming electrical serpent chow."

Dionysus grins with a mischievous glint in his eyes. "The fun part, indeed. Let's do this."

I shake my head, always bemused by his boundless energy. "Let's focus on not getting fried, okay?"

16

BRENDAN

I blink, and the world comes back into focus. My eyelids are as heavy as lead. Disjointed images skitter around in my mind, leaving behind that itchy sensation of reality scratching my brain. Man, I feel like I've been dragged backward through a hedge…no, make that a thorny rose bush. I scrub a hand down my face, rubbing the sleepy haze still dragging me down.

It comes to me in foggy pieces.

Fionn taking me for a training session.

Him teaching me to navigate the spirit plane.

Right. Today's not just any day. It's the day I flex my newly minted magic muscles and track down a wizard.

Hold up. How did I end up sprawled across my bed? The last thing I remember was being nose-deep in tomes and texts in the wizard's dusty old library.

I asked Sloan about his ring and the moment I slipped it onto my finger, I blacked out.

Was it real or a dream?

I lift my hand, and I'm still wearing Sloan's ring.

Real then.

I lay there in a mental mind mulch, sifting through what is

real and what isn't until a shiver runs down my spine. It's too quiet.

It's the kind of quiet that screams wrongness.

Something's off, and it's not only the missing snoring of Emmet from down the hall.

I'm alert in an instant, my hand slipping beneath the pillow to close around the cool polymer grip of my Glock nestled there. Sitting up in a jolt, I raise my aim, my heart pounding in a frantic rhythm.

She's there.

At the foot of my bed sits the ghost with hair as dark as the ocean depths, an apparition that seems to draw in what little light is industrious enough to fight through the slats of the blinds.

A threat? A hallucination? Something else entirely?

She's calm.

So damn calm.

Her stillness is throwing me off.

How long has she been there watching me?

My feet hit the floorboards with a thud, my movements sharp and defensive. My aim remains locked on her, my heart hammering. "Who are you? Why are you here?"

Her eyes lock with mine, lavender, haunting, and deep. She doesn't flinch at the sight of the gun, doesn't move an inch. I expect fear, confusion, something. She sits there.

"Talk to me!" She has to be a threat, right? She shoved Emmet over a banister and down the stairs. Had that been me, I wouldn't have been able to slow my fall, and I would've broken my neck.

"Are you real?" The question slips out, half-formed, a whisper of doubt. It's crazy seeing someone like her, out of myths and bedtime stories, perched casually at the foot of my bed.

It dawns on me pretty damn quick that bullets won't do me any good. I slide my gun into the back of my jeans and grab the wizard's staff propped up against my bedside table.

It has the juice to scatter a ghost into the wind.

I grip the staff like a Louisville slugger, ready to knock it out of the park. Standing ready, I tense up, every muscle coiled for a fight.

It doesn't come.

Instead of the female coming at me like she did Emmet, she frowns—a look of hurt rather than hostility swirling in her gaze.

Then she vanishes.

Alone in the room, I search in case this is a ploy. It's not. I felt her disappointment, and now the room is empty.

As the adrenaline drains away, a gnawing sense of guilt replaces it.

Did I misjudge the situation? I thought there was a connection between us. Had she felt it too? Had she come with a message rather than malice?

My mind is a tangled mess as I race through the suite. The elf's visit gnaws at me. The possibility that she might've been here to help rather than harm sparks a hot regret in my gut.

I replay our previous encounter, the way our eyes locked during the battle at the wizard's house, and can't shake the feeling there's more to her story than I know.

Why did she become tangible and solid when I touched her? Is that something I can do with any ghosts or only her?

Dammit. I should've asked Fionn.

About Fionn...was that real?

I head to the kitchen, grab a mug, and fill it with yesterday's coffee from the bottom of the pot. The bitter liquid is a fitting match for my mood as I contemplate what I recognize as a missed opportunity.

I should've read the signs better. Instead, I leaped, ready to fight. Now? I might've blown our shot at peeling back another layer of this mystery.

I take a long swig of my java sludge, letting the acrid taste jolt me awake. *Damn, that's awful.*

A rhythmic tapping on the door breaks me out of my spiral. I abandon my mug in the sink and trudge over to open things up.

Kidok stands in the hall, as stoic as ever, wearing his leather military sash from when he served the army of his homeland. "Good, you're awake. The citizens are restless, and it would help to calm them down if they see the ghosts didn't kill you." His voice carries the low rumble of distant thunder.

I blink. "They think ghosts killed me? What gave them that idea?"

His gaze narrows, and his whiskers twitch. "You weren't at the town hall meeting this morning, and that's not like you. When there is news about the city, you and Emmet deliver it together."

My mental hamster is having a hard time keeping up. "There was a town hall meeting?"

Kidok nods. "Yes, and Emmet asked the entire community to take lodging within the palace walls."

I blink. "What's that now? They're all here? Why?"

I read the confusion in his expression and sigh. "Yeah, sorry. I was away for a bit, getting trained on ghost stuff. I just got back and missed what's been going on here. Fill me in."

Kidok spends the next five minutes telling me how the attempt to summon the bones was a failure and there is currently no plan for how to stop the ghosts. Given that they feed on despair, Emmet moved everyone to the palace so Dionysus could lock down the palace and keep the whispering shadows at bay.

"Good, good. If everyone is safe, that's less to worry about." I try to sound assured. "Give me fifteen minutes to shower, change, and figure out what I'm going to say to them. I have a better handle on the ghost situation, but I need to get out there and work through a few tests before I know for certain."

Kidok nods. "Very well. I'll wait downstairs and let them know you're coming to tell them your plan."

"Perfect. Thanks, man." I close the door and scrub my fingers through my hair.

Now all I need to do is come up with a plan.

Emmet

Dionysus and I descend toward the roosting lands. Our approach is silent but swift. The floating islands are a mesmerizing maze of potential peril where one wrong decision could get us tangled in a dead-end path with lightning serpents hot on our tails.

The lands look surprisingly solid despite the appearance of being woven from pure energy. The hum of power is a constant thrum in the air. The hair on my body is raised and prickles over my skin.

Saxa and Dart move with purpose, their flight smooth and coordinated. The dragons have become such a beautiful union, the pair cutting through the air as one.

As they navigate the skies between the floating islands, I study every crevice and cranny for where Syma would've hidden the elusive fragment.

I feel the incoming attack before anything becomes apparent. The energy around us spikes with a surge of power, and a moment later, serpents arc through the air and close in.

"Incoming!" I search for the source of the electrical surge, except searching isn't necessary.

They're everywhere.

Serpents hiss and soar, their movements chaotic and hard to track. I study how they move and soon get a sense of how their ambulation works. First, they coil the length of their tails, press into the coil, and launch themselves through the air like they've been catapulted.

Once in the air, they twist and roll with incredible flexibility. They move like the elaborate beasts in a Chinese dragon dance—light and lethality that's mesmerizing and terrifying.

Dart banks sharply. A wingtip grazes the ether as we dodge a bolt of living electricity. Saxa roars and the sound vibrates through my bones as she intercepts a serpent. Her claws crackle with coruscating energy.

Dionysus astride Contessa McSparkles weaves through the maze of islands, conjuring a barrier that deflects an oncoming serpent with a burst of light.

"Emmet, above you!" Dionysus shouts, his voice barely rising above the cacophony of battle.

I jerk my head up as a serpent descends, fangs bared and crackling with deadly intent. Dart's tail whips up, and the spaded end smashes into the creature's underbelly. It recoils with a shriek. Electric sparks shower around us like deadly rain.

More serpents swarm from the clouds, their bodies coiling and uncoiling, propelling themselves with explosive force.

"Impenetrable Sphere!" I cast the protective bubble to shield myself from the spray of sparks so I can focus on finding the fragment and getting us out of here.

"Left flank, Saxa!" I throw a fireball toward a serpent that slithered into her blind spot. My offensive strike falls short of its target, but Saxa has followed the trajectory and sees the incoming threat.

With a burst of golden flame from her maw, Saxa scorches the attacker, sending it reeling back into the abyss from which it came.

Dart and Saxa move in unison, a marvel of draconic might. Their every wingbeat and claw strike are a parry to the serpents' onslaught.

"Emmet, on your six!" Dionysus calls.

I twist to see what's coming, conjure another fireball, and hurl it at the oncoming serpent. The blast hits its mark, exploding with a brilliance that momentarily blinds the creature.

Its cries echo around us as it plummets away, disoriented.

Dionysus swoops in. Contessa McSparkles beats her wings

with powerful strokes. She kicks out and strikes a serpent with incredible force.

The serpent spirals downward as more of its kin take its place. We are outnumbered but not outmatched.

Dart and Saxa twist and turn, their wings slicing the air as they evade and counterattack. I clutch the saddle, anchoring myself as we dive, ascend, and roll through the aerial battlefield with the serpents' electric hisses a constant threat all around us.

Dionysus' laughter rings out, a sound of wild joy amid the danger. "They're like the heads of a hydra—for each one we take down, two more appear!"

I'm not sure why that makes him so happy, but hey, I'm glad he's here. "Then let's make sure they regret waking up this morning!"

With a roar from Dart and a battle cry from Dionysus, we surge forward, a storm of hooves, claws, and magic. A forked tongue of lightning strikes inches from Dart's wing and the air sizzles with electricity.

Saxa banks hard, her body a bright streak against the darkening clouds. Dart follows suit, a mirror image of his mate. I grip tighter, my hair whipping against my face as the world tilts and spins.

Another serpent narrowly misses us, and I crank my head around on a pivot, doing my best to keep the attackers in sight.

My blood is thundering when I laugh, and the irony of our situation strikes me mid-dodge. "This feels like a bizarre game of snakes and ladders."

Dionysus laughs and loops around in a tight arc, narrowly dodging a serpent's snapping jaws. "Ha! I play that with the twins. Although this version is more intense."

He guides Contessa McSparkles through a corkscrew dive to avoid a particularly aggressive serpent.

This is crazy. Realizing we're getting nowhere, I realign my focus. I need to find the fragment.

After a deep breath, I sharpen my senses and attune them to the distinct energy signature of the Light Weaver sisters. I didn't spend much time with them, but the sensation of their magic was so unique that there's no way I could mistake it for anyone else's.

I close my eyes and work to filter out the chaos and find what I'm looking for.

There! A pulse, a thrumming heartbeat of power amid the battle's frenetic energy.

"Dionysus!" I point at a distant floating island, barely visible against the backdrop of the serpent storm. "The fragment's there!"

Dionysus nods, his expression set. "Onward, mac Cumhaill!"

We weave through the air, evading the lightning serpents with renewed purpose. Dart and Saxa pour on the speed, their powerful wings cutting through the air as they race toward our target.

As we get closer to the energy signature guiding me, I can practically feel the fragment waiting for me. I search the island below and lock onto my target.

There's a stone tower with no windows or doors floating in what I can only describe as a sea of electricity. Dammit. The sisters didn't want people to get this fragment without working for it.

There's no way for me to land in that energy and nowhere to enter.

What about phasing myself an entrance?

I call my power into focus and try it. I extend a hand, willing the stones to yield, to phase and grant me passage, but they stand steadfast, as unyielding as the ancient magic that binds them.

Well, crap.

With the lightning serpents still attacking, it's not like we can do this indefinitely. "Dart, take me down to get a closer look at that stone tower!"

No sooner are the words out of my mouth than Dart drops.

Butterflies flip-flop in my belly as we swoop close to the tower in what feels like a crazy g-force dive.

As we circle the fortress, I realize we can't get close enough or go slow enough for me to verify what we face.

"I'm going to jump. Cover me!"

When Dart makes the next pass, I run across his back and flying squirrel off the back of his wing.

Okay, this might've been a really stupid idea.

The freefall would've been exhilarating if I wasn't dropping at an electrical storm that I'm pretty sure will fry me if this doesn't work.

No. It will work.

I close my eyes, call to my druid abilities, and focus on transforming. While I haven't always had the best results with transfiguration—like getting stuck as a kangaroo, then a red panda—I've gained a lot of control since then.

Thankfully, the moment I focus on the form I want, my body contorts and shifts. Bones reshape, muscles contract, and feathers erupt across my skin.

I embrace the form of an eagle, majestic and free.

With a powerful beat of my new wings, I slow my descent and circle the tower. At eye level, I discover what I thought was an impenetrable structure has several small slots between stone blocks.

Too small for an eagle, though.

With another thought, I morph again, my body shrinking as my heartbeat speeds up. I am now a hummingbird, diminutive and agile, a living jewel darting through the morning sky.

I fly forward, zipping through the slender gap with ease. Inside the tower's heart, I revert to my human form. My feet touch the cold stone floor with a soft *thud*. The fragment awaits before me, a shard of crystalline blue about the length and width of a butter knife.

I chuckle at myself. In my mind's eye, I pictured this would be a door key broken into three pieces.

Nope.

I reach out, fingers trembling as they near the crystal lying on the flat surface of a podium. An invisible shield blocks my attempt to pick it up. It pops into place like a glass cake cover protecting its contents, and I sigh. "Seriously?"

The energy coming off the little dome doesn't so much feel like denial as it does caution. I press my hand flat on its surface and focus on who I am and my intention. "Syma sent me. She wanted me to find you."

The dome's energy tickles my palm. I imagine it's reading my power signature or checking my identity. I'm not sure, but I pass the test since its resistance melts away and I'm free to claim the fragment.

Yeah, baby!

Now I have to figure out how to get through that tiny slot as a hummingbird while carrying this crystal.

As I close my fingers around the cool crystal, the tower realizes what was supposed to happen. A door materializes in the wall, and swings open in a silent invitation.

I prepare to step through and back into the storm's embrace, but the air is calm now, the lightning serpents retreating as if acknowledging the completion of a trial.

Dart swoops in, his great wings spreading to catch the updraft. I don't hesitate, launching myself from the tower's threshold and falling before deftly landing on his back.

I jog to my position at his first spike, grab a firm hold of the saddle grip, and get ready to return home.

One down, two to go.

17

BRENDAN

When the elevator doors open on the palace's main floor, I walk into a zoo of turmoil the place hasn't seen since Fiona's and Sloan's wedding when all the guests realized they were prisoners of the island.

The main hall and the room of busts beyond are packed with hundreds of fae folk, all looking like someone evicted them from their treehouses.

There are more wings, glitter, fur, and pointed ears than a cosplay event.

A tug on my hair brings my attention to a pixie standing on my shoulder. "Protector Brendan, are you well? We feared the worst. It's so good to see you."

A chorus of similar statements rises from the crowd.

I raise my hands, baffled by the outpouring of affection. I barely know these people. Emmet and I do our best to make them feel welcome, but for them to be worried about me...well, it's a shock.

"Hey, everyone, thank you. Yes, I'm fine. I was getting some training to help us with the ghosts. I'm fine."

The pixie on my shoulder presses her tiny hands against my neck and exhales. "Thank the goddess."

Wow, they really are wound up.

"Everyone, I'm sure you're all anxious to get home, but Emmet was right. Your safety is our biggest concern. Give me 'til the end of the day—maybe tomorrow—and I'll know better what to tell you about when you'll all be sleeping in your regular beds."

I hope. I send a silent plea to the universe to not make me a liar.

Kidok strides into the crowd. His height and ebony fur make him stand out even in this menagerie. Without wading through the mass of bodies jostling in the press of the gathering, he tilts his head toward the exit, and I make my way out to join him.

It takes a bit to get there, but when I'm standing in the stone breezeway outside the main doors, he meets me with a solemn growl. "Do you have a plan?"

I scratch my head, trying to look more confident than I feel. "I've got a couple of new tricks up my sleeve, but need time to figure out how to make them work for us. You stay here and keep them calm. I'll have something more definite to tell you in a few hours."

He doesn't look convinced, but he doesn't argue.

I step out of the golden palace, the weight of my responsibilities heavy and with a fire kindling in my belly.

This is it—the real deal.

Fionn taught me a lot about the spirit plane and the energy it gives off. Now I need to see if I can put that into practice to weed the wizard out of our lives.

As I stride down the main street and weave through the city toward the grove, I search for any sign of whispering shadows.

Having already been caught unprepared by the despair they inspire, I don't want to fall prey to their spell a second time. I rub the ache in my chest.

It almost cost me my life.

Although I haven't been totally happy, I'm not ready to give up on things.

I go to the five-story domed house where the wizard first attacked me. This is where I first saw ghosts—a lot of ghosts.

Maybe he frequents his old home, revisiting his mortal life. Maybe he's watching me from the viewpoint of the glass dome atop his home.

I close my eyes to see if I feel his gaze on me.

That isn't magic. That's a survival instinct almost everyone has.

I don't feel him watching.

Either he's not there, or my system is singing with the excitement of what I'm about to do and drowning out the subtleties of my senses.

I can't believe how jazzed I am about being a Celtic shaman and navigating the spirit plane. It's cool, right? Hells yeah. Totally cool.

Here I've been saying I didn't want to have any magical connections to this world.

Oops. I guess I was wrong.

I shake my arms to release some of the jitters and get down to it. Fionn's words echo in my mind, a mantra to guide my senses beyond the physical.

Close yer eyes, relax, expand yer senses. Check.

Connect with the fae magic. I exhale and let it wash over me. Check.

The island's magic surges around me, coursing through the ground, radiating from the buildings and trees, and filling my lungs with every breath I take.

Ye never want to tame a stallion, lad. Ye want to gain its trust.

I relax into the energy, letting it flow through me, taking the path it chooses. Check.

With my connection made, I probe the ethereal, seeking the darkness that surrounds the necromancer.

The city is vast, its buildings, groves, and natural wonders providing numerous places for the wizard to hide. I find it twice, but it's like chasing a whisper in the wind. Every time I grasp for it, it slips away.

I tilt my head from side to side and the *pop-pop-pop* of vertebrae adjusting releases some of the tension in my neck. "I can do this."

It's not as easy by myself as it was with Fionn guiding me, but I'm a quick study. I've got this.

I try again, reaching for that dark and twisted energy that made my stomach contents curdle in my belly. There are a few muted patches of it here and there, but nothing strong enough to grab hold of to track.

I exhale and shake it off, pacing a slow lap of the clearing in front of the trees. "Okay, maybe the wizard cloaks his energy or whereabouts."

That makes sense. Why wouldn't he?

If that's what's happening, who or what can I track to get me what I want?

It strikes me then.

Maybe.

Settling down to give things another attempt, I reach out with my senses. This time, I don't focus on the sickly darkness that clings to the necromancer wizard. This time, I search for another energy source altogether.

It's almost too easy to find her.

The moment I cast my net, it's like she's the flame of a candle in a dark room. Her energy is unmistakable, vibrant, and unique —the elf with the purple hair, the one who haunts my thoughts as much as the streets of Isilon.

Her magical aura lights up my senses, a beacon in the murky waters of the spiritual plane. I focus on her presence and let her essence pull me, leading me through the twists and turns of the spectral trail.

Quietly, one step after the other, I close the distance between us, the ghostly touch of her energy guiding me. There are moments I swear I can smell the faintest hint of wildness and night breezes—the scent that clings to her like a shadow.

The farther I follow the trail, the more things solidify. Her presence becomes clearer and more tangible with every step I take.

It's working.

Fionn told me I needed to practice my skills. If this is what he meant, I'm all for it. Despite the seriousness of why I need to get good at this, it's kinda fun.

I press on, and the spiritual energy I'm tracking grows clearer. I'm close now. I can feel it.

My path winds me through the side streets and across public green spaces, leading me over ancient stone bridges that arch over the prana's fuchsia glow.

It's like chasing a ghost through the remnants of a dream, but I'm certain. This spectral thread is leading me to the enigmatic beauty with the violet hair.

When I finally find her, she's sitting poised atop a stone wall with her face raised to the morning sun as if she's absorbing the heat of the summer day.

There's a wildness about her, a fierce grace that's as intimidating as it is alluring.

I step forward. The *crunch* of gravel under my boots is the only sound in the charged silence. She tenses, and before she can bolt, I hold up my hands in a gesture of peace.

"I'm sorry about this morning," I begin, my voice sincere, every word true. "I shouldn't have threatened you. The truth is, I was surprised to find you in my space… Thrown off by… I didn't understand why you were there."

She weighs my words, her gaze piercing.

"I'm Brendan." I'm still holding up my palms. "What's your name?"

She swallows, considering. "I am Nightfall."

"Cool name." I roll my eyes at myself for that tidbit of charm and try to shake off the dust on how to speak to a beautiful woman. "I'm sure it's none of my business, but how did you end up here? Like this?"

She watches me for a long moment, and I hold my breath. She's stiff and closed off. She doesn't trust me, and after I threatened to crack her with the wizard's staff this morning, I don't blame her.

Will she vanish into the night, leaving me with more questions than answers?

"I want to understand what happened so I can help you and the other trapped spirits."

There's a shift in her demeanor, a softening around her eyes that says I might be getting through to her. Could she see me as an ally in this strange new chapter of Isilon's revitalization?

She gestures at the top of the wall beside her, and I accept the invitation to hop up and sit. I straddle the wall, facing her, because I don't want to miss a single moment of our conversation.

She's a vision, all right, with wild violet hair that sparkles in the light of the full sun. She turns to me, her eyes pale pools of lavender, and they draw me in. I can tell she's been through a lot and her struggle stirs something in me.

"Nightfall is a beautiful name." I hold her gaze. "When did you come to Isilon?"

Her mouth turns up in a rueful smile. "It was a long time ago. My kin were killed during a Dark Weaver raid, and I was brought here and offered a new home. When the Dark Weavers attacked the city a year later, I stood with the people who had taken me in, and we fought against our common enemy."

"You were trapped when Isilon locked down?"

"Like many others."

"What woke you? Was it Isilon coming out of hibernation, the necromancer's call, or what?"

Her gaze narrows. "I cannot say. The early days of coming back to myself are cloudy."

"He's got you, right? You and the others? He's controlling you?"

The glare she pegs me with is brutally cold. "We are more than what he has done to us." There's a heaviness in her words that wraps around my ribs and tightens.

"Of course you are. I'm sorry. I'm trying to understand his hold over you so I can help. My family and I are working to free you."

"Why? How is it your concern?"

I grunt. "Well, the fact that he's tethered the souls of those who already suffered an unjust death on this island aside, he's altering the ghosts into whispering shadows. That kind of negative feeding is hurting the people living in our city. He needs to be stopped."

She studies me, her gaze searching. "Do you truly believe you and your kin can best him?"

"If we can find him and figure out his weaknesses, definitely. It's kinda what we do."

She doesn't look convinced.

"We're not so different, you know. I was dead too." Okay, so that confession doesn't land as solidly in the real world as it did in my head. I really am rusty at talking to a beautiful woman. "I got a second shot at life, and I believe part of the reason I'm here is to help you and the others get *your* second chances."

Nightfall holds my gaze.

I extend my hand, wondering if I've gained enough of her trust that she might touch me. "I grabbed you when we were in the wizard's house. How did you become solid?"

She shakes her head. "I did nothing. That was you. How did *you* make me take a physical form?"

"I honestly don't know. I didn't realize I had a connection to the spiritual plane until that moment. I'm still figuring it out."

She must accept my answer because she sets her hand against mine. The moment our palms meet, the air around us shifts, and she solidifies under my touch.

I wrap my fingers around the side of her hand and marvel that she's as real and solid as the stone beneath us. "Wow, that's crazy, isn't it?"

Her lavender gaze is swirling. "How is that possible?"

"I honestly don't know."

"Is it me, or do you have this effect on the others?"

"I don't know."

She frowns. "What *do* you know?"

Fair question. "I know the wizard is a necromancer, and he gathered the bones of the dead on the island to control you and keep you from moving on. What I don't know is where the bones are or how to get them back so we can release you."

Her ethereal hair shimmers as she sighs. "There are no bones any longer. The wizard ground them to dust and used them in his spells. For the strongest of us, he added our bone dust to potions he imbibed. We are now bound to him evermore."

I clench my jaw as anger rises in me like a tide. "He consumed your bones to lock you to him?"

Another nod, more somber this time. "That is how he controls us."

The puzzle pieces fall into place, and the endgame is clear. If their existence is tied to him so inextricably, we need to ensure he is dead, salted, and burned to free the lot of them.

"I won't rest until the wizard is destroyed and I've ended his sick games. Will you help me?"

Nightfall's gaze lingers on me, a whirlpool of untold sadness. After a moment, she unfurls from her position and hops to her feet. She is grace incarnate, every motion a testament to her elven origins.

"I will show you, but know this. If he realizes you have come and calls his army to his aid, I cannot resist him. We will stand on opposite sides."

I hate that idea, but it only makes me more determined to free her and the others from his hold. "I understand. Show me where the asshole is hiding."

EMMET

When we arrive back at the dragon's lair, I thank Contessa McSparkles for her help, and after she gets another treat from Dionysus, she gallops off into the sky. "The two of you were awesome, Greek. Thanks for the assist. I wouldn't have been able to do it without you."

He glances sideways at me and frowns. "Why does it sound like there's a kiss-off coming next?"

I wave away his concern. "Not a kiss-off, dude. Never a kiss-off."

"But?"

"I'd like you to keep this fragment safe while I track down the next one."

Dionysus accepts the crystal fragment of the key to the Corestone. "You know I'll keep this safe and step back if you want me to, but being a leader of things doesn't mean you have to go it alone. Look at Garnet, your father, and your sister. They all rock the Casbah of leadership, and they all surround themselves with a strong team when things get hairy."

I consider his words, and while I would love his company, something tells me the next test isn't about the strength of my team. "I hear what you're saying, but something about Syma leaving this task to me makes me feel like I'm proving myself."

Dionysus tilts his head to one side and shrugs. "All right. You play it however you want to. If you need me, call my name. I'll listen for you and can be there in a blink if things go sideways."

I pat the side of his arm and step back. "Thanks, dude. It helps to know you're waiting in the wings."

"Then I wish you good luck on the next part of your quest, Em. Be safe. Remember, if anything happens to you, Fiona will lose her mind, and we'll all be on a shit list. So don't die, okay?"

"No one wants to be on Fi's shit list. I promise I'll try my best not to die." He snaps out with the first fragment, and I turn back to the dragons. "Dart? Can you do me one more favor?"

"Of course." Dart stretches his wings over the rocks to catch the sun. "What do you need?"

"Would you call one of your wyvern siblings and have them meet me at the beachfront? My next quest is water, and I have a feeling having a water dragon will be more beneficial than a boat."

"Any day of the week," Dart scoffs. He lifts his head, and I know by his expression that he's reaching out to speak to one of his younger siblings. After a moment, his attention returns to me, and he lowers his snout. "Tiderunner is on his way."

"Awesome. Thank you, my friend."

"My pleasure. Be well, Emmet. Fiona worries about you a great deal."

I draw a deep breath. "Yeah, I know. But I'm good. Thanks again for all your help."

The city of Isilon is hidden behind a barrier of magic on a small island off the coast of Ireland. To a human traveling the waters, there is a forested area with some rocky plateaus in the distance and a couple of waterfalls. Most impressive is the wide band of beach.

I first noticed the energy of the Light Weavers out here

during the Culling. We were in a battle to the death with dark forces of the fae realm to retain control of the island. We won, but a part of me had hoped that feeling the sisters out here meant they might be able to join the battle and help us somehow.

They didn't.

Since then, while I adjusted to being the island's champion, I have taken walks on the beach to feel close to them. I didn't understand the significance of the presence of their magical signature then, but as soon as I got thinking about the water task and needing to find the second fragment, I knew it must be out here.

The sky is blue and filled with an August summer sun as I stand on the beachfront. I stare out at the sparkling, dark blue waters of the Irish Sea and it's almost the most peaceful feeling in my life.

Or it would be if my cells weren't buzzing with adrenaline. After my adventure with the lightning serpents, I hope I don't have to take on sea monsters to secure the second fragment.

Crazy images of thrashing waves and monstrous tentacles fill my mind, and I'm tempted to call for Dionysus to join me.

Tempted, but not going to.

My instincts tell me this task is mine to take and complete.

I scan the horizon, studying the area where I feel the pull of the Light Weavers' energy. The sea seems to stretch into eternity, but that's where I need to be.

That's where my quest for the second crystal shard will begin.

Now that I've held the first fragment, I can feel its sister calling to me, an invisible thread tugging on my core.

The water's surface swirls and breaks into a rush of whitecaps as a pale blue-green dragon breaches the surface. Dart's wyvern siblings don't have the broad faces, plated scales, and barbed spines and tails like the Westerns.

The wyverns are sleeker with smooth, streamlined bodies and

softer features. Instead of wings to propel them through the air, they have webbed feet and fins to speed through the water.

"Thank you for coming, Tiderunner. I appreciate you agreeing to help me."

The massive beast lowers his chin in a reverent bow. "You are the kin of my druid mother of dragons. Therefore, you are my kin. How is Fiona? I'm told she has been gestating young."

I chuckle inwardly and remind myself to say it exactly that way to Fiona later. "She and the baby are well, thanks. Both are growing every day."

"A blessing indeed."

"Indeed. I look forward to meeting my newest little niece in a few months."

With the small talk of greetings behind us, I stride forward. Tiderunner reaches his muscled front leg onto the sand of the beach. His clawed hands are webbed and massive.

"Feline Finesse." My call for grace and coordination makes it simple to climb the shimmering scales of his arm and farther still onto the back of his neck. From there, I search for a good place to settle and drop to sit behind the jagged spikes of his frilled collar.

"I need you to take me out to sea. I'll guide you as best I can. There's something magical calling to me, and I need to retrieve it. If it's anything like the last one, there will be resistance to me getting it."

"What kind of resistance?"

"I'm not sure. Typhoons? Being attacked by sea creatures? Be ready for anything. Are you up for that?"

Unless I miss my guess, the deep bass of his chuckle is the dragon equivalent of "Bring it on."

"Will you be all right to breathe if things get challenging and I have to dive?"

"Yeah. I'm good. I'll use my druid abilities to take care of my needs. Unless something really unexpected happens, I should be fine."

With a deep breath that tastes of salt and adventure, I cast a bubble of air around my head as I did earlier and remember at the last minute to extend it all around me to keep me dry.

When Tiderunner moves, I grab a solid hold of his neck frill. He ambles backward into the water, submerges himself, and we're off.

Now all I need to do is find that fragment.

Tiderunner skims through the water. The sea embraces him like an old friend. He guides us away from land toward the magical essence. The farther out we go, the stronger I feel its pull.

How freaking cool is this? I'm out on the open sea, riding a water dragon and searching for a magical key to save a sentient city. You can't make this shit up.

All sense of time vanishes, and I'm right here, living in the moment. Then I realize I jinxed it and reality crashes around me.

The sky spews a light show of purples and oranges mixing as the midday sun and the sunset decide to throw a party without inviting the rest of the day in between.

Boom!

I grab tighter to Tiderunner, twisting in place to see what's coming at us and from where.

"Show me yer worth a damn, guardian!" Manannán Mac Lir's voice rolls in like a tidal wave, all bass and echo, shaking me right down to the bones. I've met the sea god twice before, and both times he's pretty much scared the piss out of me.

Waves throw themselves at us, one after another. It's as if the sea is his personal attack dog, which I suppose it is.

His attack dog has a vendetta.

I dodge the salt water spray, getting thrown this way and that. Tiderunner zips through the waves to keep us on course as the sea thrashes around us. As crazy as it sounds, I think my hours goofing around on the mechanical bull have been good training for this moment.

"Are you all right?" I shout to him.

"Is that all you've got?" he calls, half-laughing, half-yelling over the water's roar.

"Go left. I feel the fragment at nine o'clock."

"Left I understand. What's a nine o'clock?"

Right. Dragons don't use clocks. "Sorry. A little left. I'll tell you when to go straight."

It makes sense that the Light Weavers would leave a fragment of the key under the watchful eye of the sea god. The island is in his domain.

Each wave coming at us rises like a mountain, and after we crest the peaks, Tiderunner surfs down their slopes to climb the next one.

I'm so thankful I didn't come out here in a boat. With waves like this, a normal watercraft would never have held together.

Although I heard Manannán's voice earlier, I haven't seen him. He's likely down in the depths, watching with those age-old eyes, weighing my performance. I wonder if he's impressed or enjoying the show.

Likely the latter.

Tiderunner is brilliant, and together we match the sea's fury with stubborn pride, a fair amount of anxiety, and a lot of adrenaline—because no matter how you look at it, this is a wild ride.

We're taking everything the sea god is throwing at us, and it feels damned good.

The sea churns around me, each wave a growling beast eager to claim me as its prize. Salt spray flies. The crashing of water thunders. It's violent and powerful, testing my resolve.

"Yeah, straight ahead. We're getting close!"

Manannán's challenge is understandable. He wants to test the champion of his island. I'm totally on board with that until the mother of all waves swells before us.

It's the type of wave that would make even the most seasoned sailors offer a prayer to the sea gods.

"Come get us, you great watery beast!" I shout, more to bolster my courage than to taunt the ocean.

Tiderunner bellows and I'm unsure if he's laughing at me or annoyed that I'm challenging the god of the Irish Sea.

The wave rises above us, and I look up...*waaay* up at the wall of water about to crash down on us. The roar in my ears could be the wave or my blood pounding with adrenaline.

This is the moment of truth, the point of no return.

"Hold on!" Tiderunner shouts the warning and dives.

Down...down...deep into the depths we dive and even still, the thundering boom of that wave crashing above echoes all around us.

We get caught in a whirlpool of currents, and they tear me from my place upon the dragon. I'm dragged tumbling into the pull of the turbulent waters and must fight to keep my bearings.

I'm in the wave's clutches now.

Time slows. The only sounds are my ragged breathing and the relentless thrum of the sea. Still, with my spell of air containment intact, I can breathe, so other than being crushed by the sea god's fury, I'm okay.

Or I *will* be okay once I find that fragment.

Calming my mind, I focus on the task at hand, willing every fiber of my being to seek out the magical signature of the Light Weavers.

It's here somewhere, and I'm going to find it.

I call faerie fire to my palm, extend my arm in front of me, and search the seabed. Tiderunner got me close. I can get myself the rest of the way.

As the laughter of Manannán rolls over the waves—a deep, knowing sound that echoes from the depths of the sea—I feel the weight of his gaze upon me.

There's warmth in that laughter, and I'm relieved.

Maybe I've proven myself. Perhaps he'll let me claim what I've come for. Even as I think it, I laugh at myself. *Yeah no. Not bloody likely.*

Bring it on. A smile curls my lips. *I'm ready for whatever comes next.*

Guided by the presence of the Light Weavers' magical signature, my fingers dance across the jagged edges of the cold-water coral mounds growing along the bottom of the sea.

The faerie fire in my hand cuts through the water's murk, a blue beacon in the vast underwater night.

I'm close. I know I am.

I feel it.

I feel *them.*

A flicker of light captures my gaze. A shard of pure orange radiance lies trapped within a rough mound of oddly formed coral. The sight of it sets my pulse racing. Now to get it and get gone.

It's a good plan, but is it realistic?

Trying the direct approach first, I work at breaking the coral encapsulating it. That doesn't work.

Next, I try grabbing a rock and hammering it.

Sadly, hammering something underwater is weird and ineffective.

Then I remember how the invisible shield resisted me until it recognized me. I place both hands against the rock-hard coral and let it read my magical signature. Although I don't have nearly the same kind of power as Kyna, Syma, and their sisters, the magic we shared is what's important.

I wait and watch, my full attention locked on the fragment ensnared within its crystalline cage. With each breath, I work on slowing my breathing and getting my magical essence to sync up with the pulsating power encasing the fragment.

"It's all right." I hope I'm right about needing to have it recognize me. "I'm Emmet. I'm supposed to find this crystal. It was left for me."

The sound of my voice is strange to my ears, distorted by water and maybe by the aura of magic around me. As my words dissipate, the coral cage containing the crystal responds.

It shimmers, its structure wavering, and dissolves into a cloud of iridescent particles that drift away on the current.

The crystal fragment is free of its prison and hovers within reach. I extend my hand, my fingers closing around it. A surge of energy courses through me and for a moment, I think it's from the fragment.

It's not.

It's me.

Proud of myself, I shift to stand on the seabed and look around. "I'm going to reignite the Embers of Existence," I declare to Manannán, wherever he is. "I'm going to bring light back to the city. You'll see."

I push off the sea floor, kick my feet, and swim toward the surface.

"Well met, Guardian. The depths have tested you, and you have been found worthy." The blessing of the sea god envelopes me, and it's a warm and all-encompassing, tangible expression of Manannán's favor.

With the fragment secure, I continue upward, meeting up with Tiderunner swimming wildly in long, searching circles. "There you are. Where did you go? I've been searching everywhere for you."

"Thanks, dude. I think I was supposed to do that part by myself. I did it, and I'm good. Would you mind taking me home now?"

The dragon swoops his head beneath me, and I settle onto the back of his neck. "Happy to. It was a good time, Emmet, but you scared me. If I had lost you, my mother of dragons would never have forgiven me."

I chuckle and pat the frill of his neck. "I get that a lot, but I'm good. I don't think I've ever been better."

BRENDAN

I press two fingers under my tongue and whistle to grab everyone's attention. When the group gathered in the security room quiets down, I gesture at the holographic map of the city in front of me. "Do you guys remember the violet-haired ghost Emmet and I mentioned after the battle at the wizard's home?"

Dillan snorts. "You mean the elven goddess ghost Em's been talking about ever since?"

"Elven goddess ghost?" Fiona grins. "Do tell."

"She straight-armed him over a banister into a multistory drop. Made quite an impression on him."

"I bet she did."

Annoyance creeps into my mood, and I try not to look too closely at that. It's because I'm telling them something and they're interrupting.

That's all it is.

"Well, her name is Nightfall, and she showed me where our wizard has made his nest."

Kidok's gaze narrows. "One of the spectral soldiers of our

enemy decided to lead us to her master? Do you not find that questionable?"

I do a gut check before I answer. Nothing comes back at me. "I don't think so, no. I spoke to her, and it's hard to explain. This spirit connection I have now gives me insight into the souls of the spirit plane. Nightfall wants us to take the wizard out as much as we want to do it."

Aiden nods. "I'm sure she does, but that still doesn't mean she's showing you all her cards."

"True, but I was there. I felt his power within the building and his hold on them. Whatever her intentions, we know where the necromancer is."

Sloan presses his palms on the table and leans forward to study the tangle of streets. "Where did she lead you, exactly?"

I point out the location. "Right here. There is a community building and a bunch of old restaurants. I felt his presence strongest in that building there. It looked like it could be a theater or maybe the fae version of a religious center."

Sloan's gaze narrows, his ever-present strategist's mind ticking away behind his pale green eyes. Irish is a thinker and always sees two steps ahead of the rest of us, although I'd consider my brothers and I damned strategic.

Dionysus frowns. "Have you guys spent any time in this part of the city?"

I shake my head. "If I had my bike, I could cover more ground, but no. The city is massive, and we've barely begun to explore it."

Dillan chuckles. "Even with your motorcycle, you wouldn't get far. Where would you gas up?"

It's sad, but true. There are no motorized vehicles on the Isle of Emhain Abhlach. It's oddly peaceful but leaves me feeling bereft. My greatest indulgence in life was hitting the roads at breakneck speeds.

Still, it is what it is, and now is not the time to dwell.

"What do you guys think about raiding the building and taking out our necromancer problem?" I get us back on point.

Aiden frowns. "There's no good way to approach the building where his ghost army won't see us coming."

"And stealth of night doesn't help with ghosts lurking in the darkness," Dillan adds.

Calum meets my gaze. "How many ghosts do you think we need to get through to get inside?"

"Yeah, that's the biggest problem. There are hundreds of them. Seriously…I've never seen anything like it. You know those scenes on *The Walking Dead* when zombie herds overrun an area?"

I see the reality of that settling in on their expressions. "Now double it."

Dillan curses. "Dude, no matter how good we are at swinging iron bars, we'll never get close enough to the wizard to take him out."

"What about if Dionysus snaps us inside?" Aiden asks. "Or would that be considered godly interference?"

Dionysus tilts his head from side to side and frowns. "It could be interfering in the course of things if it's the only way for you to get in there."

"Well, we're not risking Tarzan," Fiona states. "Been there, done that. Now we play by Zeus' rules because for once, no one in the pantheon is mad at us."

Dionysus shrugs. "That's so crazy, isn't it?"

"What about asking Emmet for one of his diversions?" Calum suggests. "Something big and flashy that draws the spirits a block or two away."

Aiden squares his broad shoulders with the table, looking worried. "If Dillan has his cloak and Sloan portals a few of us to the entrance when the ruckus begins, it might work. Where is Em, anyway?"

"He's on the second leg of his Light Weaver quest," Dionysus answers. "Well, he's currently on his way back from finishing it. I told him I'd keep tabs on him in case he needed a wingman."

Fiona leans in and kisses his cheek. "Thanks, Tarzan."

He winks at her. "Of course. Before you ask, he kicked ass and was completely victorious."

"Damn straight." Fiona grins. "Yay, Em!"

"Okay, so let's assume Emmet is game for creating a diversion," Calum continues.

"Which he will be," Fiona adds.

"Yeah, he will. So, we have a diversion. It pulls a couple of hundred ghosts from around the building. What happens if the inside of the building is stuffed full too?"

"What about Eva?" Aiden asks.

"More words," Dillan prompts. "What do you mean, what about Eva?"

"Well, if she can guide the souls to where they belong, can she override the wizard's control on them, take them to their resting places, and remove them from the playing board?"

Dillan frowns. "I can ask her, but I think if it was within her power, she would've volunteered that info already."

Sloan interjects, "She can certainly lend a hand, but that's way too many ghosts for her to guide at once."

"Could she help keep them at bay?" Calum asks.

"Maybe she could call in a few friends," Fiona suggests. "Remember how many angels came during Caribana to secure the innocent?"

I don't, but it's another adventure they've had that I know nothing about.

Aiden raises a finger. "What if we can develop a containment spell that keeps ghosts in one place? Maybe we don't need to fight them. Maybe we can contain them somehow so they can't attack us, but they also can't run to the wizard and tell him we're coming."

Sloan frowns. "He'll know. A man like that will have

perimeter wards that light up like Times Square on New Year's the moment we move in."

I sigh. "What about Aiden's idea about containment, but instead of trapping the ghosts in place, we trap the wizard? Then no matter how long it takes us to get to him, he can't get away again."

I hear the words coming out of my mouth, and yeah, it sounds like wishful thinking even to me.

My siblings and I share a look that is part of our unspoken language. With all of the options floating around, we say a lot all at once.

Yeah, Emmet's diversions can be epic, but there's no way he can draw that many bodies away from the scene.

Eva is the bomb, but even she can't escort two or three hundred souls at once.

Keep thinking because nothing we've said so far will work.

Restlessness rolls off the group in waves. A collective tension grips the room, a shared frustration and understanding of what we're up against.

I groan. "We need a way in, silent as the grave, or we're gonna be up to our necks in ghosts faster than you can say boo."

Aiden grunts. "I still think there's merit in figuring out how to contain the wizard to keep him from ghosting out on us."

"What about Bruin?" Fiona suggests.

We all bristle, and she gives us all a solid stink-eyed stare. "I get that I'm not battle fit right now, you overprotective dumb-asses. I'm not suggesting I go in with him, but he could help you."

Sloan moves to pacify her, but she holds up a finger, and he knows better than to smooth things over with her when she's annoyed. "Yer right, luv. Bruin could go in, gather intel, and tell us better than anyone what we're dealin' with."

I nod. "You're right, Fi. Thanks."

"Bruin? Can you come out and play, buddy?" The moment she asks, the air stirs, and he takes form beside her. The massive

Kodiak swings his head toward the map. Fi extends her hands and flicks her wrists to signal Calum and Dillan to get out of her way.

They do.

She steps up to look at the map, and I point at the area we're focusing on. "The wizard we're after is in this building here, and the streets are crawling with his whispering shadows army."

The bear's black nose twitches and he grumbles something.

"How many ghosts do you think?" Fi translates for me.

"Three hundred?"

"What are your ideas so far?" Fi relays Bruin's next question.

"Distraction, portaling in blind, somehow binding the wizard in place so he can't phase out, but nothing feels right, yet."

"If the wizard gets wind that we're onto him, he'll bolt, and we'll be back to square one and swarmed by unfriendlies," Aiden reminds us.

There's a beat of silence while we stay quiet to let everyone think.

As bizarre as it seems, at some point over the past four years, my baby sister became the go-to warrior for all things magic and mayhem.

She nods, answering a question that isn't spoken aloud. Man, between Nikon, Dionysus, Bruin, and Dart, she could have cranial conversations with half the room.

Whatever is said, it goes in our favor.

"Sloan, *poof* home and grab the book with the blue stitching on the brown leather spine—the one I started reading during our wedding hostage weekend. I think I put it on my cedar chest or in the turret room on the shelf by the window."

Without hesitation, Sloan is gone and back a moment later holding the book.

She takes it and opens the pages. "When we were figuring out a way to get our wedding guests home, I skimmed through books that touched on the different aspects of the city. The quadrants, the wards, the portal gates, etcetera. If I remember correctly, catacombs run under many public buildings."

"Catacombs?" Calum repeats.

"Seriously?" Dillan asks.

"Uh-huh. In the days when gnomes, trolls, goblins, and incubi roamed the city's streets, there was an underground community. They carved out an entire network of tunnels beneath our feet. The southeast quadrant was riddled with them."

I crack a grin. "Yay, you, Fi."

Aiden nods. "Yeah, that's awesome, baby girl. If that's true, we can move underground and come up without tipping the ghosts off to anything."

Sloan already has his nose in the book, but I have a faster way to get our answers. "Astrid? Would you join us, please?"

Astrid materializes in all her *Tomb Raider* glory. Emmet's antics can wear on an older brother, but I'll never complain about him picking this particular image for our magically generated guide to the city.

"Yes, Brendan?" she asks.

I gesture at the map. "Can you please overlay the layout of the catacombs below the streets and mark the access points, specifically under this quadrant of the city?"

"Of course. One moment." Astrid's attention widens beyond what she sees in the room and comes back into focus. Then she moves to the war table and her fingers skim over the control pad in a blur.

A moment later, it's as if the city is sliced at ground level and lifted four inches off the table's surface, revealing a warren of tunnels beneath.

"That's what I'm talkin' about!" Dillan exclaims. "Booyah, baby."

Sloan nods. "Assuming the tunnels are still passable, if we approach on two fronts, Emmet leading the distraction over here and the rest of us coming in from there, we might be able to get in there without being detected."

"If Emmet's running the distraction, I want someone who teleports there with him," Fiona warns. "He's not luring a three-hundred-ghost swarm toward himself without a way out."

"I've got Em," Dionysus replies. "Since I can't overtly fix this for you, I can at least kill it on Team Distraction."

Fiona grins. "Thanks, Tarzan. Now, Bruin should still go in first and get the lay of the land."

"Aye, that's the wisest course, fer sure," Sloan agrees.

The bear lifts his snout and grumbles something. My siblings and Sloan all agree with what was said.

"Aye, you do that, Bear. Be careful, though. Some types of ghosts can detect other ghosts."

Bruin grunts something again.

"Damn straight." Fiona buries her fingers into the long fur of his thick coat. "No whispering shadow assholes can hold a candle to you. Still, be careful, buddy."

Bruin tilts his massive head, and she leans into him and kisses his cheek.

"Love you, too."

When the bear disappears, I check in with the others. "I take it we're waiting for an intel report from Bruin?"

Sloan nods. "Aye, so in the meantime, gear up, grab a bite to eat, and I'll come up with a spell to lock ghosts in the physical world before we leave."

I pull out my phone and text Emmet, asking him to join us at the security building to be briefed about Operation Ghostbusters. His responding text comes back a moment later. "Em's on his way."

"Excellent," Calum replies. "We'll meet back here then?"

A round of nods seal the deal.

"Let's say thirty minutes."

All righty then. Looks like we've got a plan.

<u>Emmet</u>

Since I'm already in my battle gear from my quest, when I arrive at the security office, I head over to the sofa against the wall and take a load off while we wait for everyone to suit up and get ready to roll. I could use a bite to eat, but after taking on the lightning serpents and the Irish Sea, what I need more is rest.

"You okay, Em?" Fiona follows me to the little seating area.

I flop on the sofa and lay back, sighing as my body deflates into the softness of the cushions. "Yeah, just a little knackered."

"Are you okay to go out again?"

"I will be. Give me ten minutes to catch my breath."

Fi settles into the armchair and puts her feet up on the wooden coffee table. "Gods, look how fat my ankles are. Despite what Sloan says, being pregnant is one of the least sexy states of being I've ever experienced."

I chuckle. "What does Sloan say?"

She rolls her eyes. "He doesn't stop telling me I've never been more attractive."

I snort. "Do you think he's shining you on, or does he believe that?"

She leans deep into the back of the chair, her long auburn curls bouncing against her arms. "He honestly thinks that."

"Maybe his kink is puffy ankles. I'm sure there's a freaky fetish in there somewhere. You could start an OnlyFans page."

"Hard pass."

The two of us close our eyes, and it's a comforting silence. Fi and I shared a bedroom for many of our childhood years, so existing in the same space with her is grounding and fills my well.

"Oh, I met up with Tiderunner this morning. He wanted me to give you his love and asked how your youth gestation is going."

Fiona snorts. "Did he say that?"

"Yeah."

She lays her head back and closes her eyes again. "Well, if you see him again, you can tell him it's going just fine."

"He sounded like he misses you. Have you not been to the queen's dragon lair lately?"

She shakes her head. "Sloan asked me not to go there until after the baby is born. He's worried because of how differently time moves there and how that might affect Baby Mac's gestation."

"Fair. You could be there a day, and it's been a week."

"Yeah, I get that, but between not being able to go there, not working, and not getting to participate in safeguarding our city, I'm getting pretty tired of being bubble-wrapped."

I hear the hurt in her voice, and I sigh. "Sorry. We only want to keep Baby Mac out of harm's way. If you're looking for something to do, you could spend tomorrow at the palace calming down the citizens. I'm sure they'll be going stir crazy."

"Did you get them all to agree?"

"No. Not all. A couple of the centaurs refused. A couple of gnomes too. I'm not sure everyone came to the meeting, so there's no telling. But a large majority are locked down."

"You rock socks, Em."

"Nah. I'm faking it 'til I make it."

"I don't believe that for a second. Tell me about your day. Dionysus is buzzing with tales of aerial battles with electrical serpents and all kinds of dragon acrobatics. He said you've been on a quest for Syma, yet as far as I've heard, you haven't told anyone about your success today."

I shrug. "There's been a lot going on."

"There is *always* a lot going on. That doesn't mean your triumphs get lost in the shuffle. Tell me about it. I want to hear everything."

I sit up and am surprised at how much it means to have someone ask. Over the next five minutes, I tell her about the battle with the lightning serpents, then how Tiderunner and I took on Manannán Mac Lir and the Irish Sea.

"That's incredible, Em. Congrats. Now you have the first two fragments?"

"Yeah. As soon as I get the fire fragment, I can restore the key to the Corestone and reignite the Embers of Existence."

She moves off her chair to sit next to me and hugs me. "I'm so proud of you. You're rocking this whole island guardian thing."

It's nothing she hasn't told me a dozen times before, but for some reason, this time I believe her. "I wish you were out there with me, but yeah, it felt good to do it on my own, too."

She sits back and twists on the couch to face me. "I know exactly what that feels like. Still, we're all here for you. To jump in and help as much or as little as you need us to."

"Damn straight," Calum agrees behind me.

"All you need to do is ask, bro," Dillan adds. "Fi's right. When you kick ass, we want to hear about it. Fan your peacock feathers and do a happy dance."

"Thanks, guys. I appreciate that." My stomach growls, and I regret not grabbing a bite to eat.

Fi must hear the rumble because she pulls out her phone, and Dionysus snaps in holding two plates with sandwiches and fries.

"What's this?" I ask.

Fi grins. "Hero sandwiches, obvi."

20

BRENDAN

"Okay, Bear, tell us the good news," Emmet urges once we're all assembled again.

My siblings, Eva, Dionysus, and Nikon gather around the massive bear and start in with their usual nodding. As always, it pisses me off and frustrates the hell out of me. Being the only one restricted to one-half of the conversations is annoying.

Not to mention isolating.

"Where exactly, Bruin?" Sloan moves to the city map.

I watch as Sloan traces a path with his finger and get the gist of what they're saying. Bruin did a sweep of the underground passages, and they are relatively intact.

"All right, everyone, take a couple of these." Sloan sets a black case on the table and unzips the lid. "I did my best in a pinch, and while these aren't likely to hold a spirit fer long, it should keep them from ghostin' out on ye durin' a fight."

We each grab two small vials, and I hold one up to the light. There's a pale blue powder on the bottom of the little tube and a swirling gray mist trapped inside.

I almost ask what it is, but I don't care. The only thing that matters is whether or not it'll work. Knowing Sloan, it will.

I point at the map, going over everything again. "Dionysus and Emmet, after you drop Fiona home, set up here for your diversion. Nikon will snap the rest of us to this access point, and we'll go into the tunnels to come up into the basement of the community building. Bruin, you can ghost above and below ground to keep an eye on everyone. Eva, where will you be?"

Dillan's angel bride grins. "I'll be with you to help free souls from the wizard's control. I have a few ideas that might loosen his hold on them."

"Yeah, you do." Dillan winks at her.

I'm still not used to seeing Dillan so in love. When did he morph from a hot-headed ass to a housebroken sap?

Oh, yeah, right. During the years we shall not discuss when I was dead and missed everything.

"We'll text ye when we're in place," Sloan confirms.

Emmet and Dionysus bump knuckles and straighten. "Be there or be square, boys. Good luck."

"Right and tight," I contribute.

"Nothing but net," Aiden adds.

"One and done," Dillan chimes in.

"Eye on the prize, boys," Calum finishes.

As much as I was prepared for the catacombs of a dormant city to be a little creepy and somewhat gross, my imagination didn't do it justice. I should have considered that these were the passages of goblins, incubi, and trolls. The air is thick with the scent of damp earth and ancient stone. The walls seem to close in with every step we take.

"They needed to have a cleaning lady stop in once in a while." Calum holds up his palm. A ball of blue fire glows in his hand. "Even once a century would've been good."

"Brenny? Do ghosts have full night vision?" Dillan asks. "Like, if they're down here and we have faerie fire, are we going to blind them or help them see where we are?"

"How should *I* know?"

He pegs me with a scowl. "You *are* the guy who got private tutoring from Fionn in all things spirit plane, aren't you?"

"It was more like a crash course. Speaking of—so, I drop over, and you take me back to the penthouse and dump me on my bed? Did you take me to see Wallace or anything? No one was there when I woke up."

Dillan snorts. "Are you pouting because we weren't sitting vigil at your bedside?"

Am I? Yeah, okay, maybe a little. "It might've been nice if someone was there. Or a note even. *Hey, B. Hope you're not dead again. Your brothers.*"

They all bust up laughing.

"Rude."

Aiden pats my shoulder. "Aw, don't feel bad, B. We've been through it so many times with Fiona that we knew you were fine. Fionn does that. When he had something to say, it was easier for him to pull Fiona to him than for him to come to us."

"Not only Fiona," Nikon adds. "One time, he and his sister created a portal door and sucked half a dozen of us back to be formally trained by his men. That's when we first came to this island. A sorceress was trying to take control of Emhain Ablach's power."

"Well, it was new to me, and you all suck." I shrug off their laughter and flip them all off.

It only makes them laugh harder.

Assholes.

"All right." Sloan holds up his hands. "It's best if we quiet down. By my estimation, we're only a block or two away from the community buildin'. There might well be sentries down here. Dillan, would ye care to take the lead?"

Dillan pulls the hood of his cloak up and grins like an idiot as he takes his place at the front of the party. "Watch and learn, assholes."

I roll my eyes. "Yeah, yeah, you're the shit."

The Cloak of Knowledge is not only fashionably kick-ass as outer apparel. It also gives its wearer knowledge about their surroundings, hidden entrances, traps, and dangers. Having him in front, learning the secrets of the catacombs, and guiding us through the labyrinth to get to the wizard is the smartest play.

Except I'm the ghost whisperer.

I feel them before I see them—whispers of life, flickers on the spirit plane. The catacombs are alive in more ways than one. "Hold up." I raise my fist.

The group abruptly stops, and I take stock of what I sense. The darkness ahead writhes, and for a moment, it feels like the shadows are alive.

Fae vermin scuttle out from the cracks in the walls, their eyes glowing like tiny embers in the dark.

"Just a few critters," Dillan quips, his voice a soft chuckle that bounces off the ancient bricks.

His laugh cuts short as the rat creatures scatter, and their tails grow into wild vines. As thick as a man's wrist and covered in thorns sharp enough to pierce steel, they shoot out toward us from every direction.

Although the rats are spectral, their attacks aren't.

"Motherfucking hell!" Dillan shouts, calling his twin daggers into his hands. "Those thorns hurt."

The group scrambles, and my brothers and Sloan call out druid spells in rapid fire. Their physical attacks have little effect on our spectral foes.

I reach forward and grab a section of the thing's tail. I'm uncertain if my "make ghosts solid" trick will work on ghost vermin, but like when I touched Nightfall, the rat solidifies on the physical plane.

That gives Sloan whatever he needs to take care of things. He speaks a spell in Irish and the vine recoils. As if scalded by an invisible flame, it shrinks back into being a spectral rat creature's tail, and the ugly little bugger and his friends withdraw into the wall.

"Those things were freaky." Calum releases the tension on his bow and returns the arrow to his quiver. "Tell me those things aren't in our part of the city. They're underground freaky rat things, right?"

Dillan is scowling at the line of blood welling up on his forearm. "If they know what's good for them, they'll stay down here."

Eva grips his arm, and a heavenly glow radiates beneath her palms as she heals him. "I'm sure they learned their lesson and are now cowering in their dank little dens, chittering about the big scary men who invaded their tunnels."

When she steps back, Dillan's arm is healed, and he seems less irate. "Thanks, angel."

We continue. The air grows noticeably cooler as we get closer. I'm not sure why souls of the spectral plane give off such a frosty aura, but it's a thing.

By the time my breath is frosting in the air as I breathe, I can also feel the darkness of the wizard's energy in the air, a cloying presence.

A low growl echoes through the catacombs and the six of us spin, each trying to gauge where the noise originated. There is too much of an echo down here, making it difficult to pinpoint the source.

It was close, though.

Too close.

"Anyone feel like double-timing it to put some distance between us and whatever that was?" I ask.

"Sounds good to me," Calum agrees.

"Try to keep up, boys," Dillan replies.

We book it, rushing through the last few turns of the dark tunnels by the light of faerie fire. There's no more talking until

Dillan stops and raises his fist. Then he pulls his phone out of his pocket and sends a quick text. I feel the buzz, but I don't look.

The message is for Emmet.

Dillan is telling him we're in position below the community room and he's good to start the diversion.

"What do you think he'll do?" Calum whispers.

"With Em *and* Dionysus on it, there's no telling," Nikon replies in a low tone.

Dillan whispers something to Eva, and the two chuckle.

"Will we know when it's done?" I ask.

Sloan chuckles. "Oh, I'm sure we'll know."

There's another beat of silence, and something changes. The energy of the ghosts above us becomes chaotic. I'm unsure if our team can feel it, but *I* can. "Hell is breaking loose above us."

"How so?" Sloan asks.

"The spectral energy is suddenly confused and scrambled."

"Can ye feel if they've moved out of the buildin'?"

I tilt my face up and close my eyes. The darkness isn't moving, but the spirits the wizard commands are running around like ants with an intruder stomping down their ant hill. "Yeah, the ghosts are moving outside."

Sloan nods. "Then that's our cue. Lead the way."

You don't have to tell me twice. I've wanted nothing more than to get moving on the wizard since I found him this afternoon.

I reach out with my senses and lock onto the dark energy polluting the entire area. He's here, and we need to get close enough to trap him with Sloan's potion.

We race up the narrow, rough-hewn steps cut into the earth and stone beneath the community building. I have no idea where we'll surface. There's a wooden door overhead, and I unlatch the hook and push it up and over on its hinges until it bumps flat onto the floor.

I'm out of the catacombs first, and it's pitch black. Stepping to the side, I wait for Sloan, Calum, Aiden, Eva, and Dillan to surface. With their faerie fire to guide us, I point toward the malignance I feel.

The space we're in seems to be an indoor amphitheater, the rows of seats rising in a half circle off to the right and the stage to the left.

I head left and follow the beacon of dark magic drawing me like a lighthouse on the rocks. We go through the stage area and into the corridor, getting closer to the street.

I hear it then, the unmistakable theme song for *Ghostbusters*. I roll my eyes as we race past the front entrance, and I glimpse Emmet and Dionysus in beige coveralls holding proton packs and swinging orange laser beams through the sea of ghostly protectors.

They even have the giant Stay Puft Marshmallow Man there for effect.

Dillan snorts behind me.

Calum groans. "Dammit. I should've picked distraction duty."

I have no attention to spare. Now that we're out in the open, the air is thickening with the presence of ghosts. Their forms shift in and out of focus like the static of a poorly tuned television.

"On your toes, boys," I shout, weaving through the ghostly crowd.

Specters surge forward, a relentless wave of lost souls stuck between realms. I can't get caught up with them. If they know we're here, there's a good chance the wizard will too.

My grip tightens on the wizard's staff, the wood thrumming with ancient power. There's something poetic about using his staff against him. Or, at least, I hope I get the chance to.

I swing as I go. Each arc sends shockwaves through the ghosts, shattering them with a piercing wail and an explosion of particles.

The others engage behind me, but I don't look back. I can't.

The success of this mission relies fully on my ability to take on the necromancer.

I rush through a doorway, homing in on his magical signature, and find him with his back to me. He's facing an opening in a stone wall, his arms raised as he casts a spell. *What's he doing? What is so important that he's casting instead of trying to get away?*

Not that I'm complaining, but...

I reach into my pocket, grab the two vials Sloan prepared, and throw them at the wizard's feet.

His eyes widen as he turns, and I see when he realizes he's stuck. "That's right, asshole. No ghosting out this time. You're mine."

Panic lines his face, and I love it. He deserves to be afraid. He deserves to lose his choice of when to leave. He deserves my wrath and so much more.

His lips move at a frenzied pace, spitting out spells in a desperate bid to vanish into the shadows.

I rush through the room, closing the distance until I pull my right arm back and throw a fist with the force of a concrete block. The satisfaction of my punch connecting with his jaw is such a sweet ending to the dark saga he authored.

"How?" he stammers, reeling from my hit.

"You're not so tough now, are you, dickwad? Without your army, without being able to escape into the spirit realm."

I've got him, so why does he look so smug?

I take a step back and search for what I'm missing.

The stone wall.

The doorway to the room behind the stone wall is closing. I rush sideways to look inside, and my victory blows up in my face. Bottles of gray dust fill floor-to-ceiling shelves.

It's the bone dust.

Although it's only the ground-up essence of the poor souls outside, the residual energy of their unbearable pain still echoes as loud as thunder.

It's a crypt, and he's sealing it shut.

"What have you done?" My mind is spinning.

"Once that wall is sealed, it will remain sealed for a century, a millennium, maybe longer. You won't be able to vanquish me because I will have a tether to those who serve me."

"Fuck!" I jump into the doorway, brace my back against one side of the opening, and lift my boot to keep it from closing. "Guys! I need magic help!"

The wizard laughs, and I want to shoot him dead on the spot. With everything in me, I wish that would work.

Sloan *poofs* in and starts for the wizard. He's broken free from the potion's hold and is turning tail to run.

"Let him go! I need help here." I understand Sloan's confusion, but I don't have time to argue. "Get the bone dust. He spelled the room to seal as a crypt. Get the bottles out."

Sloan runs over, curses, then *poofs* into the room and *poofs* out with two waist-high bottles of gray dust.

"Where's the wizard?" Dillan rushes in with Calum hot on his heels.

"Forget him. Help me hold this door."

The two of them race over. Dillan braces himself opposite me, but I know it's a losing battle as he lifts his boot and puts his back into it.

"Calum, try magic to stop this."

Nikon is the next to arrive. "Greek. Help Sloan get the bone dust out of this room."

The stone is too strong, and it's all but closing now. I grunt, forcing every ounce of strength into my arms.

Nikon and Sloan are snapping and *poofing* in and out, each time bringing as many bottles as they can move. It's a Herculean effort, but by the time the wall forces us to get out of the way and seals shut with a resolute *thud*, every single bottle, jar, and container of bone dust is out of the crypt.

Sloan and Nikon double over and prop their hands on their knees, panting.

Calum, Dillan, and I do the same.

We're still breathing heavily when Emmet and Dionysus jog in and frown at the five of us all but dropping on the floor.

"The wizard?" Emmet asks.

"Gone," I reply.

"What's all this?" He points at the bottles.

"Freedom for the ghosts."

Dionysus smiles. "Where shall we host the freedom party?"

I straighten. "I was thinking a bonfire in the clearing in the grove might be fitting."

Dionysus nods. "I'll take care of it."

With that, he snaps his fingers, and he—and all the containers of bone dust—are gone.

Nikon grunts. "Fuck me. Where the hell was he five minutes ago?"

"Tryin' not to cross the streams."

Dillan snorts. "Good one, Irish. Your pop culture references are really coming along."

"Yeah, Fiona will be proud," Calum agrees.

Sloan straightens. "Speaking of Fiona, if ye don't mind, I'd like to get home to my wife and have a long hot bath."

"Ditto," Nikon agrees. "Hands in, everyone. Let's call it a night."

I wave off the suggestion. "Sorry, guys, not yet. If one of you could take me to the grove, I'd like to release the ghosts as soon as possible. Their suffering is terrible, and I can't stomach calling it a night until it's done."

Sloan nods. "Aye, yer right. Nikon, if ye'll take them to the grove, I'll pop home to get Fiona and the salt."

EMMET

When the morning light bathes my sheets in warmth, I peel myself off the bed and roll to my feet. *Damn. I ache.* My muscles protest every movement, and my limbs are made of lead. Still, there's a spark in me that refuses to rest.

The thrill of yesterday's quest successes, followed by a victory against the wizard's spectral horde, has left me on a feel-good high.

We did a great thing last night.

The ceremony in the grove was short but special.

Dionysus arranged all the bone dust into a giant mound, and when we sprinkled it with salt and watched it burn, we released hundreds of trapped souls.

Eva is likely still escorting them to their resting places. It's a good thing angels don't need sleep because I'm willing to bet she didn't get any.

It's not totally over, though. There are still some ghosts tied to the wizard because he ingested their bone dust to bind their energy to him.

As sick as it sounds, it's smart too.

It's what Voldemort did with his Horcruxes.

I shuffle across my bedroom floor and stare out at the city below. The wizard is still out there somewhere, but with ninety-five percent of his army released, he won't be the fighting force he once was.

The shower's heat feels good on my aching muscles, and as I lather up, I give my body some healing energy.

Today is not a day I can afford to be tired and sore.

Today is the day I face the third trial in reinstating the fragments of the key to the Corestone—fire.

Once I'm dried off and dressed, I go to the living room and find Brendan gazing out across the rooftops of Isilon the same way I had been.

The city sprawls beneath us, a tapestry of magic and mystery, peaceful in the morning light.

"Hey," I greet Brendan, my voice still rough and deep with sleep. "Yesterday was wild, huh?"

Brendan turns with a grin spreading across his face. "For you, even more than the rest of us. I hear you were brilliant." He clasps my shoulder firmly, pride clear in his eyes. "Calum said you secured the air and water fragments from the quest Syma left for you."

"Yeah, it was something else."

We lapse into companionable silence, watching the city breathe and stretch as it wakes. I lean against the cool glass, feeling Isilon's energy seep into my bones, invigorating me.

"Sorry you felt abandoned when you woke up from your trip with Fionn. It might be old hat for us, but you're right. It was new to you, and you were probably a little freaked."

He shrugs, comes into the kitchen, and pulls out a couple of plastic sandwich bags. "I'm over it. What freaked me out more was waking up to find Nightfall on the bed with me."

I blink. "You woke up in bed with the purple-haired elven ghost goddess?"

"*On* my bed, not *in* my bed."

I shrug. "Was she released last night?"

"I don't know. If she was, I'm happy for her."

"But?"

He pulls out the salt and starts filling his little baggies. "I would've liked to say goodbye. There was something there, you know? A spark. A connection of some kind. Have you ever had that?"

I rub the place in my chest that aches almost every day, all day. "Yeah. I was handfasted to Ciara, remember?"

"Yeah, of course. Sorry."

I draw a deep breath and shake it off. "Tell me about training with Fionn. I bet it was intense."

Brendan smirks and stuffs two salt baggies into his back pocket. "He's a tough oul bugger. It's likely a good thing they don't make warriors like him anymore."

"Yeah, likely."

He leans back and crosses his arms. "I learned a lot about myself and my connection to the spirit plane. Things that are helping us now. He says I'm a Celtic shaman."

"Like Fi?"

"Not exactly. I'm not a Hunter-god or anything. I carry the family connection to the spiritual plane."

"Still, that's pretty cool." I wait to see if he thinks so. Up until now, Brendan has not only been ambivalent about magic. He's been resistant.

"Yeah, it *is* cool," he agrees.

The two of us stand there, taking in our new realities. It feels good—like our worlds have been set right after being out of sync for too long.

"I'm afraid to breathe," I whisper. "I don't want to break the bubble of this peaceful moment."

Brendan lets out a soft chuckle. "Go ahead and breathe. We both know it won't last long and it's not worth suffocating for."

I laugh and head into the kitchen to start my day. "No. I suppose not."

I'm mid-sip into my coffee when a knock at the door has me changing course. When I open the portal, Kidok is there, looking grim.

"What's happened?" I ask.

"We've got two more dead. Looks like a domestic altercation."

"Who?"

"The gnomes from the back of the meeting who stormed out. One dead in the home. His brother jumped out the window. That's how I found them."

Brendan curses behind me. "Do you think it was the whispering souls?"

Kidok nods. "Seems that way to me."

I let out a long-suffering sigh. "I tried to tell them."

Brandan holds up a hand. "No, Em. This is not your fault. You explained the situation, and they wouldn't listen. They made their choice."

"It still sucks."

"Yeah, it does."

Kidok meets my gaze. "What do you want me to do?"

I shrug and look at Brenny. "Notify next of kin and release the body for their end-of-life preparations?"

He nods. "Yeah, that's all we really *can* do."

When Kidok leaves, I resume my quest to caffeinate myself for my day. "It's stupid. If they only listened."

"But they didn't."

"We should've asked Kidok when it happened. Do you think it was before we freed the souls or one of the remaining souls that did it?"

"Does it matter?"

"No. I guess not."

A surge of familiar wayfarer energy brings Sloan and Fiona into the kitchen beside me. "Morning, brothers." She wraps me in a bear hug that could rival Bruin's. "Just came to congratulate you on a big win for both of you yesterday. In the spirit of helping but staying out of it, I think we've figured out where the quest of fire will take place."

I perk up and set my coffee down. "Seriously?"

Sloan sets down the stack of ancient-looking tomes and scrolls that would give any librarian heart palpitations. "Given what ye learned yesterday about the first two tasks, I did a little skimmin' into the possible location of the fire challenge."

I snort when I see Brendan's face and pat the texts. "For Sloan, this *is* light reading."

Sloan ignores the playful chuckles and continues. "I dove into the island's lore and read through the journals of the Light Weavers. After a long chat with Astrid, I'm convinced the last piece of yer key is hidden within the Inferno Peaks."

Inferno Peaks?

A shiver runs the length of my spine. "Well, hell. That doesn't sound daunting at all. I'm picturing a place where the ground oozes fire like an angry god's blood and the sky is a haze of soot."

"Sounds like a blast," Fiona quips.

"Right?"

Sloan waves away our commentary. "While I know ye wanted to be a one-man show yesterday, I think ye'd be better to take us along. We'll let ye handle things yer way, but a few things there have me worried."

I raise my hand. "Let's keep the horrors of the Inferno Peaks a surprise, at least until after my coffee."

Fiona meets my gaze. "All joking aside, take help, Em. You have nothing to prove, and Syma told you to rely on your team."

Honestly, after yesterday's watery escapade, I feel like a wrung-out rag. "Yeah, assemble the team and bring snacks. Definitely snacks."

Brendan doesn't look all that enthused.

"What's up?" I ask.

"Would I be a horrible brother if I let you head off with the others and I work on hunting down the wizard? I'm thinking he's got to be weak after us taking away his battery pack of power. I want to move on that before he's able to adapt."

I rest my elbows on the island countertop and take a long sip of mocha blend. "You do you, B. There are enough of us here to get the job done. It makes sense that the ghost whisperer stays on the ghost's trail. S'all good."

"Thanks, Em. If you need me, you know I'm there for you as quickly as a portal."

"I know it. Now, let's get some brekkie started. It's going to be a big day. Sloan, since you know the secret perils, I'll leave the building of our quest party to you. Let me know where and when."

Sloan nods. "Aye, we'll take care of everything."

Fiona hugs me again. "Thanks, Em. I'll worry less if you've got a team."

When they *poof* out, I wonder if Sloan building me a team is about helping me or keeping Fiona from worrying.

Likely a bit of both.

"So, this is the Inferno Peaks." We're standing at the base of a volcanic stone rise. Heat washes over me like the blast from an open oven. I stare at the smoldering gas escaping out the top. It's hot here, and the air hangs heavy with the cloying stench of sulfur.

The mountain looms, a jagged silhouette against the morning sky, and I swear I can hear it whispering my name.

Or maybe it's the sulfur getting to me.

"How did we not know this was here?" Dillan asks.

Calum chuckles. "Yeah, you'd think we would've noticed a volcano huffing and puffing on the tiny island where we live."

"Except the tiny island is enchanted," Sloan counters. "It's a see what ye need to see, when ye need to see it kind of affair."

I pat the front of my battle vest for luck. Today, the two crystal key fragments are sheathed there instead of weapons. "Then yay you, Irish, because I had no idea where the fire element to this challenge would be."

"Glad to help, Em. Whatever ye need."

I know that. Growing up the fifth boy in the Cumhaill lineup, I might have doubted myself, but I've never doubted that my family would die before they let me down. That grew to be true about our extended family, too.

Liam and Kevin have always been like brothers to us.

Then we discovered Gran and Granda.

Then Sloan, Nikon, and Dionysus.

The list goes on. Patty, Tad, Ciara, Eva…

"Hey, Em? Are you okay?" Calum is watching me, worry crinkling his brow.

I shake off the nostalgia and get back to the moment at hand. "Yeah, sorry. Taking a moment to be thankful for the people in my life. I love you guys. You know that, right?"

The worry in his expression deepens. "Yeah, of course, Em. We love you right back."

"What brought this on?" Dillan steps closer. "You're not getting any dumb ideas about mortality and the realities of this kind of quest, are you?"

I meet his gaze. "Maybe a little. It's been a tough week, but I'm good—better than I've been in a long time."

His brow tightens. "Do you want to take a day or two and come back at this when you're rested? Yesterday was a lot. No one would blink if you needed to catch your breath."

"No, I'm good. I just… It feels like I'm growing into my skin… like I finally fit in my life. Does that make any sense?"

All three of them nod, and I let out a breath.

Good, I'm glad they get it.

"Let's kick this volcano's ass and getter done, yeah? I'm in the mood for a Dionysus celebration."

Dillan pulls me in and kisses the side of my head. "You've got this, brother."

Calum pats my back. "Let's show them what you're made of."

Drawing a deep breath, I turn to Sloan. "Okay. Where do you think we start?"

He points at a plateau a couple of hundred feet up. "Do you see how the rock is darker at the far end of the plateau?"

I squint to bring it into focus. "I think so."

"That's the opening to a cavern. If I'm right, that's our way in."

"You're going to *poof* us up there, right?" Calum asks. "I didn't bring any rock-climbing gear."

Sloan chuckles. "I think yer gettin' soft, boys. What would ye do if I weren't here?"

Dillan looks up at the rock and the slope and frowns. "Likely call Nikon or Dionysus to snap us up there."

Sloan laughs. "So, I'm replaceable, am I?"

I shake my head. "Not in a million, Irish. Who else would do all our research and gray matter acrobatics? If you weren't here, we'd have to do our own homework."

Calum and Dillan both shiver and make faces.

"All right, ye eejits. Up we go." Sloan extends his arm and the moment we pile our hands on top and make contact, he portals us up to the plateau. "There, now. Dillan, if ye would?"

Dillan pulls the hood of his cloak up and takes the lead, striding into the cave's mouth. We're right behind him, but it's not long before the shadows swallow us.

I cast a ball of faerie fire every twenty feet and toss it toward the ceiling to give us some light. It will also act as a breadcrumb trail so we can Hansel and Gretel the hell out of our escape when we're done.

The deeper we delve into the cavern, the cooler it gets, and it's a relief after the sweltering heat outside. The path is dodgy, winding down as we go, with cross-corridors and switchbacks that make it hard to figure out which way we're heading.

The walls are close, rough-hewn, and jagged. There are a few places where we can walk side by side, but only a few. It's almost all single file.

We've been trekking for close to an hour when the magical energy in the air has the hair on my arms standing on end. I extend my fingers into the darkness ahead and smile. "Good one, Irish. I feel the signature of the Light Weavers up ahead. We're in the right place."

"Well, good," Dillan grumbles. "Because if we were wasting our day in here breathing this stank for no reason, I'd be getting salty."

I snort. "When are you *not* salty?"

Calum chuckles behind me. "He's got you there, D."

"Yeah, yeah, yuck it up, assholes."

The bickering of siblings is the steady heartbeat of our family, and it grounds me more than any other love language. It's totally us, and while other people might not get it looking from the outside, it works.

We're making progress as we go. Dillan and I take turns leading the way, depending on what he or I sense in the darkness. Sloan keeps our path lit with faerie fire. Calum has his bow nocked. He covers our back and watches for any surprises.

Dillan is in the middle of yet another story about how baby Han is the smartest, most talented angel baby of all angel babies when the magical signature of the sisters hits me like a tidal wave.

"Guys, hold up. There's something here." I move into a shallow alcove to press my hands to the stone. "I feel Light Weaver magic."

"Do you think it's the fragment?" Dillan steps in beside me to help me assess the wall.

I consider that and expand my senses. When I do, the two

pieces of the key sheathed against my ribs emit a blip of energy, as if searching for their final piece.

The responding blip of energy comes from off to our left. "No. I don't think so. But there's something behind this wall they focused a great deal of their magic on at some point."

"Do ye think yer meant to get inside?" Sloan asks.

"I'm not sure."

"I don't sense any opening or way to access what's beyond this wall," Dillan replies.

"Maybe the entrance is from the other side," Calum suggests. "If we keep going, maybe it'll become clear."

Something about Calum's explanation rings true. "Yeah. I say we do what we came here to do. We retrieve the third fragment to the key, then we find the Corestone and reignite the Embers of Existence."

"Easy-peasy," Dillan adds.

"Child's play," Calum agrees.

"Yeah, let's go with that." I hope positive thinking will work in our favor. "Onward to reclaiming the final fragment."

The four of us leave the mysterious alcove to its secrets and continue down the opposite tunnel, following the magical energy calling to the fragments in my possession. "Whatever happens as a challenge, I have to be the one who recovers the fragment."

"Roger that," Dillan agrees.

"We're here solely to—" Calum's words cut off short as he skitters behind us and twists back the way we came. "What the fuckety-fuck was that?"

Dillan has his dual daggers drawn. "What was what?"

"Something slithered in the shadows across the intersection." Calum's voice is a full octave higher than normal.

"Slithered how?" Sloan asks.

Dillan tosses three more balls of blue fire into the intersection to increase the lighting, and the moment they dispatch the shadows, three long, slender lizard creatures race into the light to hiss at us.

"Slithered like that!" Calum snaps.

"What the fuck are they?" Dillan widens his stance as he angles himself to get the stone wall at his back.

"Scorch wyrms." Sloan's voice is calm and smooth. "They burrow into the walls of volcanic chambers, absorbing heat they can release in powerful bursts of breath to defend their territory."

"They spit scalding heat at trespassers?" I confirm.

"Essentially, yes."

Awesomesauce. "Are they aggressive?"

"Not overly. They're usually passive if left alone," Sloan replies.

"Then I suggest Calum and Dillan lower their weapons and instead of threatening them, we leave them alone."

"Will that work, Irish?" Calum asks.

"Aye, it might."

"Or we might get bathed in burning breath and have our skin peel off our bones," Dillan snaps.

There's one in every group, amirite?

I release the fire in my palm and hold up my hands in a sign of peace. "It's worth a try. I'd rather not pick a fight if we don't have to."

Dillan grunts. It goes against the grain of his character to stand down, but we still have to go farther into this volcano and come out again.

Why burn bridges?

When Dillan moves to sheath his daggers, the wyrms hiss and advance three or four feet.

"Easy, wyrm guys." I adopt Sloan's calming tone. "No one wants you to spit scalding heat. We're cool. Everything is cool. Well, everything except you…and your breath."

Their scales shimmer coal gray as cracks of molten orange and red outline the plates of their skin.

We ease back, putting distance between us and the angry scorch wyrms. I'm about to turn and continue when a shrill scream pierces the air.

I pivot, my heart racing, and *whoosh*!

All I see is fire.

2 2

BRENDAN

I make my way through the awakening streets, my strides purposeful, my mind replaying the tumultuous events of last night. Releasing the wizard's army was a big win, but this won't be over until the ghosts are all free and the wizard is dispatched to whatever "after" awaits him.

I hope his final resting place is in the fiery pits of hell where he becomes a demon's plaything.

Turnaround is fair play, after all.

Nightfall was an unexpected ally for us. Whether she helped us to free herself or for a dozen other personal motives she might have had, I don't care.

In the end, she helped us, and it worked in our favor.

The thought that I might never see her again sends a pang of conflicting emotions through my chest. Relief that her suffering is over, regret that I didn't get to thank her or say goodbye, and maybe sorrow that the potential of something special ended so soon.

Those are thoughts for tomorrow when the job is done, and the wizard is no more.

A dog's bark has me stopping to see where it's coming from.

Emmet mentioned there was a three-legged ghost pooch hopping around. I haven't had the pleasure of meeting him yet.

He comes out from between two houses a few blocks from the security office. He's medium-sized with long hair and floppy ears. I'm no expert, but I'd say he's an Australian shepherd and sheepdog love child.

I take a knee, and he hops over, his tail wagging and his mouth open with a happy pant. "Hey, Hat Trick. I heard about you. I'm Brendan."

I hold my hand out for him to sniff. When he comes close enough, and I feel his breath on my hand, I scrub my fingers against his cheek and play with his floppy ears. "How about that, eh, boy? I make you solid. Do you like that? Do you like getting pets?"

His answer is an obvious yes because his excitement ratchets off the charts. His butt gains momentum and is waggling so much that I'm pretty sure he's about to hop off his three little paws and hurt himself.

"Whoa, you're good, buddy. I'll pet you more, but right now, we've got a wizard to find. Do you want to come along and help me?"

Another yes.

"All right. I'd be happy for the company." I brush off my palms and look around to see if anybody will see me do my ghost thing.

Not that there's anything wrong with that. It feels weird to have people look at me while I connect with the spiritual plane.

There's nobody, so we're good to go.

After a couple of deep breaths, I reach out with my senses, seeking the darkness that the necromancer's magical choices surround him with.

I don't expect much because until now, the bastard's been notoriously slippery. To my surprise, a tangible thread tugs on my awareness.

I feel his malignant energy clearly.

If I had to guess why that was possible, I'd say losing the battery power he plugged into with his ghost army has left him a shadow of his former self.

Perhaps he's not strong enough to shield his presence from me anymore. Or it's a trap, and he's luring me in because he wants me to come.

Both are legitimate possibilities, and neither of them change my next move. "It's showdown time, Hat Trick. The end. Roll credits."

The dog wags his tail, and I scrub his ears as I follow the dark energy through the streets. After I round a few corners, I have a solid idea of where I'm heading.

"He's come home to roost, buddy."

As I approach the five-story home with the glass dome on top, I cut over to stay under cover of the trees. The forested area of the grove gives me a direct line of sight to the wizard's home, and at the same time, keeps my arrival unnoticed.

When I'm tucked safely under the canopy of the grove's trees, I scan the windows of the necromancer's mansion for any movement.

There is none.

Either he's vulnerable and licking his wounds or he's finally learned he should keep his head down. Otherwise, we might chop it off.

"What do you think, boy? Should we storm the Bastille or play it smart and call for backup?"

Hat Trick pushes against my leg, and I reach down absently and stroke him.

"Yeah, you're probably right. Better to play it safe and make sure we've got the upper hand. Good call, pup." I pull out my phone and text the family WhatsApp group.

Need backup at the wizard's house by the grove. Who's available?

Seconds tick by and I watch the screen.

Anyone? Helloooo?

Fiona's avatar pops up that she's typing.

Emmet is off with Sloan, Calum, and Dillan—likely no signal inside a volcano. I'm on the baby-making bench. Dionysus is visiting his dad on Olympus. Nikon and Aiden are in Toronto, working a case for Garnet. Sending you Bruin.

Well, Bruin is the equivalent of five men, so there's that, and he can ghost out and follow spirits, so that's good too.

A moment later, the air swirls around me, and Bruin materializes beside me. He grunts something, and I fight not to roll my eyes. Not being able to talk to him is so old. It's also not helpful when preparing to go into battle.

It's the hand we've been dealt.

"Looks like it's you and me against the wizard." Bruin swings his head toward the building and grumbles something I don't understand. "Do you want to do an intel sweep?"

His boxy head bounces in the affirmative.

"Okay, that sounds good. Do your thing, and I'll wait right here."

He ghosts out, and I sigh. "Not that I'll be able to understand anything you find out when you get back."

I pat Hat Trick's side absently as I watch the house. "If Emmet's successful and this city is about to really wake up, I'm going to need my druid spark so I can communicate with the animals around here."

The dog's tail thumping against the ground probably means he agrees.

Hunkered down behind the screen of trees, Hat Trick and I keep our gazes fixed on the domed home of the wizard. I'll wait a while and see where we are. Taking time to gather intel is never a bad thing, right?

Waiting is a test of patience, which I don't have a lot of to begin with, but holding the line and working surveillance are both parts of policing.

I want to get this right.

Rushing a situation when I have the upper hand would be stupid. I don't want to give him an opportunity to get away again.

This will be our last standoff.

I'm unsure if I'm trying to convince *myself* of that, but I sense something before I have time to work it out. It's the faintest whisper on the wind, a sensation brushing against the edge of my consciousness.

It's an energy signature I wasn't sure I'd ever feel again, but I'm relieved to sense it. Nightfall.

It's off, and infused with an unmistakable undercurrent of agony.

My gut clenches as I track the source toward the wizard's home across the way.

He has her.

He's *hurting* her.

Did he figure out she helped me? Is he so angry or drained that he might consume the spectral souls he has left?

The thought of Nightfall, fierce and untamed, bound to him and writhing in torment, sends a jolt of white-hot fury surging through me.

Ready or not. Backup or not. Here I come.

I'm across the clearing, my boots pounding out a steady rhythm on the street before my mind catches up. I'm not sure what I expect to find in there or how I'll take him down.

All I know is that it's happening.

I grit my teeth and shoulder the door open, barely catching the thing before it bangs against the wall and announces my arrival.

Oops. Okay, I need to rein it in.

At least I don't need to go the Spiderman route to get inside. Dionysus broke down the wizard's wards when we were here last time. Looks like he doesn't have the juice to put them back up.

Too bad.

I'm inside, feeling for Nightfall's energy, and taking the stairs two at a time in the next racing heartbeat. By the third floor, I'm horribly aware that ditching my strength and endurance training since coming back from the dead might have been a mistake.

By the fourth floor, I'm cursing my lazy ass and contemplating using the wizard's staff in my hand as a walking stick or a prop to hold me up.

By the fifth floor, I wonder if the wizard would mind giving me five minutes to catch my breath before we begin our death match.

Is there such a thing as a time-out in a takedown?

Likely not.

Especially when your foe sees you and goes from draining his captives to downright torturing them to sucking them dry of everything they've got.

He needs to go down, and it needs to be now.

I'm relieved that it's not only Nightfall who is being drained and tortured but half a dozen ghosts he's still got his hooks into.

Wait. No. Relieved is the wrong word.

It's awful, but she hasn't been singled out as a traitor, so that's good.

I skirt the edges of the fifth-floor sanctum, searching the corners of the room, every nerve alight and ready to react to any ghostly guards he has standing sentinel.

"Back off, wizard," I shout, extending the staff between us. "Let them go."

The air's charged with magic, a tangible current against my skin. The surprised wizard scrambles to escape, but he's too slow.

I reach deep into something primal within me and slam an invisible wall down. It pins him here, in this world, where I can settle our score.

Unlike Sloan's potion that left him wiggle room to escape, my shaman connection overpowers him, and I've got him locked down tight. "You're done, asshole."

His eyes widen, and our dance begins.

His victims cry out in agony with every step I take. I feel their pain, and I know it's emotional blackmail. I'm hurting them by going after the wizard. He's using their suffering as a tool of coercion.

I stop my advance to consider my options.

There's no scenario where I let him go, but if he twists the knife with every step and kills the dozen ghosts bound to him, can I call that a win?

His form flickers in and out of view. I curse, realizing that my hold on the spirit plane is slipping. If navigating the realm of specters is a muscle, I've only been working out for two days.

I'm unsure what my next move is until a swirl of air encircles me, and it clicks into place.

I might not be able to understand Fiona's bear when he speaks, but the guy is a brutal warrior, and I know in an instant what I'm supposed to do.

"Yeah, Bear. Three…two…one."

I lunge at the wizard, racing to close the distance between us at the same moment Bruin materializes in front of him.

I don't care if you're a badass necromancer or not. When a Kodiak bear appears two feet in front of you and stands on his back paws roaring in your face, you forget to torture your minions across the room.

Using his distraction to my advantage, I grab the wizard's arm. The moment he becomes corporeal, Bruin's six-inch claws begin to slice.

Fiona makes dark jokes about how much Bruin enjoys shredding bad guys. Now I have a front-row view. As much as I'd love to back away, I have to maintain my hold to keep the wizard shreddable.

Chunks of wizard thunk to the inlaid floor. I turn my head to wear as little of him as I can manage.

I know the moment Bruin has severed enough of him to

shatter the bond holding his minions in thrall because the ghosts across the room sag, their torture ended.

Nightfall drops to her knees, her breaths coming in ragged gasps. I'm at her side in an instant with my hand outstretched. Her fingers lock with mine, and in that touch, she solidifies, her form as real as my racing pulse.

"Are you all right?"

She sits back on her knees, her gaze narrowing on the mess Bruin made across the room. "I will be if you'll help me with something."

"Anything. What do you need?"

She gets to her feet. I wait to see what she's doing, but it becomes apparent. We gather the remnants of what used to be the necromancer—or at least whatever physical remnants were created while I touched him—and make a pile in the center of the room.

I slide my hand into the back pocket of my jeans and pull out the Ziplock bags of salt I grabbed this morning. After thoroughly sprinkling the wizard heap of death, I pull out a lighter.

"You thought ahead." Nightfall watches me.

I grin. "After the past four days of trying to take this guy down, I wasn't about to be caught unprepared." I hand her the lighter. "Push this button down with your thumb and a flame will appear here."

She hesitates. "You want *me* to do it?"

"It's more your revenge than mine. I figured it might give you some peace of mind."

"That's very sweet. Thank you."

Several other ghosts hover close by as we watch unflinchingly while the wizard's form disintegrates, a pyre of justice in the dim chamber.

The air in the room grows heavy with the scent of retribution. Then, as if the universe exhales, the malevolence of his energy dissipates.

Standing there with the ghosts of Isilon's past, it's sad how lost they look. "We have an angel who will take you to your final resting place. I'll make the arrangements with her, and we'll come to the grove tonight at sundown. Does that work?"

It seems so.

One by one, they fade away until Nightfall and I are left alone, staring at a charred circle on the hardwood floor. "And that's the end of that," I remark.

She meets my gaze and smiles. "Thankfully so."

23

EMMET

I push up off the floor, brush the palms of my hands together, and check on the others. "Did someone attack us with a flamethrower?"

Sloan pats the knees of his pants and shakes his head. "No, Em. It wasn't a flamethrower."

"Then what was it?"

"It was him." Dillan's voice is much too calm. "Be cool. I don't think he likes us."

Dillan doesn't point. Instead, he tilts his head back slowly and looks toward the ceiling. Perched among the shadows of this volcanic labyrinth is an orange firebird.

Holy snarpin arseholes.

"Is that a phoenix?" I try to keep the excitement out of my tone, but my voice cracks like I'm a thirteen-year-old boy again.

"Aye, I'd say so. The question is, was he givin' us a flyby or was he makin' his intentions known?"

Calum interjects, "Irish, if he was making his intentions known, he failed because we're still having this conversation."

Good point.

213

"Given those two choices, I'd like door number one, please, Monty. A friendly flyby to make the druids crap their Calvins."

Calum nods. "Yeah, I prefer that one, too."

The way he flew down at us, I ended up at the head of the trail and the others are fifteen feet behind me. "Are we free to go?"

"I'm not sure," Sloan replies.

"Give it a try, D," Calum urges.

Dillan throws Calum a look. "Why me? Why don't *you* give it a try?"

Calum laughs. "I'm the oldest brother here. That gives me seniority. Move down the tunnel and see if the firebird tries to singe your eyebrows off."

Dillan scratches his jaw with his middle finger, flipping off Calum.

As amusing as all this is, we can't stay here all day. "It's my quest, so I'll be the crash test dummy. I'm going to act casual and not look at him. Let me know if he gets ruffled about me moving on and I need to hit the deck."

"We got you, Em," Calum replies.

I take a tentative step deeper into the tunnel, then a second. Now that I'm in motion again, the energy down the corridor is calling. "I feel the last fragment of the key up here. I'm sure this is where we're supposed to go."

Step after step, I move forward. No one shouts for me to take cover and no phoenix tries to fry me.

Winning!

When I get well into the tunnel, I turn back and whisper, "Who's next?"

Sloan lowers his chin and slowly shifts his weight. The moment he moves to join me, the phoenix squawks and flicks his fiery tail.

When Irish edges back toward Dillan and Calum, the phoenix preens his fiery feathers, and I'd swear he's laughing.

They try repeatedly, and we come up with the same result

each time. I can move on, but anytime Sloan, Dillan, or Calum tries to join me, the phoenix ruffles and gets ready to attack.

"I guess I'm supposed to take this next part on solo." I straighten, and I know I'm right when I say it out loud. "It's fine. You guys stay here. I'll be back."

"Aye, but be careful, Em."

"Will do."

The chamber is close. I feel the energy vibrating off the tunnel's walls, seeking the fragments sheathed in my battle vest.

With each step, the anticipation builds.

I toss faerie fire toward the ceiling, lighting my way, and soon after, the tunnel opens to a large chamber. It looks exactly as I would expect a chamber in the heart of a volcano to look. It's all dark stone with molten fire peeking through the cracks in the floor and a pool of thick, fiery lava in the middle, glowing as hot and bright as the heart of the sun.

Another phoenix, as majestic and terrifying as the one down the tunnel, guards the way. I'm unsure if it's my druid senses or being attuned to the island's magic, but I know this is a female.

The mate of the other phoenix.

"It's a pleasure to meet you." I incline my head. "Syma and the Light Weavers left something with you for me to reclaim."

She screeches, and the sound echoes off the cavern's walls. I'm not sure what that means, but I want to think it was, "Oh, yeah. Hey, Emmet. We've been waiting for you. Welcome."

That might be wishful thinking.

I step forward, offering my palm in case she's supposed to verify my magical energy and intentions like the other two quests.

The phoenix studies me, tilting her head to the side as if considering. A connection forms and I take a steadying breath. Okay, I think we're friends now.

With a graceful nod, the phoenix steps aside.

I exhale and step deeper into the chamber. Oppressive heat

hits me like a wave as I enter. Sweat already beads on my forehead. It's suffocating.

"Air Bubble." I draw a few deep breaths, thankful for the ability to fill my lungs. Breathing is one of those things we take for granted until it's gone.

Farther into the chamber, I glimpse an obsidian bridge spanning the lake of lava. It looks insubstantial, and considering it spans a bone-melting death pool, I'm wary.

"Is this bridge going to hold me?" I ask.

The phoenix doesn't choose to comment.

I study the lava lake, its surface a roiling dance of flames licking the air with singeing hunger. There's no doubt in my mind. Anything that touches the surface gets consumed almost instantly.

The fire fragment awaits on the far side.

I see it resting on a pedestal like in the stone tower. It's calling to the other fragments—a piece of something wishing to be whole again after over a thousand years.

I step up to the bridge's entrance and run my fingers over the runes etched there. As I trace the patterns, each one awakens with a soft glow against the dark stone.

During my training, the sisters had me poring over the ancient texts. Every rune represents something in nature and the balance between them.

These are all about fire—obviously.

The warmth of a hearth, the devastation of a blaze, the promise of renewal from ashes.

With a deep breath, I steel myself and step onto the bridge. I move quickly, exuding as much respect and intention as I can while making my way over the fiery pool of torturous death.

I swallow when my boots are firmly on the stone floor of the cavern on the other side and pat my racing heart. "That one was tough on the ticker."

The phoenix takes flight from her perch by the door and pumps her wings to close the distance between us.

I wave gently, hoping she remembers we're friends. "I'm Emmet. I'm supposed to be here, remember?"

There's no aggression in her energy as she joins me, and when she perches on a large rock, I get the sense she wants to watch.

"That's cool. I'm a voyeur too. To each their own."

The moment I stand before the pedestal, a *whoosh* of flame engulfs it. I pull my hands back, the hair on my knuckles singed.

"Dirty pool."

As I say it, I know I can get around this. Fire is nature, and I'm a druid. Hey, it's only a little unforeseen manscaping. No damage done.

"Fire Shield."

Thin, wispy flames wreath my arm and shed a brilliant fiery light. With a surprisingly steady hand, I reach through the docile fire, my flames joining those burning as the pedestal's test.

Closing my fingers around the third fragment is such a thrill. I pull back my hand and whoop.

"I did it…I did it…I got the fragment."

I do a happy dance while the phoenix watches. Then I realize I'm an adult now.

Yeah, whatever.

Resuming the happy dance, I add some sweet moonwalk moves, then drive the tractor.

The mountain groans, a deep guttural sound that rises from the bowels of the earth. I pause for a moment, clutching the fragment tight in my hand.

Its power is pulsing against my skin, happy to be claimed and so close to its other pieces.

Another groan comes from the mountain and the obsidian bridge emits a *crack*.

"Oh, nononono." I rush back the way I came.

A spiderweb of cracks is racing across its surface, and I break into a sprint. Each step is a gamble on the increasingly treacherous ground.

The thunder of my heart swallows the pounding of my boots. Then the bridge gives way. The heat from the inferno below washes over me, a blast furnace breath that threatens to sear my lungs.

I'm falling, caught in a panic about what to do.

The phoenix's screech slices through the chaos, a clarion call that's a warning and a plea. I barely have a split second to think, but I manage.

Focused on my fiery friend, I transform.

It won't be fast enough.

It's close.

When my feet hit the lava, they're already the feet of a phoenix. I kick the molten lava, pump my wings, and get the hell gone.

The mountain is angry, and I'm suddenly picturing myself as Indiana Jones in *Raiders of the Lost Ark*, where he's running through the crumbling temple being shot at by booby traps and chased by the boulder.

There's a pull amid the chaos, an invisible tether that yanks at my guts. It's the magic of the Light Weavers. It's the way into that space behind the stone wall I found with my brothers, and it's drawing me away from the exit.

I'm torn.

The logical part of my brain screams to get the hell out of Dodge to live another day. There's that other part, the guardian of this island who feels the importance of me using these fragments to reignite Isilon's Embers of Existence.

I'm airborne, flailing for balance as stones plummet into the churning lava below me. With a hiss and sizzle, they're swallowed whole by the fiery maw. Tilting this way and that, I evade the raining rocks.

My time for decision is closing, but in my heart of hearts, I know there's no choice.

The people of the island need goodness and light to win out over the dark. My friends need it. My family needs it. I think of the next generation of Clan Cumhaill—of Baby Mac, Han, and Jackson—and how they need a magical place to live in peace.

Pivoting in the air, I take the new path, ignoring my way out. The guidance of the Light Weavers got me this far. I'm not about to give up now.

With dread and determination, I turn my back on the collapsing exit and race deeper into the volcano. The air is electric, charged with an almost palpable expectancy.

The tunnels grow tighter as I go and I'm thankful I'm in bird form because it gives me the agility to navigate.

Until I reach the end of the line.

I release my phoenix form and press my hands against the stone wall at the end of the tunnel. Did I come the wrong way? I don't think so.

The power of the Light Weavers' spell cools beneath my fingertips. It's a stark contrast to the inferno raging behind me.

The fragment in my hand resonates, a vibration that matches the frequency of the wall. It's calling me, guiding me to what I hope is salvation and not a tomb.

"Of course—duh! The *key* to the Corestone."

With the fire fragment in my hand, I pull the other two out of my vest. When I hold them close together, magic takes over, and the pieces reassemble to become whole.

I can't see where to insert the key to open the wall until the stone glows, a soft luminescence that bathes me in light. It's working.

The presence of the key unlocks whatever secret the Light Weavers entrusted to this place.

The wall shimmers and parts with a sound like an exhausted breath being released.

A hidden passage reveals itself, and I don't hesitate with the volcano still belching its discomfort. I dart inside, the light from the key casting long, dancing shadows on the tunnel's walls.

Behind me, the mountain gives one last furious roar, and the passage's entrance seals shut with a definitive *thud*.

I'm plunged into semi-darkness, the only illumination coming from the key in my hand.

The Light Weavers' power thrums all around me. It prickles over my skin and feeds my cells. This is the power I felt from the other corridor, but so much stronger now that I've gained access.

Having never been in an active volcano during an eruption—which I assume is happening—I'm not sure how long I have left before things go totally FUBAR.

I race down the passage and duck as rock crumbles around me. It crashes to the ground as small stones at first and grows bigger as more of the structure gives way.

Near the end of the passage, on the other side of the stone wall, Dillan, Calum, and Sloan are shouting for me.

"I'm here! Guys, get out. You gotta get clear of this thing before it blows."

"How do we get to you?" Calum asks.

I look around, and yeah, we're all druids and I'm sure they can bypass the magic of the Light Weavers' spell and reform the stone enough to get to me, but my instincts tell me it won't be in time.

I need to be here, but *they* don't.

My job as the guardian of this island is to safeguard the island at all costs.

"Seriously, guys. Trust me. Sloan, you need to portal the three of you out. I'm supposed to be here. I feel it."

"Fuck that, Em," Dillan shouts. "We're not leaving you here to be claimed by a test those women set in place over a thousand years ago."

"You have to. This is my quest, and you're using up my time. I've gotta go, and you three do, too. Sloan, do it. Trust me."

"Don't you dare, Irish. Don't you fucking—"

When the shouting cuts off mid-rant, I send Sloan all the love and thanks I can pack into good vibes.

They're safe.

That makes what I have to do so much easier.

I return my attention to the crystal key in my hand and the hidden crevice within the ancient wall. Then I follow the path of destiny that began almost four years ago when a black witch blasted me into that prana river.

The fae magic I possess is more than the druid powers of my heritage. It's the metamorphosis that's been occurring in me for years.

"Time to break out the butterfly."

There's an almost magnetic pull as the key slots into place, and a surge of Light Weaver magic ripples through the air. The stone barrier before me shivers, then dissolves into an array of shimmering dust, revealing the lifeline of Isilon.

This is the Corestone.

I'm not sure what the Embers of Existence are, but if the nexus of our city's life force needs a reboot, I'm here to get the job done.

Prismatic lights dance across the cavernous space, and the air vibrates with the potential of the unseen. My breath catches as I step deeper into the darkness and find what is almost a garden plot of glowing coals sputtering a pitiful smattering of sparks.

Okay, yeah. That's underwhelming. There is definitely room for improvement.

With each step toward the Corestone, the key's glow intensifies. The air around me thickens the tang of magic, and it doesn't matter that Syma didn't leave me instructions because I know what I need to do.

It's like it's been imprinted within me, somehow.

The moment the key touches the embers, it begins.

A burst of light blinds me, and warmth floods my veins. The

embers flare, stoked by the power the sisters left for me. The flames rise, hungry and eager, consuming the key's energy and spreading in a glorious wave across that vast garden of embers.

The volcano emits another angry rumble, and a mirage of the sisters appears before me.

You've done well, Emmet. Your quest is almost complete. Once you perform the Ritual of the Embers of Existence, the city's core will reignite, and Isilon will thrive once more.

The shrill screeches of the phoenix couple brings them into the mix. They fly into the cavern with all their fiery majesty and dive into the flames roaring over the fiery plane of embers.

The energy they give off is joyous.

After countless centuries, they're finally free to go home. Their duty to protect the Corestone is complete.

The mirage of the sisters fades as the script of the ritual comes into focus and floats in the air before me. When I see the length of the spell, all hope of getting out of this cavern before the volcano erupts is lost.

The sisters were a wordy bunch.

I straighten, draw a deep breath, and begin the ritual, at peace with the knowledge that Isilon will live on with or without me.

24

BRENDAN

"What do you mean, he's still in the volcano? Why the fuck are you out here if he's still inside that mountain?" The gathering of family and friends at the base of the Inferno Peaks looks grim as I shout my frustration at them.

Calum looks ill, and Dillan is about to murder Sloan.

"Ye need to have more faith in Emmet," Sloan snaps. "This is his path. Allow him to walk it."

"Fine. Let him walk it," Dillan shouts. "That doesn't mean he has to walk it alone. We're family. We're there for one another. I thought you knew that by now!"

Sloan stiffens. "Och, like that, is it? Ye don't like me obeyin' his wishes, so I'm not family, and I don't understand what it means to be part of yer lot? Grow up. If ye remember, I'm the one who feels the strength of yer magical connections, and Emmet's got ye all beat ten times over. He's not yer kid brother anymore."

He might be right, but at the same time, he'll *always* be our kid brother.

"I'm going back in," Dillan snaps.

"You'll never get to him in time," Calum points out. "It took us hours to get into the belly of that beast and I'd be surprised if the thing is still standing in five minutes."

Dillan pulls out his phone. "I'm calling the Greeks. One of them will take us in."

"No, they won't," Sloan snaps. "Emmet was clear. Have some feckin' faith that he knows his own mind."

"Fuck you, Irish."

"He'll be fine." Calum frowns at the fountain of flames spewing out from the volcano's top. "Em is resourceful. He'll make it out."

"He better," Dillan snaps.

"Or what?" Sloan snaps back. "Ye want a go at me? Have at it. Yer a hot-headed ass and ye get away with it because yer family is indulgent. Maybe bein' put to the ground fer a mouthful of dirt would do ye good."

Dillan lunges, but I get to him first. I get a grip on his shoulders, but his cloak is loose and hard to hold onto. "Dillan! Stop! You're upset, and you're taking it out on Sloan. It's not his fault, and you know it."

I arch back, narrowly avoiding the right hook that whistles past my face.

Calum curses and jumps into the mix.

Too many fists fly, and I catch an elbow to the mouth. The impact splits my lip, and blood spews forth. Annoyed as I am—and I really am—it's actually kind of great.

It's been many years since we brothers have mixed it up. In that spirit, I wrap my arm around Dillan's neck and take him to the ground in a sleeper hold.

He's kicking and twisting like a Tasmanian devil.

"What the hell are you doing?" Fiona yells, arriving on the scene with Nikon and Dionysus.

The fisticuffs end, and we freeze in place.

Gods, sometimes she sounds so much like Mam that it's spooky.

"Dillan started it," Calum grunts, stepping back.

"Fuck that, Sloan started it," Dillan snaps.

Fiona frowns. "Yet Sloan is the only one not bloody and throwing fists."

"Och, but it was close," Sloan grumbles. "Another word of venom out of his mouth and I was joining the donnybrook."

Fiona frowns and shakes her head. "What happened? Where's Emmet? We came here to see how he was doing with his quest."

"Forget the family squabbles." Nikon scowls at the volcano belching up lava. "Are we far enough away from this volcano if it blows?"

"Emmet's not!" Dillan shouts. "Your genius loverboy evacuated us and left Emmet in there on his own."

Sloan throws up his hands and turns to face Fi. "It's his quest, and he told us to go. He wanted us safe so he could do what he needed."

Fiona goes still. "Emmet's still inside that volcano?"

"Aye, he is. Part of his quest was fer him alone, and he told us to trust him and leave him to it."

Dillan scoffs. "You think she'll agree with you? There's no way Fi would've left Emmet behind."

Fiona frowns. "If he asked me to trust him, I would. Emmet's been finding his way and proving himself to you four his whole life. He's been stifled in the shadow of his older brothers. If he dug in on his quest and told me to have faith in him, I would've obeyed his wishes."

Dillan's mouth falls slack. "Bullshit."

"Stop your fighting," Dionysus orders and points at where lava is sparking and spewing out the top of the cone. "You're going to miss his big moment."

The volcano lets out a deafening *crack* as three phoenixes rise from the flames, searing the mid-afternoon sky. They soar in a wide arc, then two break off and go back down the volcano's funnel while the third flies to us.

As the mythical beast nears the ground, its form shifts and Emmet lands on the grass next to us. "Hey, everybody. What's the craic?"

The next moment, we're in the palace's great hall, and Dionysus is pouring drinks at the bar. "Tons of craic." He strides over to hand Emmet a glass. "Tell us all about your adventure, Em. Leave nothing out."

***

When the excitement of Emmet's quest dies down, the group parts, the awkward tension of harsh words and hostilities still raw. Dillan walks off in a huff when he should apologize to Sloan. Fiona and Calum cover for him and explain to Irish that he'll blow it all off and wind back to his senses in a few hours, or maybe days.

Watching it unfold from across the room, I have to agree with Sloan. Dillan gets a pass on his attitude and behavior from us more often than not.

He wasn't always so angry.

Most people don't understand that he was the sweetest of us until Mam died. He took her death the hardest and the idea of losing any one of us after that became his hot button.

It might seem like he's an uncaring ass, but it's the opposite. He cares so much he doesn't always know what to do with it.

Still, he'll set himself straight and make it right in the end. He always does.

When the group dissolves, I hug Emmet and give him the apartment to clean up and have a much-needed nap.

There's something I want to do, anyway.

Using my connection with the spirit plane, I track Nightfall down to the bridge over the prana river outside the gates. She's leaning on her elbows, bent to watch the current of the fae river flow toward the cliffs where the dragons live.

"Hey. I'm glad I found you."

She turns her head to smile at me. "It seems to be one of your talents."

Yeah, my skills are new, but there are a few perks.

"I'm glad you're still here."

She stares out at the magical river and makes a noncommittal noise at the back of her throat. "Do you think it peculiar I chose not to go with your friend to my end?"

I slide in beside her and mirror her pose. "Not at all. Is that because you don't intend to go or because you're not ready yet?"

"Both." She stares out at the swirling fuchsia waters, looking sad. "My people live long lives—many centuries. To have my life spirit snuffed before I experience so many things seems wasteful. I only recently awoke. It is too soon to pass on."

"It might seem selfish, but I'm relieved. I think we made a pretty good team through all this, and I hoped to hang out with you more."

"Hang out?"

"Spend time with."

She chuckles. "Considering you are the only person who can see me, it sounds like a lonely prospect."

"I've been thinking about that. One of my sister's friends ended up a ghost but wasn't ready to leave her vampire lover. Fiona and a friend of ours crafted a ring that makes her visible to the people in her life. I could ask her how it worked. Maybe something like that could work for you."

Her frown surprises me. I thought it was a good idea.

"Or if not, you can still be seen when I touch you. That's better than nothing, right?"

Her frown deepens. "Why?"

"Why, what?"

"Why would you concern yourself with my troubles? You barely know me."

I think about that for a moment and give her an honest

answer. "There have been many times since I was given my second chance when I've felt like I barely know my siblings. Dying changes a person. Add to that the almost two years I was dead, and yeah, I'm not sure how I fit into my old life anymore."

She considers that. "It will be different from when I lived here before, and this was my home."

"I don't think it has to be."

"You think not?" She looks at me, and there are all kinds of emotions in her eyes.

Anxiety. Hope. Sadness.

Man, I want to wash away some of that pain.

"No. I don't think it has to be different. Isilon can still be your home but with different neighbors."

"Do you believe the people of Isilon will accept me as I am after what happened with the whispering shadows?"

"I think so. The reason any of us are here is because we've survived something. I expect that earns you some grace."

I brush the back of Nightfall's hand with my finger, and she solidifies into the physical world. Damn, she's beautiful from her lithe build to the points of her ears peeking out of her dark purple hair.

"If that is the case, I would very much like to stay and live a little."

I push a loose violet wave away from her cheek and lean in. Damn, she even smells good. "I'm glad."

"Speaking of living a little." Dionysus pops in and breaks the mood. "I've got a surprise for you."

Startled, I jump and straighten, and Nightfall yelps as she ghosts out again.

Dionysus seems oblivious, but after getting lectured by Emmet the last time I made him feel bad, I know better than to lay into him a second time. "What kind of surprise?"

He grins like a kid on Christmas morning. "The kind that

starts with a key and ends with you roaring through the streets of Isilon. Come on."

Without waiting for my reply, he teleports Nightfall and me to the large stone courtyard outside the palace entrance. There's a massive crowd milling around, and as we get closer, I see why.

"My bike!" My sexy black beast of a Harley is here.

"Before you ask, I made it so it doesn't need to run on fossil fuel. I gifted it a bit of my magic, so it'll run here for you."

Mind blown.

I don't even pay attention to the people I'm practically shoving out of my way to get to my bike. "Are you for real? I won't need to gas up? It'll tear up the highways forever?"

Dionysus frowns. "Well, Isilon doesn't have highways, and I don't know about forever…but I *am* immortal, so it's possible."

I pull the guy into a chest-to-chest, back-slapping hug. Then it's all about me and my bike. I kick my leg back, swing it over the seat, and settle in.

It feels as amazing as always. "Fuck, I've missed you."

I run my hands up the tank's sexy curves, across the handlebars, and out to the grips. After turning the key, I pull in the clutch and get things started. Shifting the weight between my thighs, I take it off the kickstand and twist back, ready to grip it and rip it.

"Nightfall, hop on behind me."

The moment she straddles my hips and wraps her arms around my waist, she's solid and hells yeah, there's been nothing that felt so right in years.

I meet Dionysus' expectant gaze and press a hand against my heart. "Thanks, man. I mean it. This means more than I can possibly tell you."

Dionysus grins. "You don't have to tell me. I'm a god. I already know."

Emmet

When Brendan tears off, the reverb of the Harley engine echoes off the buildings of Isilon. It's jarring, and as a fan of the peace in the city, I turn to Dionysus. "Any chance you can manipulate the sound of the Harley so Brendan hears it in all its glory, but the rest of the city hears much less of a rumble?"

Dillan snorts. "If it's too loud, you're too old."

"Maybe. I don't want to be a party pooper, but the way he rides, I'll have to cite him for disturbing the peace."

We let it go at that and return to our task of making sure everyone gets back to their homes. With the threat of the whispering shadows over, the citizens are free to resume their lives.

Although something's still bugging me.

"The magic doesn't match up."

Dillan turns to me and arches an ebony brow. "Say again? Try it with more words this time."

"I'm saying I felt the darkness in the grove when Randa's body was found, and I felt the darkness of the whispering shadows and the wizard. The magical signatures don't match up."

"You don't think we got Randa's killer?"

I check that our conversation is still private. "No, and Zxata doesn't either."

Scanning the crowd to find a nymph with bright blue hair isn't hard. Once I see him, I wave him over. We move out of the stream of citizens heading back to their homes, and I lean in. "We were talking about the energy of the darkness that desiccated Randa."

"Emmet said you don't think it was the wizard or the whispering shadows he created," Dillan adds.

Zxata purses his lips. "I mentioned to Emmet when I first got here that the trees of the grove can't create visuals when they describe something, but they communicate sensation. The feel of the darkness within the grove during Randa's attack was an isolated energy. They haven't felt anything like it since."

I sigh. "As much as I hate to think about it, I don't think this is over."

"Are we making a mistake sending these people home?" Dillan asks.

I wish I knew. "We can't keep them locked up in the palace forever. If the trees are right and what happened to Randa was an isolated attack, it might be a one-time thing or not happen again for months."

Dillan curses and whistles for Calum and Aiden to join us. They've all been helping with relocating the citizens, and I'm grateful to have them on my team.

"Did you see Brenny's face?" Calum asks. "We might have finally found a way to get through to him."

"It was a big win, Dionysus," Aiden confirms. "Thanks, Greek."

"My pleasure."

Like I always say—Dionysus is good like that.

"What's the word?" Calum asks.

Dillan takes the lead in pointing out our dark cloud. "Emmet and Zxata don't think the wizard was the one that took down the nymph in the grove."

Aiden frowns. "You said it yourself. Necromancers siphon fae energy, and to control all those souls and transform them into whispering shadows must have taken a lot of mojo."

I nod. "All true, but still, I want all of you on alert because Zxata and I don't think it was the wizard."

I know it's not what they want to hear, especially since the citizens are descending the hill from the palace and going home. "I'll have Astrid notify all households that there's a potential for more danger, just to be safe."

Aiden sighs. "I understand the importance of balance, but couldn't we have light and goodness in our home realm for the rest of our days? There's enough darkness everywhere else."

True story.

EMMET

The next few weeks mark the dawn of a new beginning for many of us. Brendan is happier than I've seen him in years. He spends a lot of time with Nightfall, is out on his bike every chance he gets, and has become the proud owner of a three-legged ghost dog who loves him because he gets belly rubs with Brendan.

Zxata claimed a bright yellow house beside the grove and has worked tirelessly to help the old oak tree through its loss. He's settling in, and from that first day, he has already made us thankful he's here.

Eva has escorted hundreds of souls to their afterlife and deserves our undying gratitude. She's amazing. We all agree she's way too good for Dillan and make a point of telling him so as often as possible.

Still, with all the things that have gone right for us, in the back of my mind, there's always that niggling worry that we're waiting for Randa's attacker to resurface.

It's been weeks, but we're caught in a "waiting for the shoe to drop" scenario.

The dragons have been doing broad sweeps over the city

while Bruin, Manx, and Doc patrol the family street. No one is letting their guard down, but reality looms.

My boots echo softly against the wood of the prana river's bridge as I make my morning jaunt to the dragons' lair. I've been taking a morning and evening patrol to stay on top of things.

There's a crispness in the air this morning.

The weather in our utopian city is always amazing, but just as in the human realm, September brings a few cooler days.

As I cross the river, the city stirs behind me, a gentle hum of life awakening. Since reigniting the Embers of Existence, Isilon, our hidden gem, pulses with renewed vigor.

The colors of the houses look brighter. The growth of nature is heartier. Everything about the city is "more."

The magic I rekindled is taking hold, stirring the ancient energies that slumbered for so long. I can feel its potential building. We all can.

It's an exciting time in the hidden city.

With a spring in my step, I climb the slope leading to the lair. The earthy scent of moss and stone fills the air. "Who's up for a morning flight? A chance to stretch those magnificent wings?"

Esym's green scales shimmer like a thousand tiny lily pads on a glittering pond. "I thought you'd never ask."

After calling *Feline Finesse*, I vault onto her broad back, feeling the familiar rush of excitement as her muscles tense beneath me. With a powerful leap, we're airborne, the city sprawling below us.

The wind tugs my hair, and the exhilaration of flight mingles with pride in everything I've accomplished here. It's been a group effort, but I'm leading the charge for the first time in my life.

Esym and I sweep over Isilon. The palace's golden cylinder gleams at the top of the hill. The green blanket of iridescent moss grows thick along the rooftops. The revitalization of the market square is coming along nicely and is bustling with early risers.

Esym dives and soars, playful in the morning light, her

laughter a deep, rumbling echo that fills the sky. I hold on tight, grinning like a fool. This is freedom. This is living. As we patrol in a circle over the streets of Isilon, I know that whatever comes, this has been my destiny all along.

We bank in the September breeze, and I notice something below that sparks my interest. Kidok is waving his arm over his head to catch my attention.

He's in the city square outside the security building, and something is amiss.

"Esym, you need to circle back and set down in the square. Something's not right."

Her muscled frame shifts beneath me and we arc in the air, turning back the way we came. As we get closer, I see Kidok is standing over two bodies lying disturbingly still by the fountain.

My guts twist, and I curse myself for jinxing things.

A swift descent has me off Esym's back before her wings fully fold. My boots hit the ground, and I run toward the grim tableau. "What have you got?"

"The dwarf and his female. Both dead and drained."

I kneel beside Thrain and Oda. My breath locks in my lungs. Like Randa, their bodies are withered husks, their fae life essence forcefully drawn out. "All they wanted was a safe place to love one another and have a family."

My sorrow rises like a river threatening to overflow its banks as I crouch beside them.

Kidok moves around the bodies with practiced care. "Unfortunately, you were right. Our killer is still out there."

I brush my fingers over Oda's sunken cheeks, her eyes, once brimming with the spark of life, now vacant pits that draw the warmth from my fingertips.

"How do you want to proceed?"

That's the question, isn't it? Really, the answer is easy. The Light Weaver sisters entrusted me to continue their work. Clan

Cumhaill might not be as experienced with the nuances of Isilon, but we know all about policing a city to keep its citizens safe.

I'll do exactly what Syma asked me to do.

Carry on.

ENDNOTE

Thank you for reading *Carry On,* book one in the Chronicles of a Hidden City. While the story is fresh in your mind, and as a favor to Michael and me, please click HERE and tell other readers what you thought.

A quick star rating and/or even one sentence can mean so much to readers deciding whether to try a book, series, or a new-to-them author.

Thank you.

If you want to continue with book two, *Back in Black,* you can find that on Amazon.

AUTHOR NOTES - AUBURN TEMPEST

SEPTEMBER 6, 2023

Thank you for being here, for giving your time to my stories. I hope you enjoyed every moment. If my Chronicles universe is new to you, I hope everything made sense. I find writing book one of related stories so difficult because I know all the characters, the relationships, and who should be there.

For the new readers, I don't want you to be lost.

For the huge fanbase that follows the stories, I don't want you to be bored or wondering where all the favorite characters have disappeared to.

It's a balance.

If you're in either of those categories and felt a bit lost, hang in there. I'll bring it together for all of us.

If you're new to this series and are interested in starting at the beginning, *Gilded Cage* is the beginning of it all. All links are posted on the pages that follow.

I've been looking forward to writing Emmet's and Brendan's story for a long time now. I envision this series as a kind of *Supernatural* brotherhood adventure.

I've given a tip of the hat to *Supernatural* with the titles. The first three books will be *Carry On, Back in Black,* and *Peace of Mind.*

All classic songs—all of them remind me of Sam and Dean adventures.

So, stay with me and if you're up for it, we'll have a little fun learning about Clan Cumhaill from two new viewpoints. And, as always, blessed be.

Blessed be,

Auburn Tempest

If you want to keep your finger on the pulse of what is happening with the series, feel free to join the Chronicles of an Urban Druid Facebook Fan page.

Or drop us a line: UrbanDruid@lmbpn.com

If you enjoyed it and want to keep your finger on the pulse, feel free to join the Facebook Fan page.

Or drop us a line: UrbanDruid@lmbpn.com

BOOKS BY AUBURN TEMPEST

Find Me

Amazon, Facebook, Newsletter,
Web page – www.auburntempest.com
Email – AuburnTempestWrites@gmail.com

Auburn Tempest—Urban Fantasy Action/Adventure

Chronicles of a Hidden City
Book 1 – Carry On
Book 2 – Back in Black
Book 3 – Peace of Mind

Chronicles of an Urban Elemental
Book 1 – Incendio: Flame Born
Book 2 – Magicae: Power Dawning
Book 3 – Potentia: Bonds Forged
Book 4 – Fidelitas: Trust Realized
Book 5 – Intellectus: Origins Discovered
Book 6 – Regeneratus: Races Rekindled

Chronicles of an Urban Druid
Book 1 – <u>A Gilded Cage</u>
Book 2 – <u>A Sacred Grove</u>
Book 3 – <u>A Family Oath</u>
Book 4 – <u>A Witch's Revenge</u>
Book 5 – <u>A Broken Vow</u>
Book 6 – <u>A Druid Hexed</u>
Book 7 – <u>An Immortal's Pain</u>
Book 8 – <u>A Shaman's Power</u>
Book 9 – <u>A Fated Bond</u>
Book 10 – <u>A Dragon's Dare</u>
Book 11 – <u>A God's Mistake</u>
Book 12 – <u>A Destiny Unlocked</u>
Book 13 – <u>A United Front</u>
Book 14 – <u>A Culling Tide</u>
Book 15 – <u>A Danger Destroyed</u>

Case Files of an Urban Druid
Book 1 – <u>Mayhem in Montréal</u>
Book 2 – <u>Sorcery in San Francisco</u>
Book 3 – <u>Necromancy in New Orleans</u>
Book 4 – <u>Hazards in the Hidden City</u>
Book 5 – <u>Hexes in Texas</u>
Book 6 – <u>Wendigos in Washington</u>
Book 7 – <u>Gods at Odds</u>

If you enjoy my writing and read sexy/steamy romance, my pen name for the books I write in Paranormal and Fantasy Romance is JL Madore.
You can find my JL books on <u>Amazon</u>.

MARCH 4, 2024

T hank you so much for reading our stories! We get to craft words for a living. It (usually) doesn't get better than this!

The Pain and Joy of New Series, Old Friends

Welcome back to the cozy little corner of our collective imagination, where characters don't just pop out of the book—they've practically moved in with us.

Rent stealing ba$tards.

We're at that spot where the familiar greets the unknown with a knowing nod. In this new series, we're hanging out again with fictional friends who've been with us through thick and thin.

Sometimes helping us out of a jam in a scene, sometimes stealing the scene from the main characters and sometimes just stealing our embittered, cold, author hearts.

Crafting a new story is a bit like catching up with an old buddy while riding a rollercoaster—comforting yet thrilling. We're tipping our hats to the characters we all know and love *while tossing them into new pickles to see how they fare.*

(Told you we are cold, embittered assholes!)

For the long-time followers, it's a chance to really get into the heads of their favorite characters, digging into nooks and crannies we've only glimpsed from afar.

But let's not forget to roll out the red carpet for you new folks. We've built this series to stand tall on its own legs—a welcoming portal into a world with layers of backstory, yet not so daunting that newbies can't jump on board and feel right at home from the get-go.

Our mission? Spin a story that feels like a fresh coat of paint on an old fence. We're playing the greatest hits of themes that never get old but also tossing in a few surprises to keep things interesting.

Gear up to see your cherished characters shine under the spotlight, tackling the kind of hurdles that can really show what they're made of.

From the writer's imagination, it's not just about pleasing ourselves—it's about hitting the right actions for our characters' growth. It's about giving them the room to stretch their legs but not losing sight of who they are at the core.

This is done with love—for the characters, for the adventure they're on, and for you, the readers, who make it all come alive with every flip of the page.

So, whether you've been with us since the beginning or just tuned in, get ready for a ride that'll echo the good old days while dialing into what's next.

We hope you enjoy our tales!

Ad Aeternitatem,
Michael Anderle

For ongoing musings, story previews, and the occasional philosophical ramble, don't forget to subscribe to the MORE STORIES with Michael newsletter HERE: https://michael.beehi iv.com/

BOOKS BY MICHAEL ANDERLE

Sign up for the LMBPN email list to be notified of new releases and special deals!

https://lmbpn.com/email/

For a complete list of books by Michael Anderle, please visit:

www.lmbpn.com/ma-books/

CONNECT WITH THE AUTHORS

Connect with Auburn

Amazon, Facebook, Newsletter

Web page – www.jlmadore.com

Email – AuburnTempestWrites@gmail.com

Connect with Michael Anderle and sign up for his email list here:

Website: http://lmbpn.com

Email List: https://michael.beehiiv.com/

https://www.facebook.com/LMBPNPublishing

https://twitter.com/lmbpn

https://www.instagram.com/lmbpn_publishing/

https://www.bookbub.com/authors/michael-anderle